Daughters of Spain

Jean Plaidy, one of the pre____ion for most of the twentieth ____ the prolific English author Eleanor Hibbert, also known as Victoria Holt. Jean Plaidy's novels had sold more than 14 million copies worldwide by the time of her death in 1993.

For further information about Jean Plaidy reissues and mailing list, please visit
www.randomhouse.co.uk/minisites/jeanplaidy

Praise for Jean Plaidy

'A vivid impression of life at the Tudor Court'
Daily Telegraph

'One of the country's most widely read novelists'
Sunday Times

'Plaidy excels at blending history with romance and drama'
New York Times

'It is hard to better Jean Plaidy . . . both elegant and exciting'
Daily Mirror

'Jean Plaidy conveys the texture of various patches of the past with such rich complexity' *Guardian*

Daughters of Spain

JEAN PLAIDY

arrow books

Published by Arrow Books in 2008

5 7 9 10 8 6 4

Copyright © Jean Plaidy, 1961

Initial lettering copyright © Stephen Raw, 2008

The Estate of Eleanor Hibbert has asserted its right
to have Jean Plaidy identified as the author of this work.

First published in the United Kingdom in 1960 by Robert Hale and Company

The Random House Group Limited
20 Vauxhall Bridge Road, London SW1V 2SA

www.rbooks.co.uk

Addresses for companies within The Random House Group Limited can be found at:
www.randomhouse.co.uk/offices.htm

The Random House Group Limited Reg. No. 954009

A CIP catalogue record for this book is available from the British Library

ISBN 9780099513544

The Random House Group Limited supports The Forest Stewardship Council (FSC),
the leading international forest certification organisation. All our titles that are printed on
Greenpeace approved FSC certified paper carry the FSC logo. Our paper procurement
policy can be found at: www.rbooks.co.uk/environment

Typeset by SX Composing DTP, Rayleigh, Essex
Printed and bound in Great Britain by
CPI Antony Rowe, Chippenham, Wiltshire

CONTENTS

❧ Chapter I ☙

THE ROYAL FAMILY

Catalina knelt on a window-seat looking out from the Palace to the purple slopes and the snowy tips of the Sierra de Guadarrama.

It would soon be Easter and the sky was cobalt, but the plain stretching out before the mountains was of a tawny bleakness.

Catalina enjoyed studying the view from the nursery window. Out there the scene always seemed a little frightening. Perhaps this was because she, who had seen bitter fighting outside Granada when she was a few years younger, was always afraid that her parents' rebellious subjects would rise again and cause distress to her beloved mother.

Here within the granite walls of the Madrid Alcazar there was a feeling of security, which was entirely due to the presence of her mother. Her father was also in residence at this time, so that they were a united family, all gathered together under this one roof.

What could be more pleasant? And yet even now her brother and sisters were talking of unpleasant matters, such as the marriages which they would have to make at some time.

'Please,' murmured Catalina to herself, 'do not do it. We are all together. Let us forget that one day we may not be so happy.'

It was no use asking them. She was the youngest and only ten years old. They would laugh at her. Only her mother would have understood if she had spoken her thoughts, although she would immediately have reminded her daughter that duty must be faced with fortitude.

Juana, who was laughing in her wild manner as though she would not in the least mind going away, suddenly noticed her young sister.

'Come here, Catalina,' she commanded. 'You must not feel left out. You shall have a husband too.'

'I don't want a husband.'

'I know. I know.' Juana mimicked her young sister: 'I want to stay with my mother all the time. I only want to be the Queen's dear daughter!'

'Hush!' said Isabella, who was the eldest and fifteen years older than Catalina. 'You must curb your tongue, Juana. It is unseemly to talk of marriage before one has been arranged for you.'

Isabella spoke from knowledge. She had already been married and had lived in Portugal. Lucky Isabella, thought Catalina, for she had not remained long there. Her husband had died and she had come home again. She had done her duty but had not had to go on doing it for long. Catalina wondered why Isabella always seemed so sad. It was as though she regretted being brought back home, as though she still pined for her lost husband. How could any husband ever make up for the companionship of their mother, the delights of being all together and part of one big happy family?

'If I wish to talk of marriage, I will,' announced Juana. 'I

2

will, I tell you, I will!' Juana stood up to her full height, tossing back her tawny hair, her eyes ablaze with that wildness which it was so easy to evoke. Catalina watched her sister in some trepidation. She was a little afraid of Juana's moods. This was because she had often seen her mother look worried when her eyes rested on Juana.

Even the mighty Queen Isabella was anxious about her second daughter. And Catalina, whose feelings for her mother were close to idolatry, was conscious of every mood, every fear, and she passionately longed to share them.

'One day,' said the Princess Isabella, 'Juana will learn that she has to obey.'

'I may have to obey some people,' cried Juana, 'but not you, sister. Not you!'

Catalina began to pray silently. 'Not a scene now ... please, please, not a scene now when we're so happy.'

'Perhaps,' said Juan who always tried to make peace, 'Juana will have such an indulgent husband that she will always be able to do as she wishes.'

Juan's beautiful face framed in fair hair was like that of an angel. The Queen's favourite name for her only son was Angel. Catalina could well understand why. It was not only that Juan looked like an angel, he acted like one. Catalina wondered whether her mother loved Angel better than all the rest of them. Surely she must, for he was not only the heir to the crown but the most beautiful, gentle and kind person it was possible to know. He never sought to remind people of his important position; the servants loved to serve him and considered it a pleasure as well as an honour to be of his household. Now he, a seventeen-year-old boy, who, one would have thought, would have wished to be with companions of his own sex, hunting or at some sport or another, was here in the old nursery with his sisters – perhaps because he knew they liked to have him or, as Catalina did, he appreciated the pleasure of belonging to a family such as theirs.

Juana was smiling now; the idea of having an indulgent husband on whom she could impose her will pleased her.

Their sister Isabella watched them all a little sadly. What children they were! she was thinking. It was a pity they were all so much younger than she was. Her mother of course had had little time for childbearing in the early part of her reign. There had been the great war and so many state matters to occupy her; so it was not surprising that Juan, who was the next in the family, was eight years younger than herself.

Isabella wished they would not talk of marriage. It brought back such bitter memories. She saw herself five years ago, clinging to her mother even as Catalina did now, terrified because she must leave her home and go into Portugal to marry Alonso, heir of the crown of that country. Then the promise of a crown had held no charm for her. She had cried for her mother even as poor little Catalina undoubtedly would when her turn came.

But she had found her young husband as terrified of marriage as she was herself, and very soon a bond had grown between them which in its turn burgeoned into love – so deep, so bitter-sweet, so short-lived.

She told herself that she would be haunted for ever by the sight of the bearers carrying his poor broken body in from the forest. She thought of the new heir to the throne, the young Emanuel who had tried so hard to comfort her, who had told her that he loved her and who had invited her to forget her dead husband and marry him, to stay in Portugal, not to

4

return, a sad widow, to her parents' dominions, but to become the bride of her late husband's cousin who was now heir to the King of Portugal.

She had turned shuddering from handsome Emanuel.

'No,' she had cried. 'I wish never to marry again. I shall continue to think of Alonso . . . until I die.'

That had happened when she was twenty; and ever since she had kept her vow, although her mother sought to persuade her to change her mind; and her father, who was so much less patient, was growing increasingly irritated with her.

She shuddered at the thought of returning to Portugal as a bride. Memories would be too poignant to be borne.

She felt tears in her eyes, and looking up she saw the grave glance of little Catalina fixed upon her.

Poor Catalina, she thought, her turn will come. She will face it with courage – that much I know. But what of the others?

Thirteen-year-old Maria was working on a piece of embroidery. She was completely unruffled by this talk of marriage. Sometimes Isabella thought she was rather stupid, for whatever happened she showed little excitement or resentment, but merely accepted what came. Life would be much less difficult for Maria.

And Juana? It was wiser not to think of Juana. Juana would never suffer in silence.

Now the wild creature had leapt to her feet and held out her hand to Juan.

'Come, let us dance, brother,' she commanded. 'Maria, take up your lute and play for us.'

Maria placidly put down her embroidery, took up the lute and played the first plaintive notes of a *pavana*.

The brother and sister danced together. They were well

5

matched and there was only a year's difference in their ages. But what a contrast they made! This thought occurred both to Isabella and Catalina. It was so marked and people often referred to it when they saw Juan and Juana together. Their names were so much alike; they were of the same height; but one would never have guessed that they were brother and sister.

Even Juana's hair seemed to grow rebelliously from her forehead; that touch of auburn was like their mother's yet it was more tawny in Juana's, so that she looked like a young lioness; her great eyes were always restless; her mood could change in a second. Juana gave the impression of never being tranquil. Even in sleep she had the appearance of restlessness.

How different was Juan with his fair face which resembled that of angels. Now he danced with his sister because she asked him to, and he knew that the thoughts of marriage and the husband she might have, had excited her. The dance would calm her; her physical exertion would help to allay the excitement of her mind.

If Juan did not want to dance when he was asked to do so, he immediately changed his mind. That was characteristic of Juan. He had a rare quality in not only wishing to please others but in finding that their wishes became his own.

Catalina went back to the window-seat, and looked out once more at the plain and the mountains and the arrivals and departures.

She found her sister Isabella standing beside her. Isabella put an arm about her as Catalina turned to smile. She had felt in that moment a need to protect the child from the ills which could befall the daughters of the House of Spain. Memories of Alonso always made her feel like this. Later she would seek out her mother's confessor and talk to him of her sorrow. She preferred to talk with him because he never gave her easy comfort, but scolded her as he would scourge himself if necessary; and the sight of his pale, emaciated face never failed to comfort her.

There were times when she longed to go into a convent and spend her life in prayer until death came to unite her with Alonso. If she were not a daughter of Spain that would have been possible.

'Look,' said Catalina, pointing to a gaunt figure in a Franciscan robe, 'there is the Queen's confessor.'

Isabella looked down at the man who with his companion was about to enter the Alcazar. She could not clearly see the emaciated features and the stern expression of the monk, but she was deeply aware of them.

'I am glad he is here,' she said.

'Isabella, he . . . he frightens me a little.'

Isabella's face grew sterner.' You must never be afraid of good men, Catalina; and there is not a better man in Spain than Ximenes de Cisneros.'

❧❦

In her apartments the Queen sat at her writing-table. Her expression was serene but it was no indication of her thoughts. She was about to perform an unpleasant duty and this was painful to her.

Here I am, she thought, with my family all about me. Spain is more prosperous than she has been for many a year; we now have a united Kingdom, a Christian Kingdom. In the past three years, since together Ferdinand and I conquered the last Moorish stronghold, the Christian flag has flown over every

Spanish town. The explorer Christobal Colon has done good work and Spain has a growing Kingdom beyond the seas. As Queen I rejoice in my country's prosperity. As a mother I know great happiness because at this moment I have my entire family with me under one roof. All should be well and yet . . .

She smiled at the man who was sitting watching her.

This was Ferdinand, her husband; a year younger than herself he was still a handsome man. If there was a certain craftiness in the eyes, Isabella had always refused to recognise it; if his features were touched with sensuality Isabella was ready to tell herself that he was indeed a man and she would not have him otherwise.

He was indeed a man – a brave soldier, a wily statesman; a man who loved little on this Earth as he loved gold and treasure. Yet he had affection to spare for his family. The children loved him. Not as they loved their mother of course. But, thought Isabella, it is the mother who bore them who is closer to them than any father could be. That was not the answer. Her children loved her because they were aware of the deeper devotion which came from her; they knew that, when their husbands were chosen, their father would rejoice at the material advantages those marriages would bring; his children's happiness would rank only as secondary. But their mother, who would also wish grand marriages for them all, would suffer even as they did from the parting.

They loved their mother devotedly. They alone knew of the tenderness which was so often hidden beneath the serenity, for it was only for them that Queen Isabella would lift the veil with which she hid her true self from the world. Now she was staring at the document which lay on the table before her and she was deeply conscious of Ferdinand's attention which was riveted on it.

They must speak of it. She knew that he was going to ask her outright to destroy it.

She was right. His mouth hardened and for a moment she could almost believe that he hated her. 'So you intend to make this appointment?' Isabella was stung by the coldness of the tone. No one could convey more hatred and contempt in his voice than Ferdinand.

'I do, Ferdinand.'

'There are times,' went on Ferdinand, 'when I wish you would listen to my advice.'

'And how I wish that I could take it.'

Ferdinand made an impatient gesture. 'It is simple enough. You take the document and tear it in two. That could be an end to the matter.'

He had leaned forward and would have taken it, but Isabella's plump white hand was immediately spread across it, protecting it.

Ferdinand's mouth was set in a stubborn line which made him look childish.

'I am sorry, Ferdinand,' said Isabella.

'So once again you remind me that you are Queen of Castile. You will have your way. And so . . . you will give this . . . this upstart the highest post in Spain, when you might . . .'

'Give it to one who deserves it far less,' said the Queen gently; 'your son . . . who is not my son.'

'Isabella, you talk like some country wife. Alfonso is my son. I have never denied that fact. He was born when you and I were separated . . . as we were so often during those early days. I was young . . . hot blooded . . . and I found a mistress as young men will. You must understand.'

'I have understood and forgiven, Ferdinand. But that does not mean that I can give your bastard the Archbishopric of Toledo.'

'So you're giving it to this half-starved monk . . . this simple man . . . this low . . .'

'He is of good family, Ferdinand. It is true he is not royal. But at least he is the legitimate son of his father.'

Ferdinand brought his fist down on the table. 'I am weary of these reproaches. It has nothing to do with Alfonso's birth. Confess it. You wish to show me . . . as you have so often . . . that you are Queen of Castile and Castile is of greater importance to Spain than is Aragon; therefore you stand supreme.'

'Oh Ferdinand, that has never been my wish. Castile . . . Aragon . . . what are they compared with Spain? Spain is now united. You are its King; I its Queen.'

'But the Queen will bestow the Archbishopric of Toledo where she wishes.'

Isabella looked at him sadly.

'Is that not so?' he shouted.

'Yes,' said Isabella, 'that is so.'

'And this is your final decision on the matter?'

'It is my final decision.'

'Then I crave Your Highness's permission to retire.' Ferdinand's voice was heavy with sarcasm.

'Ferdinand, you know . . .' But he would not wait. He was bowing now and strutting from the room.

Isabella remained at her table. This scene was reminiscent of so many which had occurred during their married life. There was this continual jostling for the superior position on Ferdinand's part; as for herself, she longed to be the perfect wife and mother. It would have been so easy to have said: Have it your own way, Ferdinand. Give the Archbishopric where you will.

But that gay young son of his was not suited to this high post. There was only one man in Spain whom she believed to be worthy of it, and always she must think first of Spain. This was why she was now determined that the Franciscan Ximenes should be Primate of Spain, no matter how the appointment displeased Ferdinand.

She rose from the table and went to the door of the apartment.

'Highness!' Several of the attendants who had been waiting outside sprang to attention.

'Go and discover whether Fray Francisco Ximenes de Cisneros is in the Palace. If he is, tell him that it is my wish that he present himself to me without delay.'

❧❧

Fray Francisco Ximenes de Cisneros was praying silently as he approached the Palace. Beneath the rough serge of his habit the hair shirt irritated his skin. He took a fierce delight in this. He had eaten nothing but a few herbs and berries during his journey to Madrid from Ocaña, but he was accustomed to long abstinence from food.

His nephew, Francisco Ruiz, whom he loved as dearly as he could love anyone, and who was closer to him than his own brothers, glanced anxiously at him.

'What,' he asked, 'do you think is the meaning of the Queen's summons?'

'My dear Francisco, as I shall shortly know, let us not waste our breath in conjecture.'

But Francisco Ruiz was excited. It had so happened that the great Cardinal Mendoza, who had occupied the highest post in Spain – that of the Archbishop of Toledo – had recently died and the office was vacant. Was it possible that such an honour was about to be bestowed on his uncle? Ximenes might declare himself uninterested in great honours, but there were some honours which would tempt the most devout of men.

And why not? Ruiz demanded of himself. The Queen thinks highly of her confessor – and rightly so. She can never have had such a worthy adviser since Torquemada himself heard her confessions. And she loves such men, men who are not afraid to speak their minds, men who are clearly indifferent to worldly riches.

Torquemada, suffering acutely from the gout, was now an old man with clearly very little time left to him. He was almost entirely confined to the monastery of Avila. Ximenes on the other hand was at the height of his mental powers.

Ruiz was certain that it was to bestow this great honour on his uncle that they were being thus recalled to Madrid.

As for Ximenes, try as he might, he could not thrust the thought from his mind.

Archbishop of Toledo! Primate of Spain! He could not understand this strange feeling which rose within him. There was so much about himself which he could not understand. He longed to suffer the greatest bodily torture, as Christ had suffered on the cross. And even as his body cried out for this treatment, a voice within him asked: 'Why, Ximenes, is it because you cannot endure that any should be greater than yourself? None must bear pain more stoically. None must be more devout. Who are you, Ximenes? Are you a man? Are you a God?

'Archbishop of Toledo,' the voice gloated within him. 'The power will be yours. You will be greater than any man under the Sovereigns. And the Sovereigns may be swayed by your influence. Have you not had charge of the Queen's conscience; and is not the Queen the real ruler of Spain?

'It is for your own vanity, Ximenes. You long to be the most powerful man in Spain; more powerful than Ferdinand whose great desire is to fill his coffers and extend his Kingdom. Greater than Torquemada who has set the holy fires scorching the limbs of heretics throughout the land. More powerful than any. Ximenes, Primate of Spain, the Queen's right hand. Ruler of Spain?'

I shall not take this post if it is offered to me, he told himself.

He closed his eyes and began to pray for strength to refuse it, but it was as though the Devil spread the kingdoms of the Earth at his feet.

He swayed slightly. There was little nourishment in berries, and when he travelled he never took food or money with him. He relied on what he could find growing by the wayside, or the help from the people he met.

'My Master did not carry bread and wine,' he would say, 'and though the birds had their nests and the foxes their lairs there was no place in which the Son of Man might lay his head.'

What his Master had done Ximenes must do also.

When they entered the Palace the Queen's messenger immediately called to him.

'Fray Francisco Ximenes de Cisneros?'

'It is I,' answered Ximenes. He felt a certain pride every time he heard his full title; he had not been christened

Francisco but Gonzalo, and had changed his first name that he might bear the same one as the founder of the Order in which he served.

'Her Highness Queen Isabella wishes you to wait upon her with all speed.'

'I will go to her presence at once.'

Ruiz plucked at his sleeve. 'Should you not wipe away the stains of the journey before presenting yourself to the Queen's Highness?'

'The Queen knows I have come on a journey. She will expect me to be travel-stained.'

Ruiz looked after his uncle in some dismay. The lean figure, the emaciated face with the pale skin tightly drawn across the bones were in great contrast to the looks of the previous Archbishop of Toledo, the late Mendoza, sensuous, good-natured epicure and lover of comfort and women.

Archbishop of Toledo! thought Ruiz. Surely it cannot be!

Isabella gave a smile of pleasure as her confessor entered the apartment.

She waved her hand to the attendant and they were alone.

'I have brought you back from Ocaña,' she said almost apologetically, 'because I have news for you.'

'What news has Your Highness for me?'

His manner lacked the obsequiousness with which Isabella was accustomed to being addressed by her subjects, but she did not protest. She admired her confessor because he was no great respecter of persons.

But for the truly holy life this man led, it might have been said that he was a man of great pride.

'I think,' said Isabella, 'that this letter from His Holiness the Pope will explain.' She turned to the table and took up that document which had caused such displeasure to Ferdinand, and put it into the hands of Ximenes.

'Open it and read it,' urged Isabella.

Ximenes obeyed. As he read the first words a change passed across his features. He did not grow more pale – that would have been impossible – but his mouth hardened and his eyes narrowed; for a few seconds a mighty battle was raging within his meagre frame.

The words danced before his eyes. They were in the handwriting of Pope Alexander VI himself, and they ran as follows:

'To our beloved son, Fray Francisco Ximenes de Cisneros, Archbishop of Toledo . . .'

Isabella was waiting for him to fall on his knees and thank her for this great honour; but he did no such thing. He stood very still, staring before him, oblivious of the fact that he was in the presence of his Queen. He was only aware of the conflict within himself, the need to understand what real motives lay behind his feelings.

Power. Great power. It was his to take. For what purpose did he want power? He was unsure. He was as unsure as he had been years ago when he had lived as a hermit in the forest of Castañar.

Then it seemed to him that devils mocked him. 'You long for power, Ximenes,' they said. 'You are a vain and sinful man. You are ambitious, and by that sin fell the angels.'

He put the paper on to the table and murmured: 'There has been a mistake. This is not for me.' Then he turned and strode from the room, leaving the astonished Queen staring after him.

Her bewilderment gave way to anger. Ximenes might be a holy man but he had forgotten the manner in which to behave before his Queen. But almost immediately her anger disappeared. He is a good man, she reminded herself. He is one of the few about me who do not seek personal advantage. This means he has refused this great honour. What other man in Spain would do this?

❧❧

Isabella sent for her eldest daughter.

The young Isabella would have knelt before her mother but the Queen took her into her arms and held her tightly against her for a few seconds.

Holy Mother of God, thought the Princess, what can this mean? She is suffering for me. Is it a husband that I shall be forced to take? Is that why she is so sorry for me?

The Queen put the Princess from her and composed her features.

'My dearest,' she said, 'you do not look as well as I would wish. How is your cough?'

'I cough now and then, Highness, as I always have.'

'Isabella, my child, now that we are alone together, let us throw aside all ceremony. Call me Mother. I love to hear the word on your lips.'

The Princess began: 'Oh, my Mother . . .' and then she was sobbing in the Queen's arms.

'There, my precious child,' murmured Isabella. 'You still think of him then? Is it that?'

'I was so happy . . . happy. Mother, can you understand? I was so frightened at first, and when I found that . . . we loved . . . it was all so wonderful. We planned to live like that for the rest of our lives . . .'

The Queen did not speak; she went on stroking her daughter's hair.

'It was cruel . . . so cruel. He was so young. And when we went out into the forest that day it was like any other day. He was with me but ten minutes before it happened . . . laughing . . . with me. And then there he was . . .'

'It was God's will,' said the Queen gently.

'God's will? To break a young body like that! Wantonly to take one so young, so full of life and love!'

The Queen's face set into stern lines. 'Your grief has unnerved you, my child. You forget your duty to God. If it is His wish to make us suffer we must accept suffering gladly.'

'Gladly! I will never accept it gladly.'

The Queen hastily crossed herself, while her lips moved in prayer. Isabella thought: She is praying that I may be forgiven my wicked outburst. However much *she* suffered she would never give way to her feelings as I have done.

She was immediately contrite. 'Oh, Mother, forgive me. I know not what I say. It is like that sometimes. The memories come back and then I fear . . .'

'You must pray, my darling, for greater control. It is not God's wish that you should shut yourself away from the world as you do.'

'It is not my father's wish, you mean?' demanded Isabella.

'Neither the wish of your heavenly nor your earthly father,' murmured the Queen soothingly.

'I would to God I could go into a convent. My life finished when his did.'

'You are questioning the will of God. Had He wished you to end your life He would have taken you with your husband. This is your cross, my darling; think of Him and carry it as willingly as He carried His.'

'He had only to die. I have to live.'

'My dearest, have a care. I will double my prayers for you this night and every night. I fear your sufferings have affected your mind. But in time you will forget.'

'It is four years since it happened, Mother. I have not forgotten yet.'

'Four years! It seems long to you because you are young. To me it is like yesterday.'

'To me it will always be as though his death happened yesterday.'

'You must fight against such morbid thoughts, my darling. It is a sin to nurse a grief. I sent for you because I have news for you. Your father-in-law has died and there is a new King of Portugal.'

'Alonso would have been King had he lived . . . and I his Queen.'

'But he did not live, yet you could still be Queen of Portugal.'

'Emanuel . . .'

'My dear daughter, he renews his offer to you. Now that he has come to the throne he does not forget you. He is determined to have no wife but you.'

Emanuel! She remembered him well. Kindly, intelligent, he was more given to study than his gay young cousin Alonso had been; but she had known that he envied Alonso his bride. And now he was asking for her hand once more.

'I would rather go into a nunnery.'

'We might all feel tempted to do that which seems easier to us than our duty.'

'Mother, you are not commanding me to marry Emanuel?'

'You married once, by the command of your father and

myself. I would not command you again; but I would have you consider your duty to your family . . . to Spain.'

Isabella clenched her hands tightly together. 'Do you realise what you are asking of me? To go to Lisbon as I did for Alonso . . . and then to find Emanuel waiting for me and Alonso . . . dead.'

'My child, pray for courage.'

'I pray each day, Mother,' she answered slowly. 'But I cannot go back to Portugal. I can never be anything but Alonso's widow as long as I live.'

The Queen sighed as she drew her daughter down to sit beside her; she put an arm about her and as she rested her face against her hair she was thinking: In time she will be persuaded to go to Portugal and marry Emanuel. We must all do our duty; and though we rebel for a while it avails us little.

❧❧

Ferdinand looked up as the Queen entered. He smiled at her and his expression was slightly sardonic. It amused him that the Franciscan monk who, in his opinion so foolishly, had been offered the Archbishopric of Toledo, should merely have fled at the sight of his title in the Pope's handwriting. This should teach Isabella to think before bestowing great titles on the unworthy. The fellow was uncouth. A pleasant prospect! The Primate of Spain a monk who was more at home in a hermit's hut than a royal Palace. Whereas his dear Alfonso – so handsome, so dashing – what a Primate he would have made! And if he were unsure at any time, his father would have been at hand to help him.

Ferdinand could never look at his son Alfonso without

remembering voluptuous nights spent with his mother. What a woman! And her son was worthy of her.

Fond as he was of young Juan he almost wished that Alfonso was his legitimate son. There was an air of delicacy about Juan, whereas Alfonso was all virility. Ferdinand could be sure that this bastard of his knew how to make the most of his youth, even as his father had done.

It was maddening to think that he could not give him Toledo. What a gift that would have been from father to son.

Still, he did not despair. Isabella might admit her folly now that the monk had run away.

'I have spoken to Isabella,' said the Queen.

'I hope she realises her great good fortune.'

'She does not call it such, Ferdinand.'

'What! Here's Emanuel ready to do a great deal for her.'

'Poor child; can you expect her to *enjoy* returning to the place where she has once been so happy?'

'She'll be happy there again.'

Isabella studied her husband quizzically. Ferdinand would be happy were he in his daughter's place. Such a marriage would mean to him a kingdom. He could not see that it made much difference that the bridegroom would be Emanuel instead of Alonso.

The Queen stifled the sorrow which such a thought roused. It was not for her to feel regrets; she was entirely satisfied with her fate.

'You made our wishes known to her, I hope?' went on Ferdinand.

'I could not command her, Ferdinand. The wound has not yet healed.'

Ferdinand sat down at the polished wood table and beat his

fist on it. 'I understand not such talk,' he said. 'The alliance with Portugal is necessary for Spain. Emanuel wants it. It can bring us great good.'

'Give her a little time,' murmured Isabella; but in such a way that Ferdinand knew that, whatever he wished, their daughter would be given a little time.

He sighed. 'We are fortunate in our children, Isabella,' he said. 'Through them we shall accomplish greatness for Spain. I would we had many more. Ah, if we could have been together more during those early years of our marriage . . .'

'Doubtless you would have had more legitimate sons and daughters,' agreed Isabella.

Ferdinand smiled slyly, but this was not the moment to bring up the matter of Alfonso and the Archbishopric of Toledo.

Instead he said: 'Maximilian is interested in my proposals.'

Isabella nodded sadly. At such times she forgot she was ruler of a great and expanding country; she could only think of herself as a mother.

'They are young yet . . .' she began.

'Young! Juan and Juana are ready for marriage. As for our eldest, she has had time enough in which to play the widow.'

'Tell me what you have heard from Maximilian.'

'Maximilian is willing for Philip to have Juana and for Juan to have Margaret.'

'They would be two of the grandest marriages we could arrange for our children,' mused Isabella. 'But I feel that Juana is as yet too young . . . too unsteady.'

'She will soon be too old, my dear; and she will never be anything but unsteady. No, the time is now. I propose to go ahead with my plans. We will tell them what we propose.

There is no need to look gloomy. I'll warrant Juana will be excited at the prospect. As for your angel son, he'll not have to leave his mother's side. The Archduchess Margaret will come to Juan. So it is only your poor unsteady Juana who will have to go away.'

'I wish we could persuade Philip to come here . . . to live here.'

'What, Maximilian's heir! Oh, these are great matches, these marriages of our son and daughter to Maximilian's. Have you realised that Philip's and Juana's offspring will hold the harbours of Flanders, and in addition will own Burgundy and Luxembourg, to say nothing of Artois and Franche Comté? I would like to see the face of the King of France when he hears of this match. And when Isabella marries Emanuel we shall be able to relax our defences on the Portuguese frontier. Oh yes, I should like to see the French King's face.'

'What do you know of Maximilian's children . . . Philip and Margaret?'

'Nothing but good. Nothing but good.' Ferdinand was rubbing his hands together and his eyes gleamed.

Isabella nodded slowly. Ferdinand was right, of course. Both Juan and Juana were due for marriage. She was allowing the mother to subdue the Queen when she made wild plans to keep her children with her for ever.

Ferdinand had begun to laugh. 'Philip will inherit the Imperial crown. The house of Habsburg will be bound to us. France's Italian projects will have little success when the German dominions stand with us against them.'

He is always a statesman first, thought Isabella, a father second. To him Philip and Margaret are not two human beings – they are the House of Habsburg and the German Dominions.

But she had to admit that his plan was brilliant. Their empire overseas was growing, thanks to their brilliant explorers and adventurers. But Ferdinand's dream had always been of conquests nearer home. He planned to be master of Europe; and why should he not be? Perhaps he would be master of the world.

He was the most ambitious man she had ever known. She had watched his love of power grow with the years. Now she asked herself uneasily whether this had happened because she had found it necessary so often to remind him that she was the Queen of Castile, and in Castile her word should be law. Had his *amour propre* been wounded to such a degree that he had determined to be master of all the world outside Castile?

She said: 'If these marriages were made it would seem that all Europe would be your friend with the exception of that little island – that pugnacious, interfering little island.'

Ferdinand kept his eyes on her face as he murmured: 'You refer to England, do you not, my Queen. I agree with you. That little island can be one of the greatest trouble spots. But I have not forgotten England. Henry Tudor has two sons, Arthur and Henry. It is my desire to marry Arthur, Prince of Wales, to our own little Catalina. Then, my dear, the whole of Europe will be bound to me. And what will the King of France do then? Tell me that.'

'Catalina! She is but a child.'

'Arthur is young also. This will be an ideal match.'

Isabella covered her face with her hands.

'What is the matter with you?' demanded her husband. 'Will you not congratulate your children on having a father who makes such good matches for them?'

Isabella could not speak for a moment. She was thinking of

Juana – wild Juana whose spirits no amount of discipline had been able to subdue – of Juana's being torn from her and sent to the flat, desolate land of Flanders, there to be wife of a man whom she had never seen but who was so suitable because he was the heir of the Habsburgs. But chiefly she thought of Catalina . . . tender little Catalina . . . taken from her family to be the bride of a foreign Prince, to live her life in a bleak island where, if reports were true, the sun rarely shone, and the land was frequently shrouded in mists.

It had to come, she told, herself. I always knew it. But that does not make it any easier to bear now that it is upon me.

The Queen had finished her confession and Ximenes enumerated her penances. She was guilty of allowing her personal feelings to interfere with her duty. It was a weakness of which she had been guilty before. The Queen must forget she is a mother.

Isabella meekly accepted the reproaches of her confessor. He would never stray from the path of duty, she was sure. She looked at his emaciated face, his stern straight lips which she had never seen curved in a smile.

You are a good man, Ximenes, she was thinking; but it is easier for you who have never had children. When I think of my little Catalina's eyes fixed upon me I seem to hear her pleading with me: Don't send me away. I do not want to go to that island of fogs and rains. I shall hate Prince Arthur and he will hate me. And for you, Mother, I have a love such as can never be given to any other person.

'I know, my love, I know,' Isabella whispered. 'If it were in my power . . .'

But her thoughts were straying from her sins and, before she had earned forgiveness, she was falling into temptation once more.

When she next saw Catalina she would remind the child of her duty.

She rose from her knees. Now she was no longer a penitent but the Queen. Regality fell like a cloak about her and she frowned as her eyes rested on the monk.

'My friend,' she said, 'you still refuse the honour I would give you. How much longer will you hold out?'

'Your Highness,' answered Ximenes, 'I could not take office for which I felt myself to be unfitted.'

'Nonsense, Ximenes, you know that the position fits you as a glove. I could command you to accept, you know.'

'If Your Highness should adopt such a measure there would be nothing for me to do but retire to my hut in the forest of Castañar.'

'I believe that is what you wish to do.'

'I think I am more suited to be a hermit than a courtier.'

'We do not ask you to be a courtier, Ximenes, but Archbishop of Toledo.'

'They are one and the same, Your Highness.'

'If *you* took the office I am sure they would be quite different.' Isabella smiled serenely. She was certain that within the next few days Ximenes would accept the Archbishopric of Toledo.

She dismissed him and he went back to the small chamber which he occupied in the Palace. It was like a monk's cell. There was straw on the floor; this was his bed, and his pillow was a log of wood. There would be no fire in this room whatever the weather.

It was said in the Palace: Fray Francisco Ximenes enjoys punishing himself.

As he entered this cell-like apartment he found a Franciscan monk awaiting him there and, as the hood of this newcomer fell back, Ximenes saw that his visitor was his own brother Bernardín.

The grim face of Ximenes was as near to expressing pleasure as it could be. It delighted him that Bernardín had entered the Franciscan brotherhood. Bernardín had been a wild boy and the last thing to have been expected of him was that he should enter the Order.

'Why, brother,' he said, 'well met. What do you do here?'

'I come to pay a call on you. I hear that you are highly thought of at Court.'

'The man who is highly thought of at Court one day is often in disgrace the next.'

'But you are not in disgrace. Is it true that you are to be Archbishop of Toledo?'

Bernardín's eyes sparkled with pleasure, but Ximenes said quickly: 'You have been misinformed. I am not to be Archbishop of Toledo.'

'It can't be true that the post has been offered to you and you refused it! You wouldn't be such a fool.'

'I have refused it.'

'Ximenes! You . . . idiot! You crass . . . stupid . . .'

'Have done. What do you know of these matters?'

'Only what good you could have brought to your family if you had become the most important man in Spain.'

'I feared they had not made a monk of you, Bernardín. Tell me, what advantages should a good Franciscan hope for from the most important man in Spain?'

'You don't expect an answer to such a stupid question. Any man would hope for the highest honours. Whom should an Archbishop honour if not his own family?'

'Is this my brother speaking?'

'Don't be an old hypocrite!' burst out Bernardín. 'Do you think you can hide your true feelings from *me*? You've refused this, have you not? Why? So that you can be pressed more strongly. You'll take it. And then, when you see what power is yours, perhaps you'll give a little something to a needy fellow Franciscan who also happens to be your own brother.'

'I should prefer you to leave me,' said Ximenes. 'I do not like the way you talk.'

'Oh, what a fool I have for a brother!' wailed Bernardín. His expression changed suddenly. 'You have forgotten, have you not, that there are so many wrongs that you can put right. Why, even within our own Order there is much that you dislike. Some of our fellows love luxury too much. You would like to see us all tormenting our bodies with our hair shirts; you would like to see us all using planks as our pillows; starvation should be our lot. Well, it is in your power to bring all these discomforts to us, oh holy brother.'

'Get you gone,' cried Ximenes. 'You are no brother of mine . . . nay, even though our mother bore us both and you wear the habit of the Franciscans.'

Bernardín bowed ironically. 'Even though you are a hypocrite, even though you are so holy that you will not take the honours which would enable you to help your family, it is not a bad thing to be the brother of Francisco Ximenes de Cisneros. Men already are wary how they treat me, and seek my favour.' Bernardín came closer to his brother and whispered: 'They all know that in good time you will not be able to resist this honour. They all know that I, Bernardín de Cisneros, will one day be the brother of the Archbishop of Toledo.'

'They shall not have that gratification,' Ximenes told him.

Bernardín laughed slyly and left his brother. When he was alone Ximenes fell to his knees and began to pray. The temptation was very great.

'Oh Lord,' he murmured, 'if I accepted this great honour there are so many reforms I could bring about. I would work in Thy name. I would work for Thy glory and for that of Spain. Might it not be my duty to accept this honour?

'No, no,' he admonished himself. 'It is temporal power which you are seeking. You want to wear the robes of the Archbishop, to see the people kneel before you.'

But that was not true.

What did he want? He did not know.

'I will never accept the Archbishopric of Toledo!' he said aloud.

It was but a few days later when he was summoned to the Queen's apartment.

Isabella received him with a gracious smile which held a hint of triumph.

She put a document into his hand. 'It is for you, Fray Francisco Ximenes,' she said. 'You will see it is from His Holiness and addressed to you.'

Once more the Pope had addressed Ximenes as Archbishop of Toledo, and this document contained direct instructions from Rome.

There must be no more refusals. Alexander VI wrote from the Vatican that Fray Francisco Ximenes de Cisneros was henceforth Archbishop of Toledo, and any refusal on his part to accept the post would be regarded as disobedience to the Holy See.

The decision had been made for him.

Ximenes wondered whether the feeling he experienced was exultation. The Kingdoms of the world were no longer merely shown to him. He was forced by the Holy Father himself to accept his destiny.

✌⃝✌

Isabella sat with her children. Whenever she could spare the time from her state duties she liked to be with them, and it was comforting to know that they enjoyed this intimacy as she did.

Juan put a shawl about her shoulders. 'There is a draught coming from the window, dear Mother.'

'Thank you, Angel.' She offered a silent prayer of thankfulness because, whoever else was taken from her, Angel would always be near.

Catalina was leaning against her knee, dreamily happy. Poor defenceless little Catalina, who was the baby. Isabella remembered well the day the child had been born, a miserably cold December day in Alcalá de Henares. Little did she think then that this, her fifth child, would be her last.

Juana could not cease chattering. 'Mother, what are the women like in Flanders? They have golden hair, I hear . . . most of them. They are big women with great breasts.'

'Hush, hush!' said the Princess Isabella. She was sitting on her stool, her fingers caressing her rosary. The Queen believed she had been praying. She was constantly praying. And for what? A miracle which would bring her young husband back to life? Was she praying that she would not have to leave home and go once more as a bride to Portugal? Perhaps that would be as much a miracle as the return to life of Alonso would have been.

'But,' cried Juana, 'the Queen said there was to be no cere-mony. There never is ceremony when we are together thus.'

'That is so, my daughter,' said the Queen. 'But it is not seemly to discuss the size of the breasts of the women in your future husband's country.'

'But Mother, why not? Those women might be of the utmost importance to me.'

Has she been hearing tales of this handsome philanderer who is to be her husband? the Queen wondered. How could she? Has she second sight? What strangeness is this in my Juana? How like her grandmother she grows . . . so like that I never look at her without feeling this fear twining itself about my heart like ivy about a tree . . . strangling my contentment.

'You should listen to your sister, Juana,' the Queen said. 'She is older than you and therefore it is very possible that she is wiser.'

Juana snapped her fingers. 'Philip will be a greater King than Alonso ever could have been . . . or Emanuel will be.'

The younger Isabella had risen to her feet; the Queen noticed how she clenched her hands, and the colour flooded into her pale cheeks.

'Be silent, Juana,' commanded the Queen.

'I will not. I will not.' Juana had begun to dance round the room while the others watched her in dismay. None of them would have dreamed of disobeying the Queen. Juana must be bordering on one of her odd moods or she would not have dared.

The Queen's heart had begun to beat wildly but she smiled, outwardly serene. 'We will ignore Juana,' she said, 'until she has learned her manners. Well, Angel, so soon you are to be a husband.'

'I hope I shall be a satisfactory one,' he murmured.

'You will be the most satisfactory husband there ever was,' said Catalina. 'Will he not, Mother?'

'I believe he will,' answered the Queen.

Juana had danced up to them. She had flung herself at her mother's feet and now lay on her stomach, propping her face in her hands.

'Mother, when shall I sail? When shall I sail for Flanders?'

The Queen ignored her and, turning to Catalina, she said: 'You are looking forward to the festivities of your brother's wedding, eh, my child?'

Juana had begun to beat her fist on the floor. 'Mother, when . . . when . . . ?'

'When you have apologised to your sister for what you have said, we shall be ready to talk to you.'

Juana frowned. She glared at Isabella and said: 'Oh, I'm sorry. Philip will be as great a King as Alonso would have been if he had lived. And I'll be as good a Queen as you would have been if Alonso's horse had not kicked him to death.'

The Princess Isabella gave a little cry as she went to the window.

'My dear child,' the Queen patiently said to her wild daughter, 'you must learn to put yourself into the place of others, consider what you are about to say and ask yourself how you would feel if it were being said to you.'

Juana's face crinkled up and she burst out: 'It is no use, Mother. I could never be like Isabella. I don't think Philip could ever be like Alonso either.'

'Come here,' said the Queen and Juana came to her mother.

The Queen put her arms about this daughter who had caused her many a sleepless night. How can I part with her? she asked herself. What will happen to her in a strange country where there will be no one to understand her as I do?

'Juana,' she said, 'I want you to be calm. Soon you will be going among people who do not know you as we do. They may not make allowances as we do. Soon you will be travelling to Flanders with a great fleet of ships. There you will meet your husband Philip, and the ships which take you to him will bring his sister Margaret home for Juan.'

'I shall be left behind in Flanders where the women have big breasts . . . and Philip will be my husband. He will be a great ruler, will he not, Mother . . . greater than Father. Is that possible?'

'It is only at the end of a ruler's life that his greatness can be judged,' murmured the Queen. Her eyes were on her eldest daughter and she knew by the rigid position of her body that she was fighting back her tears.

She took Juana's hand and said: 'There is much you will have to be taught before you go away. It is regrettable that you cannot be as calm as your brother.'

Catalina spoke then. 'But Mother, it is easy for Angel to be calm. He is not going away. His bride will come *here* for him.'

The Queen looked down at the solemn little face of her youngest daughter; and she knew then that the parting with Catalina was going to be the most heartbreaking of them all.

I will not tell her just yet that she is to go to England, she mused. It will be years before she must leave us. There is no point in telling her now.

Ferdinand came into the room and the effect of his presence was immediate. He could not even regard his children without betraying his thoughts of the brilliant future he had planned for them. Now, as his eldest daughter came first to greet him, the Queen knew that he saw her as the link to friendship with Portugal . . . a peaceful frontier which would enable him to continue with greater ease his battles against his old enemies, the French. Now Juan – and Juana. The Habsburg alliance. And Maria. He scarcely glanced her way, for no grand schemes for a profitable alliance had yet formed in his mind regarding her.

The Queen put her hand on Catalina's arm, as though to protect her. Poor little Catalina! She would mean to her father friendship with England. She had been chosen as the bride of Arthur, Prince of Wales, because she was only a year older than he was, and therefore more suitable than Maria who was four years Arthur's senior.

Ferdinand surveyed his family. 'I see you merry,' he said.

Merry! thought the Queen. My poor Isabella with the grief on her face; the resignation of my Angel; the wildness of Juana; the ignorance of Catalina. Is that merriment?

'Well,' went on Ferdinand, 'you have good reason to be!'

'Juana is eager to learn all she can about Flanders,' the Queen said.

'That is well. That is well. You must all be worthy of your good fortune. Isabella is fortunate. She knows Portugal well. How singularly blessed is my eldest daughter. She thought to lose the crown of Portugal and finds it miraculously restored to her.'

The Princess Isabella said: 'I cannot return to Portugal, Father. I could not . . .' She stopped, and there was a short but horrified silence in the room. It was clear that in a few moments the Princess Isabella was going to commit the terrible indiscretion of weeping before the King and Queen.

The Queen said gently: 'You have our leave to retire, daughter.' Isabella threw her mother a grateful glance and curtsied.

'But first . . .' Ferdinand was beginning.

'Go now, my dear,' interrupted the Queen firmly, and she did not look at the angry lights which immediately shot up in Ferdinand's eyes.

For the sake of her children, as for her country, Isabella was ready to face the wrath of her husband.

Ferdinand burst out: 'It is time that girl was married. The life she leads here is unnatural. She is continually at her prayers. What does she pray for? Convent walls! She should be praying for children!'

The children were subdued with the exception of Juana, in whom any conflict aroused excitement.

'I am praying for children already, Father,' she cried.

'Juana,' warned her mother; but Ferdinand gave a low laugh.

'That's well enough. You cannot start your prayers too early. And what of my youngest daughter? Is she eager to learn the manners of England?'

Catalina was staring at her father in frank bewilderment.

'Eh, child?' he went on, looking at her lovingly. Little Catalina, the youngest, only ten years old – and yet so important to her father's schemes.

Isabella had drawn her little daughter close to her. 'Our youngest daughter's marriage is years away,' she said. 'Why, Catalina need not think of England for many a year.'

'It will not be so long,' declared Ferdinand. 'Henry is an impatient man. He might even ask that she be educated over there. He'll be wanting to turn her into a little Englishwoman at the earliest possible moment.'

Isabella felt the tremor run through her daughter's body. She wondered what she could do to appease her. That it should have been broken like this! There were times when she had to restrain her anger against this husband who could be so impetuous in some matters, so cold blooded in others.

Could he not see the stricken look in the child's face now? Could he not understand its meaning?

'I have a little matter to discuss with your mother,' he went on. 'You may all leave us.'

The children came forward in order of seniority and took their leave of their parents. The coming of Ferdinand into the apartment had brought with it the return of ceremony.

Little Catalina was last. Isabella leaned towards her and patted her cheek. Those big dark eyes were bewildered; and the fear was already beginning to show in them.

'I will come to you later, my child,' whispered the Queen, and for a moment the fear lifted. It was as it had been in the days of the child's extreme youth when she had suffered some slight pain. 'Mother will come and make it well.' It was always so with Catalina. Her mother's presence had such an effect on her that its comfort could always soothe her pain.

Ferdinand was smiling the crafty smile which indicated that he had some fresh scheme afoot and was congratulating himself on its shrewdness.

'Ferdinand,' said Isabella when they were alone, 'that is the first indication that Catalina has had that she is to go to England.'

'Is that so?'

'It was a shock to her.'

'H'm. She'll be Queen of England one day. I can scarcely wait to get those marriages performed. When I think of the great good which can come to our country through these alliances I thank God that I have five children and wish I had five more. But it was not of this that I came to speak to you. This man Ximenes . . . this Archbishop of yours . . .'

'And yours, Ferdinand.'

'Mine! I'd never give my consent to setting up a humble monk in the highest office in Spain. It has occurred to me that, as a humble man who will suddenly find himself a very rich one, he will not know how to manage great riches.'

'You can depend upon it, he will not change his mode of life. He will give more to the poor, I'll swear, and I believe it has always been a great dream of his to build a University at Alcalá and to compile a polyglot Bible.'

Ferdinand made an impatient gesture. There came into his eyes that acquisitive gleam which Isabella now knew so well and which told her that he was thinking of the rich revenues of Toledo, and she guessed that he had some scheme for diverting them from the Archbishop to himself.

'Such a man,' said Ferdinand, 'would not know what to do with such a fortune. It would embarrass him. He prefers to live his hermit's life. Why should we prevent him? I am going to offer him two or three *cuentos* a year for his personal expenses, and I do not see why the rest of the revenues of Toledo should not be used for the good of the country generally.'

Isabella was silent.

'Well?' demanded Ferdinand impatiently.

'Have you put this matter before the Archbishop?' she asked.

'I thought it would be wiser if we did so together. I have sent for him to come to us. He should be here very shortly. I shall expect you to support me in this.'

Isabella did not speak. She was thinking: I shall soon need to oppose him with regard to Catalina. I shall not allow him to send my daughter away from home for some years. We must not continually pull one against the other. The Archbishop, I am sure, is more able to fight his battles than my little Catalina.

'Well?' repeated Ferdinand.

'I will see the Archbishop with you and hear what he has to say on this matter.'

'I need money . . . badly,' went on Ferdinand. 'If I am going to pursue the Italian wars with any success I must have more men and arms. If we are not to suffer defeat at the hands of the French . . .'

'I know,' said Isabella. 'The question is, is this the right way to get the money you need?'

'Any way to get the money for such a purpose is the right way,' Ferdinand sternly told her.

It was shortly afterwards when Ximenes came to the apartment.

'Ah, Archbishop!' Ferdinand stressed the title almost ironically. Anyone looking less like an Archbishop there could not possibly be. Why, in the day of Mendoza the title had carried much dignity. Isabella was a fool to have bestowed it on a half-starved holy man.

'Your Highnesses,' murmured Ximenes, making obeisance before them.

'His Highness the King has a suggestion to make to you, Ximenes,' said the Queen.

The pale eyes were turned on Ferdinand, and even he felt a little disturbed by their cold stare. It was disconcerting to come face to face with someone who was not in fear of one. There was nothing this man feared. You could strip him of office and he would shrug his shoulders; you could take him to the faggots and set them alight and he would delight in his agony.

Yes, it was certainly disturbing for a King, before whom men trembled, to find one so careless of his authority as Ximenes.

'Ah,' Ferdinand was blustering in spite of himself, 'the Queen and I have been speaking of you. You are clearly a man of simple tastes, and you find yourself burdened with great revenues. We have decided that you shall not be burdened with these. We propose to take them from you and administer them for the good of the country. You shall receive an adequate allowance for your household and personal expenses . . .'

Ferdinand stopped, for Ximenes had lifted a hand as though demanding silence; he might have been the sovereign and Ferdinand his subject.

'Your Highness,' said Ximenes, addressing himself to Ferdinand, for he knew that this was entirely his idea, 'I will tell you this. It was with great reluctance that I accepted my Archbishopric. Nothing but the express orders of the Holy Father could induce me to do so. But I have accepted it. Therefore I will do my duty as I see it should be done. I know that I shall need these resources if I am to care for the souls in my charge. And I must say this without more ado: If I remain in this post I and my Church must be free; and what is mine must be left to my jurisdiction, in much the same way as Your Highness has charge of your kingdoms.'

Ferdinand's face was white with anger. He said: 'I had thought that your mind was on holy matters, Archbishop, but it seems it is not unaffected by your revenues.'

'My mind is on my duty, Your Highness. If you persist in taking the revenues of Toledo you must also remove its Archbishop from his post. What has Her Highness the Queen to say of this matter?'

Isabella said quietly: 'It must be as you wish, Archbishop. We must find other means for meeting the requirements of the state.'

Ximenes bowed. 'Have I your leave to retire, Your Highnesses?'

'You have our leave,' answered Isabella.

When he had gone she waited for the storm to break. Ferdinand had gone to the window; his fists were clenched and she knew that he was fighting to control his anger.

'I am sorry, Ferdinand,' she said, 'but you cannot rob him of his rights. The revenues are his; you cannot take them merely because he is a man of holy habits.'

Ferdinand turned and faced her. 'Once again, Madam,' he said, 'you give an example of your determination to thwart and flout me.'

'When I do not fall in with your wishes it is always with the utmost regret.'

Ferdinand bit his lips to hold back the words which were struggling to be spoken. She was right, of course. She was indeed happy when they were in agreement. It was her perpetual conscience which came between them. 'Holy Mother,' he murmured, 'why did you give me such a *good* woman for my wife? Her eternal conscience, her devotion to duty, even when it is opposed to our good, is the cause of continual friction between us.'

It was no use being angry with Isabella. She was as she always had been.

He said in such a low voice that she could scarcely hear him: 'That man and I will be enemies as long as we live.'

'No, Ferdinand,' pleaded Isabella. 'That must not be. You both wish to serve Spain. Let that be a bond between you.

What does it matter if you look at your duty from different angles when the object is the same?'

'He is insolent, this Archbishop of Toledo!'

'You must not blame Ximenes because he was chosen instead of your natural son, Ferdinand.'

Ferdinand snapped his fingers. 'That! That is forgotten. Have I not grown accustomed to seeing my wishes disregarded? It is the man himself . . . the holy man, who starves himself . . . and walks the Palace in his grubby serge. I think of Mendoza's day . . .'

'Mendoza is dead now, Ferdinand. This is the day of Ximenes.'

'The pity of it!' murmured Ferdinand; and Isabella was wondering how she was going to keep her husband and her Archbishop from crossing each other's paths.

But her mind was not really on Ximenes, nor on Ferdinand. From the moment Catalina had left the apartment with her brother and sisters she had been thinking of the child.

She must go to her without delay. She must explain to her that marriage into England was a long way off.

'I do not believe,' said Ferdinand, 'that you are giving me your attention.'

'I was thinking of our daughter, of Catalina. I am going to her now to tell her that I shall not allow her to leave us until she is much older.'

'Do not make rash promises.'

'I shall make none,' said Isabella. 'But I must comfort her. I know how badly she needs such comfort.'

With that she left him, frustrated as he so often was, admiring her as he had such reason for doing, realising that although she often exasperated him beyond endurance he owed a great deal to her of what was his.

He thought ruefully that she would seek to protect Catalina from his marriage plans in the same way as she had stubbornly refused to give Toledo to his son Alfonso. Yet he was bound to her as she was to him. They were one; they were Spain.

Isabella was thinking only of her daughter as she hastened to the children's apartments. It was as she had expected: Catalina was alone. The child lay on her bed and her face was buried in the pillows as though, thought Isabella tenderly, by hiding her eyes she need not see what was too unpleasant to be borne.

'My little one,' whispered the Queen.

Catalina turned, and her face was illumined with sudden joy.

Isabella lay down and took the child in her arms. For a few moments Catalina clung childishly to her mother as though by doing so she could bind them together for ever.

'I did not mean you to know for a long, long time,' whispered the Queen.

'Mother . . . when shall I go away from you?'

'My dearest, it will not be for years.'

'But my father said . . .'

'Oh, he is an impatient man. He loves his daughters so much and is so happy in the possession of them that he longs to see them with children of their own. He forgets how young you are. A little girl of ten to be married!'

'Sometimes they are taken away from their mothers to live in foreign courts . . . the courts of their bridegrooms.'

'You shall not leave me for many years. I promise you.'

'How many, Mother?'

'Not until you are grown up and ready for marriage.'

Catalina snuggled closer to her mother. 'That is a long, long time. That is four years, or five years perhaps.'

'It is indeed. So you see how foolish it would be to worry now over what may happen in four or five years' time. Why, by then you will be almost a woman, Catalina . . . wanting a husband of your own perhaps, not so eager to cling to your mother.'

'I shall always cling to my mother!' Catalina declared passionately.

'Ah,' sighed Isabella, 'we shall see.'

And they lay silently side by side. Catalina was comforted. To her, four or five years seemed an eternity. But to her mother it seemed a very little time.

But the purpose was achieved, the blow was softened. Isabella would talk to her young daughter about England. She would discover all she could about the Tudor King who, some said, had usurped the throne of England. Though of course it would be well if the child did not hear such gossip as that. She would talk to her about the King's children, the eldest of whom was to be her husband . . . a boy a year younger than herself. What was there to fear in that? There was another boy, Henry; and two girls, Margaret and Mary. She would soon learn their ways and in time forget about her Spanish home.

That was not true, she knew. Catalina would never forget.

She is closer to me than any of the others, I believe, thought Isabella. How happy I should be if this English marriage came to nothing and I were able to keep my little Catalina at my side until the day I die.

She did not mention such a thought. It was unworthy of the Queen of Spain and the mother of Catalina. At this time it seemed that Catalina's destiny lay with the English. As a daughter of Spain, Catalina would have to do her duty.

❧ Chapter II ❧

XIMENES AND TORQUEMADA

The cavalcade had come to rest at last in the port of Laredo which stood on the eastern borders of the Asturias. During the journey from Madrid to Laredo the Queen's anxieties had kept pace with her daughter's increasing excitement.

Isabella had determined to remain with Juana until that moment when she left Spanish soil. She would have liked to accompany her all the way to Flanders, for she was very fearful of what would await her wild daughter there.

Isabella had left her family and her state duties to be with her daughter, and during that long and often tedious journey she had never ceased to pray for Juana's future and to ask herself continually: What will become of her when she reaches Flanders?

Isabella had spent a night on board that ship in which Juana would sail. She now stood on deck with her daughter, awaiting the moment of departure when she must say farewell to Juana. About them was a fine array of ships, a fleet worthy of the Infanta's rank which would carry her to Flanders and bring back the Archduchess Margaret to be Juan's bride. There were a hundred and twenty ships in this magnificent armada, some large, some small. They carried means of defending themselves, for they had been made ready to fight against the French. Ferdinand, however, had been willing to put them to this use, because in conveying his unstable daughter to Flanders they were prosecuting the war against the French as certainly as if they went into battle.

Ferdinand himself was not with them on this occasion. He had gone to Catalonia to make ready for an attack on the French. Isabella was rather pleased that she was alone to say goodbye to Juana. So great were her anxieties that she could not have borne to see the pleasure which she knew would shine from her husband's eyes as he watched their daughter's departure.

Juana turned to her mother, her eyes sparkling, and cried: 'To think that all that is for me!'

Isabella continued to look at the ships, because she could not bear to look into her daughter's face at that moment. She knew that she was going to be reminded of her own mother, who was living out her clouded existence at the castle at Arevalo, unable to distinguish between past and present, raging now and then against those who were long since dead and had no power to harm her. There had been times when Isabella had dreaded her mother's outbreaks of violence, even as she now dreaded those of her daughter.

How will she fare with Philip? was another question she asked herself. Will he be kind to her? Will he understand?

'It is a goodly sight,' murmured the Queen.

'How long before I reach Flanders, Mother?'

'So much will depend on the weather.'

'I hope there will be storms.'

'Oh, my child, no! We must pray for calm seas and a good wind.'

'I should like to be delayed a little. I should like Philip to be waiting for me . . . rather impatiently.'

'He will be waiting for you,' murmured the Queen.

Juana clasped her hands across her breasts. 'I long for him, Mother,' she said. 'I have heard that he is handsome. Did you know that people are beginning to call him Philip the Handsome?'

'It is pleasant to have a handsome bridegroom.'

'He likes to dance and be gay. He likes to laugh. He is the most fascinating man in Flanders.'

'You are fortunate, my dear. But remember, he is fortunate too.'

'He must think so. He *shall* think so.'

Juana had begun to laugh; it was the laughter of excitement and intense pleasure.

'Soon it will be time to say goodbye,' said the Queen quickly. She turned impulsively to her daughter and embraced her, praying as she did so: 'Oh God, let something happen to keep her with me. Let her not go on this long and hazardous journey.'

But what was she thinking! This was the grandest marriage Juana could have made. It was the curse of Queens that their daughters were merely lent to them during their childhood. She must always remember this.

Juana was wriggling in the Queen's arms. It was not her mother's embrace that she wanted; it was that of her husband.

Will she be too eager, too passionate? wondered the Queen. And Philip – what sort of man is he? How I wish I could have met him, had a word with him, warned him that Juana is not quite like other girls.

'Look!' cried Juana. 'The Admiral is coming to us.'

It was true. Don Fadrique Enriquez, Admiral of Castile, had appeared on deck and Isabella knew that the moment was at hand when she must say goodbye.

'Juana,' she said, grasping her daughter's hands and forcing the girl to look at her, 'you must write to me often. You must never forget that my great desire is to help you.'

'Oh no, I will not forget.' But she was not really listening. She was dreaming of 'Philip the Handsome', the most attractive man in Europe. As soon as this magnificent armada had carried her to Flanders she would be his wife, and she was impatient of everything that kept her from him. She was already passionately in love with a bridegroom whom she had never seen. The desire which rose within her was driving her to such a frenzy that she felt that if she could not soon satisfy it she would scream out her frustration.

The ceremony of the farewell was almost more than she could endure. She did not listen to her mother's gentle advice; she was unaware of the Queen's anxiety. There was only one need within her: this overwhelming hunger for Philip.

Isabella did not leave Laredo until the armada had passed out of sight. Then only did she turn away, ready for the journey back to Madrid.

'God preserve her,' she prayed. 'Give her that extra care which my poor Juana so desperately needs.'

※

Young Catalina was watching for her mother's return.

This, she thought, is what will happen to me one day. My mother will accompany me to the coast. Perhaps not to Laredo. To what town would one go to embark for England?

Juana had gone off gaily. Her shrill laughter had filled the Palace during her last days there. She had sung and danced and talked continually of Philip. She was shameless in the way she talked of him. It was not the way Catalina would ever talk of Arthur, Prince of Wales.

But I will not think of it, Catalina told herself. It is far away. My mother will not let me go for years and years . . . even if the King of England does say he wishes me to be brought up as an English Princess.

Her sister Isabella came into the room and said: 'Still watching, Catalina?'

'It seems so long since Mother went away.'

'You will know soon enough when she returns. Watching will not bring her.'

'Isabella, do you think Juana will be happy in Flanders?'

'I do not think Juana will be happy and contented anywhere.'

'Poor Juana. She believes she will live happily for ever when she is married to Philip. He is so handsome, she says. They even call him Philip the Handsome.'

'It is better to have a good husband than a handsome one.'

'I am sure Prince Arthur is good. He is only a boy yet. It will be years before he marries. And Emanuel is good too, Isabella.'

'Yes,' agreed Isabella, 'Emanuel is good.'

'Are you going to marry him?'

Isabella shook her head and turned away.

'I am sorry I mentioned it, Isabella,' said Catalina. 'It reminds you, doesn't it?'

Isabella nodded.

'Yes,' said Catalina, 'you were happy, were you not? Perhaps it was better to have found Alonso such a good husband even though he died so soon . . . better than to have married a husband whom you hated and who was unkind to you.'

Isabella looked thoughtfully at her young sister. 'Yes,' she said, 'it was better than that.'

'And you have seen Emanuel. You know him well. You know he is kind. So, Isabella, if you should have to marry him, perhaps you will not be so very unhappy. Portugal is near home . . . whereas . . .'

Isabella suddenly forgot her own problems and looked into the anxious eyes of her little sister. She put her arm about her and held her tightly.

'England is not so very far away either,' she said.

'I have a fear,' Catalina answered slowly, 'that once I am there I shall never come back . . . never see you all again. That is what I think would be so hard to bear . . . never to see you and Juan, Maria and our father . . . and mother . . . never to see *Mother* . . .'

'I thought that. But, you see, I came back. Nothing is certain, so it is foolish to say "I shall never come back." How can you be sure?'

'I shall not say it. I shall say: "I *will* come back," because only if I did could I bear to go.'

Isabella put her sister from her and went to the window. Catalina followed.

They saw two men riding fast up the slope to the Palace.

Catalina sighed with disappointment, because she knew they were not of the Queen's party.

'We shall soon discover who they are,' said Isabella. 'Let us go to Juan. The messengers will have been taken to him if they have important news.'

When they reached Juan's apartments, the messengers had already been conducted to him and he was ordering that they be taken away and given refreshments.

'What is the news?' Isabella asked.

'They come from Arevalo,' said Juan. 'Our grandmother is very ill and calls constantly for our mother.'

⧈⧈

The Queen entered the familiar room, the memory of which she felt would haunt her with sadness for as long as she lived.

As soon as she had arrived at Madrid she had set out for Arevalo, praying that she would not be too late and yet half hoping that she would be.

In her bed lay the Dowager Queen of Castile, Isabella's ambitious mother, that Princess of Portugal who had suffered from the scourge of her family and whose mental aberrations had darkened her daughter's life.

It was because of her mother that Isabella felt those shocks of terror every time she noticed some fresh wildness in her daughter Juana. Had this madness in the royal blood passed one generation to flower in the next?

'Is that Isabella . . .?'

The blank eyes were staring upwards, but they did not see the Queen, who leaned over the bed. They saw instead the little girl Isabella had been when her future was the greatest concern in the world to this mother.

'Mother, dear Mother. I am here,' whispered Isabella.

'Alfonso, is that you, Alfonso?'

One could not say: Alfonso is dead, Mother . . . dead these many years. We do not know how he died, but we believe he was poisoned.

49

'He is the true King of Castile . . .'

'Oh, Mother, Mother,' whispered Isabella, 'it is all so long ago. Ferdinand and I rule all Spain now. I became more than the Queen of Castile.'

'I do not trust him . . .' the tortured woman cried.

Isabella laid a hand on her mother's clammy forehead. She called to one of the attendants. 'Bring scented water. I would bathe her forehead.'

The sick woman began to laugh. It was hideous laughter, reminding Isabella of those days when she and her young brother, Alfonso, had lived here in this gloomy palace of Arevalo with a mother who lost a little more of her reason with the passing of each day.

Isabella took the bowl of water from the attendant.

'Go now and leave me with her,' she said; and she herself bathed her mother's forehead.

The laughter had lost its wildness. Isabella listened to the harsh breathing.

It could not be long now. She would call in the priests who would administer the last rites. But what would this sadly deranged, dying woman know of that? She had no idea that she was living through her last hours; she believed that she was a young woman again, fighting desperately for the throne of Castile that she might bestow it upon her son Alfonso or her daughter Isabella.

Still it was just possible that she might realise that it was Extreme Unction that was being administered; she might for a few lucid seconds understand the words of the priest.

Isabella stood up and beckoned one of the attendants who had been hovering in a corner of the apartment.

'Your Highness . . .' murmured the woman.

'My mother is sinking fast,' said Isabella. 'Call the priests. They should be with her.'

'Yes, Highness.'

Isabella went back to the bed and waited.

The Dowager Queen Isabella was lying back on her pillows, her eyes closed, her lips moving; and her daughter, trying to pray for her mother's soul, could only find the words intruding into her prayers: 'Oh God, You have made Juana so like her. I pray You, take care of my daughter.'

❧❧

Catalina was eagerly awaiting the return of her mother from Arevalo, but it was long before she could be alone with her.

Since the little girl had learned that she was to go to England she could not spend enough time in her mother's company. Isabella understood this and made a point of summoning Catalina to her presence whenever this was possible.

Now she dismissed everyone and kept Catalina with her; the joy on the face of the child was rewarding enough; it moved Isabella deeply.

Isabella made Catalina bring her stool and sit at her feet. This, Catalina was happy to do; she sat leaning her head against her mother's skirts, and Isabella let her fingers caress her youngest daughter's thick chestnut hair.

'Did it seem long that I was away then?' she asked.

'So long, Mother. First you went away with Juana, and then as soon as you had returned you must leave for Arevalo.'

'We have had little time together for so long. We must make up for it. I rejoiced to be with my mother for a little while before she died.'

'You are unhappy, Mother.'

'Are you surprised that I should be unhappy now that I have no mother? You who, I believe, love your own mother, can understand that, can you not?'

'Oh yes. But your mother was not as *my* mother.'

Isabella smiled. 'Oh, Catalina, she has caused me such anxieties.'

'I know it, Mother. I hope never to cause you one little anxiety.'

'If you did it would be solely because I loved you so well. You would never do aught, I know, to distress me.'

Catalina caught her mother's hand and kissed it fiercely. Such emotion frightened Isabella.

I must strengthen her, this tender little child, she thought.

'Catalina,' she said, 'you are old enough to know that my mother was kept a prisoner, more or less, at Arevalo because . . . because her mind was not . . . normal. She was unsure of what was really happening. She did not know whether I was a woman or a little girl like you. She did not know that I was the Queen but thought that my little brother was alive and that he was the heir to Castile.'

'Did she . . . frighten you?'

'When I was young I was frightened. I was frightened of her wildness. I loved her, you see, and I could not bear that she should suffer so.'

Catalina nodded. She enjoyed these confidences; she knew that something had happened to make her relationship with her mother even more poignantly precious. This had taken place when she had discovered she was destined to go to England; and she believed that the Queen did not want her to go as an ignorant child. She wanted her to understand something of the world so that she would be able to make her own decisions, so that she would be able to control her emotions – in fact, so that she would be a grown-up person able to take care of herself.

'Juana is like her,' said Catalina.

The Queen caught her breath. She said quickly: 'Juana is too high spirited. Now that she is to have a husband she will be more controlled.'

'But my grandmother had a husband; she had children; and she was not controlled.'

The Queen was silent for a few seconds, then she said: 'Let us pray together for Juana.'

She took Catalina's hand and they went into that small ante-room where Isabella had set up an altar; and there they knelt and prayed not only for the safe journey of Juana but for her safe and sane passage through life.

Afterwards they went back to the apartment and Catalina sat once more on her stool at the Queen's feet.

'Catalina,' said Isabella, 'I hope you will be friends with the Archduchess Margaret when she comes. We must remember that she will be a stranger among us.'

'I wonder whether she is frightened,' Catalina whispered, trying not to think of herself setting out on a perilous journey across the sea to England.

'She is sixteen years old, and she comes to a strange country to marry a young man whom she has never seen. She does not know that in our Juan she will have the kindest, dearest husband anyone could have. She has yet to learn how fortunate she is. But while she is discovering this I want you and your sisters to be very kind to her.'

'I shall, Mother.'

'I know you will.'

'I would do anything you asked of me . . . gladly I would do it if you commanded me.'

'I know it, my precious daughter. And when the time comes for you to leave me you will do so with good courage in your heart. You will know, will you not, that wherever I am and wherever you are, I shall never forget you as long as I live.'

Catalina's lips were trembling as she answered: 'I will never forget it. I will always do my duty as you would have me do it. I shall not whimper.'

'I shall be proud of you. Now take your lute, my dearest, and play to me awhile; for very soon we shall be interrupted. But never mind, I shall steal away from state duties and be with you whenever it is possible. Play to me now, my dearest.'

So Catalina brought her lute and played; but even the gayest tunes sounded plaintive because Catalina could not dismiss from her mind the thought that time passed quickly and the day must surely come when she must set out for England.

❧❦

Those were sad weeks for the Queen. She was in deep mourning for her mother, and there had been such tempests at sea that she feared for the safety of the armada which was escorting Juana to Flanders.

News came that the fleet had had to put into an English port because some of the ships had suffered damage during the tempest. Isabella wondered how Don Fadrique Enriquez was managing to keep the wild Juana under control. It would not be easy and the sooner she was married to Philip the better.

But travelling by sea was a hazardous affair and it might well be that Juana would never reach her destination.

A storm at sea might rob Ferdinand of his dearest dream. If Juana were lost on her way to Flanders, and Margaret on her way to Spain, that would be the end of the proposed Habsburg alliance. Isabella could only think of the dangers to her children, and her prayers were constant.

She tried to concentrate on other matters, but it was not easy to shut out the thought of Juana in peril; and since the recent death of her mother she had had bad dreams in which the sick woman of Arevalo often changed into the unstable Juana.

She was fortunate, she told herself, in her Archbishop of Toledo. Others might rail against him, criticise him because he had taken all the colour and glitter from his office, because he was as stern and unrelenting in his condemnation of others as he was of himself. But for him Isabella had that same admiration which she had had – and still had – for Tomás de Torquemada.

Tomás had firmly established the Holy Inquisition in the land, and Ximenes would do his utmost to maintain it. They were two of a kind and men whom Isabella – as sternly devout as they were themselves – wished to have about her.

She knew that Ximenes was introducing reforms in the Order to which he belonged. It had always seemed deplorable to him that many monks, who appeared in the Franciscan robes, did not follow the rules which had been set down for them by their Founder. They loved good living; they feasted and drank good wine; they loved women, and it was said that many of them were the fathers of illegitimate children. This was something to rouse fury in a man such as Ximenes and, like Torquemada, he was not one to shrug aside the weaknesses of others.

Therefore Isabella was not entirely surprised when, one day

while she mourned her mother and waited anxiously for news of Juana's safe arrival in Flanders, she found herself confronted by the General of the Franciscan Order who had come from Rome especially to see her.

She received him at once and invited him to tell her his grievance.

'Your Highness,' he cried, 'my grievance is this: the Archbishop of Toledo seeks to bring reforms into our Order.'

'I know it, General,' murmured the Queen. 'He would have you all following the rules laid down by your Founder. He himself follows those rules and he deems it the duty of all Franciscans to do the same.'

'His high position has gone to his head, I fear,' said the General.

The Queen smiled gently. She knew that the General was a Franciscan of the Conventual Order while Ximenes belonged to the Observatines, a sect which believed it should follow the ways of the Founder in every detail. The Conventuals had broken away from these rigid rules, believing that they need not live the lives of monks to do good in the world. They were good-livers, some of these Conventuals, and Isabella could well understand and sympathise with the desire of Ximenes to abolish their rules and force them to conform with the laws of the Observatines.

'I crave Your Highness's support,' he went on. 'I ask you to inform the Archbishop that he would be better employed attending to his duties than making trouble within the Order of which he is honoured to be a member.'

'The Archbishop's conduct is a matter for his own conscience,' said Isabella.

The General forgot he was in the presence of the Queen of

Spain. He cried out: 'What folly is this! To take such a man and set him up in the highest position in Spain! Archbishop of Toledo! The right hand of the King and Queen. A man who is more at home in a forest hut than in a Palace. A man without ability, without noble birth. Your Highness should remove him immediately from this high office and put someone there who is worthy of the honour.'

'I think,' said Isabella quietly, 'that you are mad. Have you forgotten to whom you speak?'

'I am not mad,' replied the General. 'I know I am speaking to Queen Isabella – she who will one day be a handful of dust . . . even as I or anyone else.'

With that he turned from her and hurried out of the room.

Isabella was overcome by astonishment, but she did not seek to punish this man.

She was astounded though at the hatred which Ximenes engendered, but she was more certain than she had ever been that, in making him Archbishop of Toledo, she had made a wise choice.

≈❧≈

Francisco Ximenes de Cisneros lay in his bed in his house at Alcalá de Henares. He preferred this simpler dwelling to the Palace which could have been his home at Toledo, and there were often times when he yearned for his hermit's hut in the forest of Our Lady of Castañar.

His thoughts were now on Bernardín, that erring brother of his who would come to him soon; he had sent for him and he did not believe even Bernardín would dare disobey.

It was disconcerting to have to receive his brother while in bed, but he was now enduring one of his spells of illness, which some said were due to his meagre diet and the rigorous life he led. He spent most of his time in a cell-like room, the floor of which was uncovered and which he kept unheated during the coldest weather. He felt great need to inflict punishment on himself.

It was true that he now lay in this luxurious bed, because here he must receive those who came to see him on matters of State and Church. At night he would leave this luxury and lie on his hard pallet bed with a log for his pillow.

He longed to torture his body, and deplored the fact that orders had come from the Pope commanding him to accept the dignity of his office. There had been many to lay complaints against him. They complained because he was often seen in his shabby Franciscan robe, which he had patched with his own hands. Was this the way for the Archbishop of Toledo to conduct himself? many demanded.

It was useless to tell them that it was the way of a man who wished to follow in the footsteps of his Master.

But instructions had come from Rome.

'Dear brother,' Alexander had written, 'the Holy and Universal Church, as you know, like heavenly Jerusalem, has many and diverse adornments. It is wrong to seek them too earnestly, so it is also wrong to reject them too contemptuously. Each state of life has its appropriate conditions, which are pleasing to God and worthy of praise. Everyone, therefore, especially prelates of the Church, must avoid arrogance by excessive display, and superstition by excessive humility; for in both cases the authority of the Church will be weakened. Wherefore we exhort and advise you to order your life suitably to the rank which you hold; and since the Holy Father has raised you from humble station to that of Archbishop, it is reasonable that as you live in your conscience according to the rules of God (at which we feel great joy), so in your external life you should maintain the dignity of your rank.'

That was the command of the Pope and not to be ignored. So Ximenes had since worn the magnificent garments of an Archbishop, though beneath them had been the robe of the Franciscan, and beneath that the hair shirt itself.

Ximenes felt that there was something symbolic about the manner in which his emaciated body appeared to the public. The people saw the Archbishop, but beneath the Archbishop was the real man, the Franciscan friar.

But which was the real man? Often his fingers itched to deal with problems of State. He longed to see Spain great among the nations and himself at the helm guiding the great ship of state from one triumph to another until the whole world was under the domination of Spain . . . or Ximenes.

'Ah,' he would cry swiftly when such a thought came to him. 'It is because I wish to see the Christian flag flying over all the Earth.' He wished all lands to be governed as Spain was being governed since Torquemada had set the fires of the Inquisition burning in almost every town.

But now his thoughts must turn to Bernardín, for soon his brother would be with him and he would have to speak to him with the utmost sternness.

He rehearsed the words he would say: 'You are my brother, but that does not mean that I shall treat you with especial leniency. You know my beliefs. I hate nepotism. I shall never allow it to be used in any of my concerns.'

And Bernardín would stand smiling at him in that lazy cynical way of his, as though he were reminding his powerful brother that he did not always live up to his own rigid code.

It was true that he had made exceptions. There was the case of Bernardín for one. He had taken him into his household with a lucrative post as steward. What folly!

'Yet this was my brother,' said Ximenes aloud.

And how had Bernardín shown his gratitude? By giving himself airs, by stirring up trouble, by extricating himself from those difficult situations which were of his own making, by truculently reminding those who sought justice: 'I am the brother of the Archbishop of Toledo. I am greatly favoured by him. If you dare to bring any complaints against me, it will go ill with you.'

'Oh shame!' cried Ximenes. 'This was the very weakness I deplore in others.'

And what had he done with Bernardín? Banished him to a monastery, and there Bernardín had drawn up complaints against his brother in which he had been supported by the Archbishop's enemies – who were numerous.

There had been nothing to do but send Bernardín to prison. And how his conscience had suffered. 'My own brother . . . in prison?' he had demanded of himself. 'Yes, but he deserves his fate,' was the answer. 'Your own brother! Oh, it is only little Bernardín who was always one for mischief.'

So he had brought him out of prison and taken him back as a steward, and had talked to him sternly, imploring him to lead a better life.

But what had been the use? Bernardín would not mend his ways. It had not been long before news had come to Ximenes that his brother had interfered with the justice of the Courts, threatening that if a judge did not give a certain verdict he would incur the displeasure of the Archbishop of Toledo.

This was the final disaster. For this reason he had sent for Bernardín, for all his peccadilloes of the past seemed slight compared with this interference with the justice of the Courts.

Ximenes raised himself and called Francisco Ruiz.

His nephew came hurrying to his bedside. How he wished that his brother were like this trustworthy man.

'Francisco, when Bernardín comes, have him brought to me at once and leave us together.'

Ruiz bowed his head and, when Ximenes waved a hand, immediately left the sickroom.

'I would be alone,' Ximenes said gently as he went. 'I want to pray.'

He was still praying when Bernardín was brought to him.

Ximenes opened his eyes and regarded his wayward brother, looking in vain for a sign of penitence in Bernardín's face.

'Well, brother,' said Ximenes, 'as you see I have been forced to take to my bed.'

'I pray you do not ask for my sympathy,' cried Bernardín. 'You are ill because of this ridiculous life you lead. You could be well and strong if you allowed yourself to live in comfort.'

'I have not summoned you to me that you may advise me on *my* way of life, Bernardín, but to remonstrate with you regarding your own.'

'And what sins have I committed now?'

'You will know so much better than I.'

'In your eyes, brother, all human actions are sin.'

'Not all, Bernardín.'

'All mine. Your own, of course, are virtues.'

'I found it necessary recently to have you imprisoned.'

Bernardín's eyes glittered and he came nearer to the bed. 'Do not attempt to do such a thing again. I swear to you that if you do you will live to regret the day.'

'Your threats would never make me swerve from my duty, Bernardín.'

Bernardín leaned over the bed and seized Ximenes roughly by the shoulder. Ximenes tried to throw him off but failed to do so and lay panting helplessly on his pillows.

Bernardín laughed aloud. 'Why, 'tis not I who am at your mercy, but you at mine. What is the Archbishop of Toledo but a skin full of bones! You are sick, brother. Why, I could put these two hands of mine about your neck and press and press . . . In a matter of seconds the Sovereigns would find themselves without their Archbishop of Toledo.'

'Bernardín, you should not even think of murder.'

'I will think what I will,' cried Bernardín. 'What good will you ever do me? What good have you ever done? Had you been a normal brother to me I should have been a Bishop by now. And what am I? Steward in your household! Brought before my Lord Archbishop to answer a charge. What charge? I ask you. A charge of getting for myself what most brothers would have given me.'

'Have a care, Bernardín.'

'Should I have a care? I . . . the strong man? It is you who should take care, Gonzalo Ximenes . . . I beg your pardon . . . The name our parents gave you is not good enough for such a holy man. Francisco Ximenes, you are at my mercy. I could kill you as you lie there. It is you who should plead with me for leniency . . . not I with you.'

A lust for power had sprung up in Bernardín's eyes. What he said was true. At this moment his brilliant brother was at his mercy. He savoured that power, and longed to exercise it.

He will never do anything for me, he told himself. He is no good to our family . . . no good to himself. He might just as well have stayed in the hermitage at Castañar. A curse on him! He has no natural feeling.

All Bernardín's dreams were remembered in that second. Ximenes could have made them come true.

Ximenes had recovered his breath and was speaking.

'Bernardín, I sent for you because what I heard of your conduct in the Courts distressed and displeased me . . .'

Bernardín began to laugh out loud. With a sudden movement he pulled the pillow from under his brother's head and laughing demoniacally he held it high. Then he pushed Ximenes back on the bed and brought the pillow down over his face and held it there.

He could hear Ximenes fighting for his breath. He felt his brother's hands trying to pull at the pillow. But Ximenes was feeble and Bernardín was strong.

And after a while Ximenes lay still.

Bernardín lifted the pillow; he dared not stop to look at his brother's face, but hurried from the room.

❧

Tomás de Torquemada had left the peace of his monastery of St Thomas in Avila and was travelling to Madrid. This was a great wrench for him as he was a very old man now and much of the fire and vitality had gone from him.

Only the firm belief that his presence was needed at Court could have prevailed upon him to leave Avila at this time.

He loved his monastery – which was to him one of the greatest loves in his life. Perhaps the other was the Spanish

Inquisition. In the days of his health they had fought together for his loving care. What joy it had been to study the plans for his monastery; to watch it built; to glory in beautifully sculptured arches and carvings of great skill. The Inquisition had lured him from that love now and then; and the sight of heretics going to the *quemadero* in their hideous yellow *sanbenitos* gave him as much pleasure as the cool, silent halls of his monastery.

Which was he more proud to be – the creator of St Thomas in Avila or the Inquisitor General?

The latter was more or less a title only nowadays. That was because he was growing old and was plagued by the gout. The monastery would always stand as a monument to his memory and none could take that from him.

He would call first on the Archbishop of Toledo at Alcalá de Henares. He believed he could rely on the support of the Archbishop for the project he had in mind.

Painfully he rode in the midst of his protective cavalcade. Fifty men on horseback surrounded him, and a hundred armed men went on foot before him and a hundred marched behind.

The Queen herself had implored him to take adequate care when he travelled. He saw the wisdom of this. People whose loved ones had fed the fires of the Inquisition might consider revenge. He could never be sure, as he rode through towns and villages or along the lonely roads, whether the men and women he met bore grudges against him.

Fear attacked him often, now that he was growing infirm. A sound in the night – and he would call to his attendants.

'Are the doors guarded?'

'Yes, Excellency,' would be the answer.

'Make sure to keep them so.'

He would never have anyone with Jewish blood near him. He was afraid of those with Jewish blood. It was but a few years ago that all Jews who would not accept the Christian faith had been mercilessly exiled from Spain on his decree. Many Jews remained. He thought of them sometimes during the night. He dreamed they stole into his room.

He had every dish which was put before him first tasted in his presence before he ate.

When a man grew old he contemplated death often, and Torquemada, who had sent thousands to their deaths, was now afraid that someone who had suffered through him would seek to hurry him from life.

But duty called; and he had a plan to lay before the Sovereigns.

He reached Alcalá in the late afternoon. The residence of Ximenes was very sombre.

Ruiz received Torquemada in the place of his master.

'Does aught ail Fray Francisco Ximenes de Cisneros?' Torquemada asked.

'He is recovering from an illness which has been most severe.'

'Then perhaps I should not delay but continue my journey to Madrid.'

'Let me tell him that Your Excellency is here. If he is well enough he will certainly wish to see you. Allow me to inform him of your arrival after I have shown you to an apartment where you can rest while I have refreshment sent to Your Excellency.'

Torquemada graciously agreed to this proposal and Ruiz hurried to the bedside of Ximenes who had not left his bed since that horrifying encounter with Bernardín.

He opened his eyes and looked at Ruiz as he entered. To this nephew he owed his life. Ruiz had dashed into the apartment as Bernardín had hurried out because Ruiz, who knew Bernardín well, had feared he might harm his brother. It was Ruiz who had revived his half-dead uncle and brought him back to life.

Ximenes had since been wondering what action to take. Clearly he could not have Bernardín back in his household, but justice should be done. There should be punishment for such a crime. But how could he denounce his own brother as a would-be murderer?

Ruiz came to stand by the bed.

'Uncle,' he said, 'Tomás de Torquemada is with us.'

'Torquemada! Here!' Ximenes attempted to raise his weakened body. 'What does he want?'

'To have a word with you if you are well enough to see him.'

'It must be some important business which brings him here.'

'It must be. He is a sick man and suffering greatly from the gout.'

'You had better bring him to me, Ruiz.'

'If you do not feel strong enough I can explain this to him.'

'No. I must see him. Have him brought to me.'

Torquemada entered Ximenes's bedchamber and coming to the bed embraced the Archbishop.

They were not unalike – both had the stern look of the man who believes himself to have discovered the righteous way of life; both were ascetic in the extreme, emaciated through hardship; both were well acquainted with semi-starvation and the hair shirt – all of which they believed necessary to salvation. Both had to fight with their own particular demon, which was a pride greater than that felt by most men.

'I am sad to see you laid low, Archbishop,' said Torquemada.

'And I fear you yourself are in no fit state to travel, Inquisitor.' Inquisitor was the title Torquemada enjoyed hearing more than any other. It was a reminder that he had set up an Inquisition the like of which had never been seen in Spain before.

'I suffer from the gout most cruelly,' said Torquemada.

'A strange sickness for one of your habits,' answered Ximenes.

'Strange indeed. And what is this latest illness of yours?'

Ximenes answered quickly: 'A chill, I suspect.'

He was not going to tell Torquemada that he had been almost suffocated by his own brother, for if he had Torquemada would have demanded that Bernardín should be brought to trial and severely punished. Torquemada would doubtless have behaved with rigorous justice if he had been in the place of Ximenes.

Perhaps, thought Ximenes, I lack his strength. But he has had longer in which to discipline himself.

Ximenes went on: 'But I believe you have not come here to talk of illness.'

'No, I am on my way to Court and, because I know I shall have your support in the matter which I have decided to bring to the notice of the Sovereigns, I have called to acquaint you with my mission. It concerns the Princess Isabella, who has been a widow too long.'

'Ah, you are thinking that with the Habsburg marriages, the eldest daughter should not be forgotten.'

'I doubt she is forgotten. The Princess is reluctant to go again into Portugal.'

'Such reluctance is understandable,' said Ximenes.

'*I* cannot understand it,' Torquemada retorted coldly. 'It is clearly her duty to make this alliance with Portugal.'

'It has astonished me that it has not been made before,' Ximenes put in.

'The Queen is a mother who now and then turns her face from duty.'

They, who had both been confessors to Isabella the Queen, exchanged nods of understanding.

'She is a woman of great goodness,' Torquemada acceded, 'but where her children are concerned she is apt to forget her duty in her desire to please them.'

'I know it well.'

'Clearly,' Torquemada went on, 'the young Isabella should be sent immediately into Portugal as the bride of Emanuel. But there should be one condition, and it is this which I wish to put before the Sovereigns.'

'Condition?'

'When I drove the Jews from Spain,' said Torquemada, 'many of them found refuge in Portugal.' His face darkened suddenly; his eyes gleamed with wild fanaticism; they seemed like living things in a face that was dead. All Torquemada's hatred for the Jewish race was in his eyes, in his voice at that moment. 'They pollute the air of Portugal. I wish to see them driven from Portugal as I drove them from Spain.'

'If this marriage were made we should have no power to dictate Emanuel's policy towards the Jews,' Ximenes pointed out.

'No,' cried Torquemada triumphantly, 'but we could make it a condition of the marriage. Emanuel is eager for this match. He is more than eager. It is not merely to him a grand marriage . . . union with a wealthy neighbour. This young King is a weak and emotional fellow. Consider his tolerance towards the Jews. He has strange ideas. He wishes to see all races living in harmony side by side in his country following their own faiths. You see he is a fool; he is unaware of his duty to the Christian Faith. He wishes to rule with what he foolishly calls tolerance. But he is a love-sick young man.'

'He saw the Princess when she went into Portugal to marry Alonso,' murmured Ximenes.

'Yes, he saw her, and from the moment she became a widow he has had one plan: to make her his wife. Well, why not? Isabella must become the Queen of Portugal, but on one condition: the expulsion of the Jews from that country as they have been expelled from our own.'

Ximenes lay back on his pillows exhausted and Torquemada rose.

'I am tiring you,' he said. 'But I rely on your support, should I need it. Not that I shall.' All the fire had come back to this old man who was midway in his seventies. 'I shall put this to the Queen and I know I shall make her see her duty.'

When Torquemada had taken his leave of Ximenes the Archbishop lay back considering the visit.

Torquemada was a stronger man than he was. Neither of them thought human suffering important. They had sought to inflict it too often on themselves to be sorry for others who bore it.

But at this time Ximenes was more concerned with his own problem than that of Isabella and Emanuel. He had decided what he must do with Bernardín. He would send his brother back to his monastery; he would give him a small pension; but it should be on condition that he never left his monastery and never sought to see his brother again.

I am a weak man where my own are concerned, thought Ximenes. And he wondered at himself who could contemplate undisturbed the hardships which would certainly befall the Jews of Portugal if Emanuel accepted this new condition, yet must needs worry about a man who, but for chance, might have committed fratricide – and all because that man happened to be his own brother.

❧ ❧

The Princess Isabella looked from her mother to the stern face of Torquemada.

Her throat was dry; she felt that if she had tried to protest the words would not come. Her mother had an expression of tenderness yet determination. The Princess knew that the Queen had made up her mind – or perhaps that this stern-faced man who had once been her confessor had made it up for her as he had so many times before. She felt powerless between them. They asked for her consent, but they did not need it. It would be as they wished, not as she did.

She tried once more. 'I could not go into Portugal.'

Torquemada had risen, and she thought suddenly of those men and women who were taken in the dead of night to his secret prisons and there interrogated, until from weariness – and from far worse, she knew – agreed with what he wished them to say.

'It is the duty of a daughter of Spain to do what is good for Spain,' said Torquemada. 'It is sinful to say "I do not wish that." "I do not care to do that." It matters not. This is your duty. You must do your duty or imperil your soul.'

70

'It is you who say it is my duty,' she answered. 'How can I be sure that it is?'

'My daughter,' said the Queen, 'that which will bring benefit to Spain is your duty and the duty of us all.'

'Mother,' cried the Princess, 'you do not know what you are asking of me.'

'I know full well. It is your cross, my dearest. You must carry it.'

'You carry a two-edged sword for Spain,' said Torquemada. 'You can make this marriage which will secure our frontiers, and you can help to establish firmly the Christian Faith on Portuguese soil.'

'I am sure Emanuel will never agree to the expulsion of the Jews,' cried Isabella. 'I know him. I have talked with him. He has what are called liberal ideas. He wants freedom of thought in Portugal. He said so. He will never agree.'

'Freedom for sin,' retorted Torquemada. 'He wishes for this marriage. It shall be our condition.'

'I cannot do it,' said Isabella wearily.

'Think what it means,' whispered her mother. 'You will have the great glory of stamping out heresy in your new country.'

'Dearest Mother, I do not care . . .'

'Hush, hush!' It was the thunderous voice of Torquemada. 'For that you could be brought before the tribunal.'

'It is my daughter to whom you speak,' the Queen put in with some coldness.

'Highness, it is not the first time I have had to remind *you* of your duty.'

The Queen was meekly silent. It was true. This man had a more rigorous sense of duty than she had. She could not help it

71

if her love for her family often came between her and her duty.

She must range herself on his side. Ferdinand would insist on this marriage taking place. They had indulged their daughter too long. And, if they could insist on this condition, that would be a blow struck for Holy Church, so she must forget her tenderness for her daughter and put herself on the side of righteousness.

Her voice was stern as she addressed her daughter: 'You should cease to behave like a child. You are a woman and a daughter of the Royal House. You will prepare yourself to accept this marriage, for I shall send a dispatch to Emanuel this day.'

Torquemada's features were drawn into lines of approval. He did not smile. He never smiled. But this expression was as near to a smile as he could come.

When her mother spoke like that, Isabella knew that it was useless to protest; she lowered her head and said quietly: 'Please, may I have your leave to retire?'

'It is granted,' said the Queen.

Isabella ran to her apartment. She did not notice little Catalina whom she passed.

'Isabella, Isabella,' called Catalina, 'what is wrong?'

Isabella took no notice but ran on; she had one concern – to reach her bedroom before she began to weep, for it seemed to her in that moment the only relief she could look for was in tears.

She threw herself on to her bed and the storm burst.

Catalina had come to stand by the side of her bed. The child watched in astonishment, but she knew why Isabella cried. She shared in every sob; she knew exactly how her sister felt. This was like a rehearsal of what would one day happen to her.

At length she whispered very softly: 'Isabella!'

Her sister opened her eyes and saw her standing there.

'It is Catalina.'

Catalina climbed on to the bed and lay down beside her sister.

'It has happened then?' asked the little girl. 'You are to go?'

'It is Torquemada. That man . . . with his schemes and his plots.'

'He has made this decision then?'

'Yes. I am to marry Emanuel. There is to be a condition.'

'Emanuel is a kind man, Isabella. He loves you already. You will not be unhappy. Whereas England is a strange place.'

Isabella was silent suddenly; then she put her arms about Catalina and held her close to her.

'Oh Catalina, it is something we all have to endure. But it will be years before you go to England.'

'Years do pass.'

'And plans change.'

Catalina shuddered, and Isabella went on: 'It is all changed now, Catalina. I wish I had gone before. Then Emanuel would have loved me. He did, you know, when I was Alonso's wife.'

'He will love you now.'

'No, there will be a shadow over our marriage. You did not know what happened here when the Jews were driven out. You were too young. But I heard the servants talking of it. They took little children away from their parents. They made them leave their homes. Some died . . . some were murdered. There was great suffering throughout the land.

Emanuel will hate to do in his country what was done in ours . . . and if he does not do it there will be no marriage.'

'Who said this?'

'Torquemada. He is a man who always has his way. You see, Catalina, if I go to Portugal it will not be the same any more. There will be a great shadow over my marriage. Perhaps Emanuel will hate me. They cursed us . . . those Jews, as they lay dying by the roadside. If I go to Portugal they will curse me.'

'Their curses cannot hurt you, for you will be doing what is good.'

'Good?'

'If it is what our mother wants, it will be good.'

'Catalina, I'm frightened. I think I can hear their curses in my ears already.'

They lay in silence side by side. Isabella was thinking of the roads of Portugal filled with bands of exiles, broken-hearted men and women looking for a home, prepared to find death on the highway, at the hands of murderers or from exposure.

'This is my marriage with Emanuel,' she whispered.

Catalina did not hear her; she was thinking of a ship which would sail away to a land of fogs and strangers; and she was a passenger on that ship.

❧ Chapter III ❧

THE ARCHDUCHESS MARGARET

The Archduchess Margaret clung to the ship's bulwarks. The wind was rising; the storm clouds loured.

Was the middle of winter a good time to make a perilous sea journey? She was sure that it was not. Yet, she thought, what would it have availed me had I asked to wait for the spring?

There had already been much delay, and her father was anxious for her marriage; so, it seemed, were the King and Queen who were to be her parents-in-law.

'It is their will, not mine,' she murmured.

Some girls of sixteen might have been terrified. There were so many events looming ahead of her which could be terrifying. There was to be a new life in a strange country, a new husband; even closer was a threatening storm at sea.

But the expression on the face of the Archduchess was calm. She had been sufficiently buffeted by life to have learned that it is foolish to suffer in anticipation that which one may or may not have to suffer in fact.

She turned to the trembling attendant at her side and laid a hand on the woman's arm.

'The storm may not touch us,' she said. 'It may break behind us. That can happen at sea. The strong wind is carrying us fast to Spain.'

The woman shuddered.

'And if we are to die,' mused Margaret, 'well then, that is our fate. There are worse deaths, I believe, than drowning.'

'Your Grace should not talk so. It is tempting God.'

'Do you think God would change His plans because of the idle chatter of a girl like myself?'

The woman's lips were moving in prayer.

I should be praying with her, thought Margaret. This is going to be a bad storm. I can feel it in the air. Perhaps I am not meant to be a wife in reality.

Yet she did not move, but stood holding her face up to the sky – not with defiance but with resignation.

How can any of us know, she asked herself, when our last hour will come?

She turned her comely face to the woman. 'Go to my cabin,' she said. 'I will join you there.'

'Your Grace should come with me now. This is no place for you.'

'Not yet,' said Margaret. 'I will come when the rain starts.'

'Your Grace . . .'

'That was an order,' said Margaret with a quiet firmness, and a few seconds later she was smiling to see with what alacrity the woman left her side.

How terrified people were of death, mused Margaret. Was it because they remembered their sins? Perhaps it was safer to die when one was young. At sixteen a girl, who had been watched over as she had been, could not have committed a great many sins.

She held up her face to the rising anger of the wind.

How far are we from the coast of Spain? she wondered. Can we reach it? I have a feeling within me that I am destined to die a virgin.

It was unusual that a young girl could feel so calm when she was leaving her home for a strange country. But then her father's dominions had not been home to her for so long. She scarcely knew Maximilian, for he was a man of many engagements. His children were to him as counters in a great game to be used in winning him possessions in the world. He was fortunate to have a son and a daughter both strong and healthy, both comely enough; in the case of Philip extremely so. But it was not the appearance of men that was so important. Nevertheless Maximilian had nothing of which to complain in his children. He had a worthy son and a daughter with whom to bargain in the markets of the world.

Margaret smiled. The men were the fortunate ones. They did not have to leave their homes. Arrogant Philip had merely to wait for his bride to be delivered to him. It was the women who must suffer.

And for that, thought Margaret, I should be grateful, since I suffer scarcely at all. Does it matter to me whether I am in France, in Flanders or in Spain? None has seemed to be home to me. I am too young to have had so many homes, and as I quickly learned that my hold on any of them lacked permanence, I learned also not to attach myself too tenderly to any one of them.

She faintly remembered her arrival in France. She had been barely three years old at the time and had been taken from her home in Flanders to be brought up at the French Court because, through her mother, Mary of Burgundy, she had inherited Burgundy; and the French King, Louis XI, had sought to bring Burgundy back to France by betrothing her to his son, the Dauphin Charles.

So to Amboise she had come. She often thought of the great château which had been her home for so many years. Even now, with the storm imminent, she could imagine that she was not on this deck but within those thick walls. She recalled the great buttresses, the cylindrical towers and the rounded roofs, which looked as if they could defy the wind and rain to the end of time.

Within those walls she had been prepared to meet her betrothed – a rather terrifying experience for a little girl of three and a half whose bridegroom was a boy of twelve.

That ceremony of betrothal was an occasion which would never be obliterated from Margaret's memory. Clearly she could recall meeting her bridegroom at a little farm near the town of Amboise, which was afterwards called *La Métairie de la Reyne*, whither she had been carried in a litter. It was a strange ceremony, doubtless considered fitting for children of such tender years. She remembered being asked if she would take Monsieur le Dauphin in marriage, and how the Grand Sénéchal, who stood close to her, prodded her and told her she must say that she would.

Then she had been put into the arms of young Charles and told to kiss him. She was to be a wife to the future King of France, and the people of Amboise showed their pleasure by hanging scarlet cloth from their windows and putting up banners which were stretched across the streets.

After that she had been taken back to the château, and her sister-in-law, Anne, the Duchess of Bourbon who was the eldest daughter of the reigning King and past her twentieth birthday, had been her guardian.

Margaret had quickly adjusted herself and had pleased her tutors by her love of learning. She will make a good Queen of France, they often said; she is the best possible wife for the Dauphin.

Charles had very soon become King, and that meant that she, Margaret, was an even more important person than before.

Yet she had never been Charles's wife in reality, for eight years after her arrival in France, while she was still a child, Charles decided that he preferred Anne, Duchess of Brittany, to be his wife.

So, to the wrath of Margaret's father, Charles sent her back to Flanders, ignoring the vows he had taken in the *Métairie de la Reyne* on that day eight years before.

Maximilian was infuriated by the insult, but Margaret had felt philosophical.

She thought of Charles now. He was far from the handsome husband a girl might long for. He was short and, because his head was enormous, his lack of inches was accentuated. His expression was blank and his aquiline nose so enormous that it overpowered the rest of his features. He seemed to find it difficult to keep his mouth closed, for his lips were thick and coarse and he breathed heavily and took a long time to consider what he was going to say; whereas Margaret herself was quick-witted and fluent.

He was kind enough; but he had little interest in books and ideas, which made him seem dull to her; she could not share his interest in sport and jousting.

So, she thought, perhaps it was not such a tragedy that he shipped me back to Flanders.

And now she was being shipped to Spain. 'If I ever reach there,' she murmured.

Two of the ship's high-ranking officers had approached her, and so deep was she in her thoughts that she had not noticed them.

'Your Grace,' said one, bowing low, 'it is unsafe for you to remain on deck. The storm is about to break and we must ask you to seek the shelter of your cabin.'

Margaret inclined her head. They were anxious about her, she knew. She was the most important cargo they had ever carried. She represented all the advantages that union with a daughter of Maximilian could bring to Spain.

They were right too. She was almost blown off her feet, as she started across the deck. The two men held her, and laughing, she accepted their assistance.

❧❧

The ship tossed and rolled, and the din was terrific. As she sheltered in her cabin with two of her attendants she occasionally heard the shouts of the sailors above the roar of the wind.

She saw two of her attendants clinging together. They were terrified. Their orders had been not to leave her if there was any danger, and their fear of Maximilian was greater than their fear of the storm.

She saw the tears on their faces as their fingers clutched their rosaries and their lips moved in continual prayer.

'How frail a thing is a ship,' said Margaret.' How fierce is an ocean!'

'You should pray, Your Grace. I fear some of the smaller ships will have been lost and we shall never come out of this alive.'

'If it is the end, then it is the end,' said Margaret.

The two women looked at each other. Such calmness alarmed them. It was unnatural.

'We shall die without a priest,' sighed one of the women, 'with all our sins on us.'

'You have not sinned greatly,' Margaret comforted her. 'Pray now for forgiveness, and it will be granted you.'

'You pray with us.'

'I find it difficult to ask God to spare my life,' said Margaret, 'for, if He has decided to take it, I am asking Him to go against His wishes. Perhaps we shall hate living so much that it will be more intolerable than death.'

'Your Grace! Do not say such things!'

'But if we are to find bliss in Heaven why should we be so distressed at the thought of going there? I am not distressed. If my time has come, I am ready. I do not think that my new father and mother-in-law are going to be very pleased with me. Perhaps they will already have heard of the manner in which Philip is treating their daughter.'

She was thinking of Philip – golden haired and handsome. What a beautiful boy he had always been. Everyone had made much of him, especially the women. She suspected that he had been initiated into the arts of love-making at a very early age, for some lusty young serving girl would surely have found the good looks of Philip impossible to resist; and Philip would be so eager to learn; he had been born to philander.

At an early age he had had his mistresses and had not been greatly interested in the wife he was to have. He had accepted her in his free and easy Flemish way – for Philip had the Flanders easy manners – as one of a group. Margaret knew he would not give up his mistresses merely because he had a wife.

And it was said that the Spaniards were a dignified people. Their ways would certainly not be the ways of Flanders. Poor Juana. Her future was not an enviable one. But perhaps, thought Margaret, she has a temperament like my own. Then she will accept what is, because it must be, and not ask for what it is impossible for life to give her.

Did they know in Spain that Philip had made no haste to greet his bride, that he had dallied with his gay friends – so many of them voluptuous women – and had laughingly declared that there was time enough for marriage?

I am afraid Juana is not getting a good husband, mused Margaret. I must say this even though that husband is my own brother.

So perhaps there would not be a very enthusiastic welcome for Philip's sister when she reached Spain; and if she never did, who could say at this stage that that would not be a fortunate outcome?

The women in her cabin were moaning.

'Our last hour has come,' whispered one of them. 'Holy Mother of God, intercede for us.'

Margaret closed her eyes. Surely the ship was being rent asunder.

Yes, she thought, this is the end of my father's hopes through me. Here on the ocean bed will lie the bones of Margaret of Austria, daughter of Maximilian, drowned on her way to her wedding with the heir of Spain.

She began to compose her epitaph. It helped her not to catch the fear of those about her; she had discovered that it was all very well to talk lightly of death when it was far off; when you felt its breath in your face, when you heard its mocking laughter, you could not resist a certain fear. How could anyone

be sure what was waiting on the other side of that strange
bridge which joined Life with Death?

   '*Ci gist Margot,*' she murmured, '*la gentil' damoiselle*
   Qu'a deux maris, et encore est pucelle.'

✈ Chapter IV ✈

THE MARRIAGE OF JUAN

O
n a bright March day what was left of the battered fleet came into the port of Santander.

Waiting to greet it were Ferdinand the King and by his side his son, Juan, the bridegroom to be.

Juan was nervous. His thoughts were for the young girl who had come perilously near to death at sea and had been miraculously brought to him. He must try to understand her; he must be gentle and kind.

His mother had talked to him about her, although she knew of course that she had no need to ask her son to show indulgence. Kindness came naturally to him. He hoped that she was not a flighty, senseless girl. Although if she were he would try to understand her ways. He would try to be interested in her interests. He would have to learn to enjoy dancing perhaps; he would have to pay more attention to sports. It was hardly likely that she would share his interests. She was young and doubtless she was gay. One could not expect her to care for books and music as he did.

Well then, he must suppress his inclinations. He must try

above all to put her at ease. Poor child! How would she feel, leaving her home?

Ferdinand was smiling at him.

'Well, my son, in a short while now you will see her,' he said.

'Yes, Father.'

'It reminds me of the first day I saw your mother.' Ferdinand wanted to say: If she does not please you, you should not take it to heart. There are many women in the world and they'll be ready enough to please the heir to my crown.

But of course one would not say such things to Juan. He was quite unlike the gay Alfonso on whom Ferdinand had wished to bestow the Archbishopric of Toledo. Ferdinand felt a little wistful. It would have been pleasant had this son of his been a little more like himself. There was too much of Isabella in him. He had too strong a sense of duty. He looked almost frail in the spring sunshine. We should try to fatten him up, harden him, thought Ferdinand. And yet he was always a little abashed in the presence of his son; Juan made him feel earthy, a little uneasy about the sins he had committed throughout a long and lusty life. Angel was a good name for him; but the company of an angel could sometimes be a little disconcerting.

Even now Ferdinand guessed that, instead of impatiently waiting to size up the girl's personal attributes – which was all he need concern himself with, her titles and inheritance being good enough even for the heir to Spain – he was thinking how best he could put her at ease.

Odd, thought Ferdinand, that such as I should have a son like that.

'She is coming ashore now,' said Juan; and he was smiling.

They rode side by side on their way to Burgos where Queen Isabella and the rest of the royal family would be waiting to greet them.

They were pleased with each other, and they made a charming pair. The people, who had lined their route to watch them pass, cheered them and called out their blessings.

They loved their heir. He was not so much handsome as beautiful, and his sweet expression did not belie the reports they had heard of him. It was said that any petition first submitted to Juan would be certain to receive attention, no matter if it came from the most humble. Indeed the more humble the petitioner, the more easily the Prince's sympathies were aroused.

'Long live the Prince of the Asturias!' cried the people. 'Long live the Archduchess Margaret!'

Ferdinand, riding with them, had graciously hung back. He was ready on this occasion to take second place to his heir and the bride. He would not have had it otherwise. He was congratulating himself. The girl looked healthy and none would guess she had been almost drowned at sea a week ago.

Margaret wished to talk to Juan. His Spanish manners were to her somewhat dignified, and she, after some years in Flanders, knew no such restraint.

'The people love you,' she said.

'They love a wedding,' he answered. 'It means feasting and holidays.'

'Yes, no doubt they do. But I think they have a special regard for you personally. Is my Spanish intelligible to you?'

'Completely. It is very good.'

She laughed. 'You would say it was good, no matter how bad it was.'

'Nevertheless it is very good indeed. I trust my sister Juana speaks her husband's language as well as you speak that of the man who will be yours.'

'Ah . . . Juana,' she said.

'Did you see much of my sister?' he asked anxiously.

'No. She travelled to Lille, you know, for the wedding. I had to prepare myself to return with the fleet.'

He was quick to notice that she found the subject of Juana disconcerting, so changed it immediately although he was anxious to hear news of Juana.

'Tell me, what pastimes please you most?'

She gave him a grateful look. 'I'm afraid you will find me rather dull,' she said.

'I cannot believe it.'

She laughed aloud again, and he noticed – though she did not – that the attendants were astonished at her displays of mirth. Flemish manners! they were thinking. It was not fitting to show such lack of dignity in Spain.

But Juan liked that laughter; it was fresh and unaffected.

'Yes,' she said, 'I do not greatly care for games and dancing and such diversions. I spend a great deal of time reading. I am interested in the history of countries and the ideas of philosophers. I think my brother deemed me a little odd. He says that I have not the right qualities to please a husband.'

'That is not true.' She saw the sudden gleam in Juan's eyes. 'I am not good at sport and games either. I frankly dislike hunting.'

Margaret said quickly: 'I too. I cannot bear to hunt animals

87

to the death. I picture myself being hunted to death. My brother laughs at me. He said that you would.'

'I would never laugh at you nor scorn your ideas if they differed from my own. But, Margaret, I think that you and I are going to think alike on many things.'

'That makes me happy,' she said.

'And you are not afraid . . . coming to a strange land . . . to a strange husband?'

'No,' she answered seriously, 'I am not afraid.'

Juan's heart began to beat wildly as he looked at her clean-cut young profile and her fair, fine skin.

She has all that I could have wished for in a wife, he told himself. Surely I am the luckiest of Princes. How serene she is! She looks as though she would never be ruffled. It is going to be so easy . . . so pleasant . . . so wonderful. I need not have been afraid. I shall not be shy and awkward with her. She is so young, and yet she has a calmness almost equal to that of my mother. What a wonderful person my wife will be.

'You are smiling,' she said. 'Tell me what amuses you.'

He answered seriously: 'It is not amusement which makes me smile. It is happiness.'

'That,' she replied, 'is the best possible reason for smiling.'

So, thought Juan, I am beginning to love her already.

Margaret also began to smile. She was telling herself that she had been fortunate as she remembered the flabby lips of Charles VIII of France.

She was glad that she had been sent to France and affianced to Charles. It was going to make her realise how lucky she was to have come to Spain to marry Juan.

So on they rode to the shouts of 'Long live the Prince! Blessings on him and his bride!'

They were already serenely contented as they thought of the years ahead.

❧❧

In the Palace at Burgos the arrival of the cavalcade, headed by Ferdinand, his son and the bride, was awaited with eagerness.

In the children's apartments the Princess Isabella watched the servants busy at the toilet of her sisters, Maria and Catalina.

How quiet they were! It would have been so different if Juana had been with them. She would have been speculating about the bride, shouting her wild opinions to them all.

Isabella felt rather pleased that Juana was no longer with them.

She was praying – she spent a great deal of time praying – that this young girl would make Juan happy. She hoped that she would be a gentle, religious girl. It would be heartbreaking if she were a wanton; and Isabella knew that stories were already reaching Spain of this girl's brother's conduct.

The Queen was very anxious about Juana, and the Flemish marriage was her greatest concern at the moment. Their father of course was only congratulating himself because the alliance had been made, and that Juana would be the mother of the Habsburg heirs. It would seem unimportant to him if she were wretchedly unhappy while she was producing them.

Maria was placidly relaxed while her attendants dressed her. She was as emotionless as ever. Stolid Maria, who lacked the imagination to wonder what Margaret felt on coming into a new country, to wonder whether she herself would not be doing the same in a future which was not really very distant!

How different it was with Catalina. Her little face was set

and anxious, and it was not difficult to guess at the thoughts which went on behind those big dark eyes.

Poor little Catalina! She was going to suffer a terrible wrench if she ever went to England.

An attendant came to the apartment and whispered to Isabella that the Queen's Highness wished to see her without delay, and she was to present herself in the Queen's bed-chamber.

Young Isabella left her sisters at once and went to her mother's apartment.

The Queen was waiting for her, and Isabella's heart sank as she looked at her, for she guessed what she had to say.

The Queen kissed the Princess and said: 'There is news from Portugal. I wanted to tell you myself. I wanted to prepare you. Your father will doubtless be speaking of this matter when he sees you.'

Isabella's mouth had gone dry. 'Yes, Mother,' she said.

'Emanuel writes that since we insist on this condition he is ready to accept it.'

Isabella's pale cheeks were suddenly flushed. She cried out: 'You mean he will drive all those people out of his country just because . . .'

'Just because he is so eager for this marriage. So, my dear, you should really begin to plan your departure for Portugal.'

'So . . . soon?' stammered Isabella.

'I'm afraid your father wishes the marriage to take place this year.'

'Oh . . . no!'

'It is so. Dear Isabella, I shall insist that we meet again soon after you leave us. If you do not come to me here in Spain, I will come to you in Portugal.'

'Mother, do you promise this?'

'I swear it.'

Isabella was silent. Then she burst out: 'Is there nothing I can do . . . ? I did not think he would agree to this . . .'

'He wants this marriage. You should rejoice. It is more than a good marriage. On his side it is a love-match.'

'But there is my side, Mother.'

'You will love him in time. I know, my child. I am sure of it. He is a good and gentle man and he loves you dearly. You have nothing to fear.'

'But, Mother, this condition . . .'

'But shows how much he loves you.'

'I know that he does it against his will.'

'That is because, good as he is, he has a certain blindness. That holy man, Tomás de Torquemada, sees in this the hand of God.'

Isabella shuddered. She wanted to shout that she did not like Torquemada, that she feared him, and when her cough kept her awake at night she fancied she heard the curses of the exiled Jews.

Her mother would not understand such flights of fancy. How could she explain to her? Her emotions seemed to choke her, and she feared that if she did not calm herself one of her bouts of coughing would overtake her.

She tried not to cough in front of her mother, because she knew how it worried the Queen. It was enough that Juana gave her such anxieties.

She said: 'Mother, if you will excuse me, I will go back to my apartment. I have some more preparations to make if I am to be ready when the party arrives.'

The Queen nodded assent and, when her daughter had

gone, murmured to herself: 'All will be well. This is the best thing that could happen to my Isabella.'

❦

Isabella the Queen took the daughter of Maximilian in her arms and embraced her.

There were tears in Isabella's eyes. The girl was charming; she was healthy; and it seemed to her that Juan was already very happy with his bride.

Ferdinand looked on, his eyes agleam. It was very pleasant to be able to share in the general delight.

'We welcome you to Burgos,' said the Queen. 'I could not express how eager we have been for your coming.'

'I am happy to be here, Your Highness.'

The girl's smile was perhaps too warm, too friendly.

I must remember, the Queen told herself, that she has lived long in Flanders and the Flemish have little sense of decorum.

The Princesses Isabella, Maria and Catalina came forward and formally welcomed Margaret.

They thought her strange with her Flemish clothes, her fresh complexion and her familiar manners; but they liked her. Even Maria seemed to grow a little animated as she watched her. As for Catalina, she took great courage from this girl, who seemed quite unperturbed that she had come to a land of strangers to marry a man whom she had only recently met.

A banquet had been prepared, and Juan and his bride sat with the King and Queen; and they talked of the jousting and festivities which had been arranged to celebrate the marriage.

'It is a pity that it is Lent,' said the Queen. 'But as soon as it is over the nuptials shall be solemnised. We think that the third of April shall be the day of the wedding.'

Catalina looked quickly at the face of the Flemish Archduchess; she was relieved to see that the mention of a date for her wedding did not seem to disturb her.

❧

It was the most magnificent spectacle seen in Spain for many years.

This was, after all, the wedding of the heir to the throne. It seemed more than the celebration of a wedding. Spain had never seemed to hold out such hopes of a prosperous future for her people. The prospects for peace were brighter than they had been for many years. No more taxes to pay for useless battles! No more forcing men from their peaceful labours to fight in the armies! Peace meant prosperity – and it seemed that here it was at last.

The charming young bridegroom would be the first heir of the whole of Spain, and the people had come to realise that a united Spain was happier to live in than a country divided into kingdoms which were continually warring with each other.

Even the frugal Isabella was determined that this marriage of her only son should be an occasion which all should remember, and she was therefore ready to spend a great deal of money in making it so.

All over the country there were tourneys and fêtes. Towns were gaily decorated throughout the land. Across the narrow streets in the smallest villages banners hung.

'Long life to the heir!' cried the people. 'Blessings on the Prince of the Asturias and his bride!'

The marriage was celebrated with the greatest dignity and ceremony. The Archbishop of Toledo performed it, and with him were the grandees of Castile and the nobility of Aragon. It was a sight of great magnificence and splendour.

And as Margaret made her vows once more she compared her bridegroom with that boy of twelve to whom she had been betrothed in a farmhouse near the château of Amboise, and again she rejoiced in her good fortune.

❧❧

Juan had dreaded the moment when they would be alone together. He had imagined the terrors of a young girl who might not fully understand what would be required of her, and himself explaining as gently as he could; he had not relished the task.

When they lay in the marriage bed it was Margaret who spoke first.

'Juan,' she said, 'you are afraid of me.'

'I am afraid that I might distress you,' he answered.

'No,' she told him. 'I shall not be distressed.'

'Are you never distressed, Margaret?'

'Not by that which must be.'

Juan lifted her hand and kissed it. 'I am sorry,' he said. 'As you say, what must be, must be.'

Then she laughed suddenly and, pulling her hand away from him, she put her arms about him.

'I am so glad that you are as you are, Juan,' she said. 'I am sure nothing you do could possibly distress me. When I think that it might have been Charles lying beside me at this moment . . .' She shivered.

'Charles? The King of France?'

'He has thick lips, and he grunts. He is not unkind but he would be coarse and . . . he would never understand me.'

94

'I hope to understand you, Margaret.'

'Call me Margot,' she said. 'It is my special name . . . the name I like those whom I love to call me by.'

'Do you love me then, Margot?'

'I think so, Juan. I think I must, because . . . I am not afraid.'

And so the difficulty was soon over, and that which had alarmed them became a pleasure. She taught him to laugh in her gay Flemish way, and he found himself fascinated by her familiar talk which might have seemed coarse on some lips, never on hers.

'Oh Juan,' she cried, 'I thought my bones would now be lying on the sea bed and the big fishes would have eaten my flesh, and the little ones sport about my skeleton and swim in and out of the sockets of my eyes.'

'Don't say such things,' he said, kissing her eyes.

'I said, "Here lies Margot. She was twice married but she died a virgin."' Then she began to laugh afresh. 'That can never be my epitaph now, Juan. For here lies Margot . . . beside you . . . but she is no longer a virgin . . . and she is not displeased.'

So they made love again, without fear or shame.

And in the morning Juan said: 'We have given our parents what they wanted.'

Margaret interrupted: 'The crown of Spain.'

Juan chanted: 'The Habsburg inheritance.'

Then they laughed and began to kiss in a sudden frenzy of passion. Margaret drew herself away from him and kneeling on the bed bowed her head as though before the thrones of the King and Queen.

'We thank Your Gracious Majesties. You may keep the crown of Spain . . .'

'And the Habsburg inheritance . . .' added Juan.

'Because . . .' began Margaret, smiling at him.

'Because,' added Juan, 'you gave us each other.'

❦

The wedding celebrations continued. The most popular person in the whole of Spain was the young Prince Juan. It was said of him that since the coming of Margaret he looked more like a man than an angel, but his sweetness of expression had not grown less. His bride was clearly a happy girl. It was small wonder that wherever they went there was rejoicing.

The Queen discussed with her husband her pleasure in this marriage.

'You see,' said Ferdinand, 'how well it has turned out. This was a marriage of my making. You will admit that I knew what I was about.'

'You have acted with the utmost wisdom,' Isabella agreed. 'You have given our Juan a share in the Habsburg inheritance – and happiness.'

'Who would not be happy with a share in the Habsburg inheritance?' demanded Ferdinand.

Isabella's face was anxious. 'I do not like these rumours I hear about Juana. She is so far from home . . .'

'Nonsense! All will be well. She will adjust herself. The Flemings have different manners from our own. *I* have heard that she is passionately attached to her husband.'

'Too passionately attached.'

'My dear Isabella, can a wife love her husband too much?'

'If he is not kind to her it would be easier for her to bear if she did not love him dearly.'

'Strange words on your lips! You seem to imply it is a virtue that a wife should not love her husband dearly.'

'You misunderstand me.'

'Ah, have no fear for Juana. Rumour often lies.'

The Queen knew that he could not think of their daughter, Juana, without remembering all the advantages her marriage had brought to Spain. It was no use expecting him to see the personal view. He was quite incapable of that. He had hardened with the years. Have I softened? Isabella asked herself. No, it is merely that having so many loved ones I have become more vulnerable.

Ferdinand said abruptly: 'Why should there be this delay with our daughter Isabella? Emanuel grows impatient.'

'Should she not wait until her brother's wedding celebrations are over?'

'But we planned that these ceremonies should continue for a long time. The people expect it. Soon however I want Juan and Margaret to go on a long pilgrimage through the country, showing themselves in the various towns. There will be feasting and celebrations wherever they halt. There is nothing like a progress for winning the devotion of the people. And when you have a pair like Juan and Margaret . . . young, handsome and in love . . . the people will be their devoted slaves for ever.' Ferdinand's eyes blazed. 'When I think of all that young man of ours is heir to, I could sing for joy.'

'Perhaps Isabella could accompany them on their pilgrimage.'

'And thus delay her departure for Portugal?'

'It would remind the people of all that we are doing for them with these alliances.'

'Quite unnecessary. Isabella must prepare to leave Spain for Portugal at once.'

The Queen was about to protest, but Ferdinand's mouth was stubborn.

These are my children as well as yours, he was reminding her. You may be Queen of Castile, but I remain the head of the family.

It was useless to protest, the Queen decided. And a short postponement would make little difference to Isabella in the long run. She was sure that when her daughter was in Portugal she would be as happy with Emanuel as Margaret was with Juan.

❧❧

The coming of Margaret to Spain had brought an immense relief to Catalina. It seemed to her that here she saw, played out before her eyes, that drama which had begun to dominate her life. The transference of a foreign Princess to the home of her bridegroom could be a happy event.

It was exhilarating therefore to watch the happiness of Margaret and Juan.

Margaret was very friendly with her husband's sisters. She was amusing and clever, and her manner of never hesitating to say what she meant was extraordinary.

Catalina knew that the Princess Isabella was a little shocked by her sister-in-law. But Isabella could not share in the general rejoicing, because her own departure was imminent.

'How cruel of us,' said Catalina to Maria, 'to be happy when soon Isabella is going to leave us.'

Maria looked astonished. Like her father she could not understand why Isabella should be so distressed. She was going to have a wedding, as Juan had; she was going to be the centre of attraction. That seemed a very fine thing to Maria.

Catalina often left the company, which Margaret was enlivening with some story of the manners of the Flemish, that she might sit with her sister, Isabella.

Isabella had changed in the last weeks. She had become resigned. She seemed a little thinner than usual but there was a hectic flush on her cheeks which made her look very pretty. Her cough worried her still but she continually sought to control it.

One day Catalina crept to her sister's apartments and found her at the window, looking out wistfully on the scene below.

'May I come in, Isabella?'

'But of course.'

Isabella held out her hand and Catalina took it.

'Why do you come to me?' Isabella asked. 'Is it not more fun to be with the others?'

Catalina was thoughtful. Yes, it was more fun. Margaret was amusing and it was pleasant to watch her and remind oneself that this was what it was like going to a strange country to be married; but Catalina could not enjoy the stories of Margaret while she must be thinking of Isabella.

'I wished to be with you,' she explained.

'There will not be many more days when we can be together, for I shall soon be setting out for Portugal. Juan and Margaret will be starting on their journey, so you will miss them also. But of course they will be coming back.'

'You will come back too.'

'Yes. Our mother has promised that I shall return to see you all or she will come to me. If she does, I hope she will bring you with her, Catalina.'

'I will implore her to.'

They were silent for a while and then Isabella said: 'Catalina, you are the youngest, yet I think you are the wisest. You understand my feelings more than any of the others.'

'It is because one day I too shall have to go away.'

'Why yes, Catalina. How selfish I am, to think of myself all the time. But it will be different for you. Catalina, how I wish that I had gone before.'

'Then you would not have been here now.'

'You are too young to remember what happened in this country; and because of me it will happen in Portugal. Emanuel has agreed that it shall.'

'They will drive out the Jews, Isabella; but is that not a good thing? Then Portugal will be an all-Christian country, even as Spain is.'

'I think of those men, women and children driven from their homes.'

'But they are Jews, Isabella. I have heard the servants talking about them. They poison wells. They destroy the crops with their incantations and, do you know, Isabella, they do something far worse. They kidnap Christian boys and crucify them as Christ was crucified.'

'I have heard these stories too, but I wonder if they are true.'

'Why should you wonder?'

'Because when people do great injustice they always seek to convince themselves that what they have done is just.'

'But it is surely just to bring all people to the Christian Faith. It is for their good.'

'I believe that, but I am haunted by them, Catalina. I see them in my dreams. Terrible things happen to them. When they reached barbarous foreign countries they were robbed and murdered. Little girls like you were violated before the very eyes of their parents. And when they had raped them they slit open their bodies because it was rumoured that they had swallowed their jewels that they might take them away with them. You see, they were not allowed to take what belonged to them.'

'Isabella, you must pray. You must be serene, as Margaret is. You must not think of these things.'

'It is easy for her. She does not come to her husband with this guilt upon her.'

'Nor should you, Isabella.'

'But I do, Catalina. I hear their voices in my dreams. I see them . . . rows and rows of angry, frightened faces. I see terrible things in my dreams, and I feel that a curse is upon me.'

There was little that Catalina could do to comfort Isabella.

❧ Chapter V ❧

TRAGEDY AT SALAMANCA

Juan and Margaret had started on their triumphal journey, and the time had come for the Princess Isabella to set out for the meeting with Emanuel.

She was glad that her mother was travelling with her. Ferdinand also accompanied them, but the Princess had little to say to her father; she was aware of his impatience for the marriage to take place.

The Queen understood her daughter's reluctance to return as a bride to the country of the man she had loved so tenderly; but she had no idea of the horrors which filled her daughter's mind. It was inconceivable to the Queen that young Isabella could be so concerned about the fate of a section of the community who refused the benefits of Christianity.

The marriage was to be performed without the pomp which usually accompanied royal marriages. Isabella was a widow. The people were still rejoicing over the marriage of Juan and Margaret. A great deal had been spent on that ceremony, and important as this marriage with Portugal was, it must be performed with the minimum outlay. Neither Ferdinand nor

Isabella were spendthrifts and they were not eager to spend unless it was necessary.

So the ceremony which was to take place at Valencia de Alcantara would be a quiet one. In this little town Emanuel was waiting for his bride.

Strange emotions filled the young Isabella's heart as she lifted her eyes to her bridegroom's face. Memories came back to her of the Palace in Lisbon where she had first seen him standing beside the King, and she remembered thinking at that moment that he was Alonso.

He had been her friend afterwards; he had shown clearly his desire to be in Alonso's place; and after that unhappy day when Alonso died he had been the kindest and most sympathetic of her friends. It was then that he had suggested that she stay in Portugal as his wife.

Now he was the King of Portugal – an honour which could never have come to him but for that accident in the forest, for had Alonso lived she and he would have sons to come before Emanuel.

But it had happened differently, tragically so. And here she was, the bride of Emanuel.

He lifted her hand to his lips and kissed it. He loved her still. How wonderful that this young man should have remained faithful to her all those years. While she had mourned in her widowhood and declared that she would never marry again, he had waited.

And so she had come to him at last, but now it was with a hideous burden about her neck, the misery of thousands of Jews.

There was pain behind his smile. He too was thinking that it was a terrible price – the denial of his own beliefs – which he had to pay for her.

The ceremony was performed, while Ferdinand exulted and the Queen smiled graciously. All was well. The Infanta Isabella of Spain was now the Queen of Portugal.

❧❧❧

Isabella was glad that it had not been the usual exhausting ceremony. That was something she could not have endured.

When she was with Emanuel, when she was aware of his tenderness for her, his gentleness, his determination to make her happy, she felt a quiet contentment. She thought, I am fortunate, even as Margaret has been in Juan.

She had been foolish in delaying so long. She could have married him a year . . . two years . . . why, three years before. If she had done so she might have had a child by now.

'What a faithful man you are,' she told her husband, 'to wait all those years.'

'Did you not understand that, once I had seen you, I should be faithful?' he answered.

'But I am not young any more. I am twenty-seven. Why, you could have married my sister Maria. She is twelve years younger than I, and a maiden.'

'Does it seem strange to you that it was Isabella I wanted?'

'Oh, yes,' she said, 'very strange.'

He took her hands and kissed them. 'You will soon learn that it is not strange at all. I loved you when you first came to us. I loved you when you went away; and I love you more than ever now that you have come to me.'

'I shall try to be all that you deserve in a wife, Emanuel.'

He kissed her then with passion, and she had a feeling that he was trying to shut something from his mind. She knew what it was. He had not mentioned 'the condition', but it was there between them, she felt, between them and complete happiness.

To lie beside Emanuel, to know that she had a husband once more, did not bring back the bitter memories of Alonso which she had so feared. She realised now that this was the quickest way to obliterate the memory of that long ago honeymoon which had ended in tragedy.

Emanuel was not unlike his dead cousin. And if she could not feel the wild exultation which she had enjoyed with Alonso she believed that this quieter contentment was something to which she and Alonso would have come in time.

In those first days of marriage, Alonso and Emanuel had begun to mingle strangely in her mind. They had become as one person.

During those first days they forgot. Then she noticed that one of Emanuel's attendants had a Jewish cast of feature, and when it seemed to her that she caught this man's gaze fixed upon her malevolently, a terrible fear shot through her.

She said nothing of this at the time, but that night she woke screaming from a frightening dream.

Emanuel sought to comfort her but she could not remember what the dream was.

She could only sob out her terror in Emanuel's arms.

'It is my fault,' she said. 'It is my fault. I should have come to you earlier. I should never have let this happen.'

'What is it, my dearest? Tell me what is on your mind.'

'It is what we are going to do to those people. It is the price you had to pay for our marriage.'

She felt his body stiffen, and she knew that this terrible thing was on his mind as surely as it was on her own.

He kissed her hair and whispered: 'You should have come before, Isabella. You should have come long ago.'

'And now?'

'And now,' he answered, 'the deed must be done. I have given my word. It is a condition of the marriage.'

'Emanuel, you hate this. You loathe it. It haunts you . . . even as it does me.'

'I wanted you so much,' he said. 'It was the price that was asked of me and I paid it . . . because I wanted you so much.'

'Is there no way out?' she whispered.

It was a stupid question. As she asked it, she saw the stern face of Torquemada, the serene one of her mother, the shrewd one of her father. They had made this condition. They would insist on its being carried out.

They were silent for a while, then she went on: 'It is like a blight upon us. Those strange people, with their strange religion, will curse us for what we have done to them. They will curse our House. Emanuel, I am afraid.'

He held her tightly against him and when he spoke his voice sounded muffled: 'We must do the deed and then forget. It was not our fault. I was weak in my need of you. But we are married now. We will do this thing and then . . . we will begin again from there.'

'Is it possible?'

'It is, my Isabella.'

She allowed herself to be comforted; but when she slept her dreams were haunted by a thousand voices – voices of men, women and children who, because of their faith, would be driven from their homes. These voices cursed her, cursed the united Houses of Spain and Portugal.

Salamanca was celebrating the arrival of the heir of Spain and his bride. The people had come in from miles around; men, women and children moved like ants across the plain on their way to the town of the University.

The students were *en fête*; they were of all nationalities for, next to Paris, this was the foremost seat of learning in the world. The town was rich, as many noblemen had bought houses there that they might live near their student sons and watch over them during their years at the University.

Through the streets the students swaggered in their stoles, the colour of which indicated their faculties. Salamanca was often gay, but it had never seen anything to equal this occasion. The bells of the churches rang continually; its streets and courtyards were filled with laughter; the bulls were being brought in – there must always be bulls; and in the Plaza Mayor the excitement was at its height. On the balconies of the houses sat beautiful women, and the students watched them with gleaming eyes. Now and then a brilliant cavalcade would sweep through the streets, and the crowd would cheer because they knew this was part of the Prince's retinue.

On their way to the balls and banquets, which were given in their honour, the Prince and his bride would pass through the streets, and the people of Salamanca were given an opportunity to show their delight in the heir to the throne.

In Salamanca there was nothing but gaiety and loyalty to the royal pair.

Margaret looked on with serene eyes.

It was pleasant to know that the people loved her and her husband. She suspected that they loved the excitement of ceremony even more, but she did not tell Juan this. She was perhaps a little more cynical than he was.

He delighted in the people's pleasure, not because he wanted adulation – this worried him because he did not think himself worthy of it – but because he knew that his parents would hear of the reception which was being given them and how much it would please them.

They had danced at the ball given in their honour and were now in their own apartment.

Margaret was not tired; she could have danced all night because she was happier than she had ever been in her life. She looked at Juan and thought: Now this is the time to share this happiness with him, for it is his as well as mine and will please him as much as it pleases me.

She had not wanted to tell him until she was sure, but now she believed there could not be a doubt.

She sat down on the bed and looked at him. She had waved away the attendants who would have helped them to bed, wanting none of their ceremonies. She shocked them, she knew; but it was not important. Juan accepted her free Flemish manners and others must do the same. Those attendants who had come with her from Flanders found it difficult to settle happily in Spain. 'The continual ceremonies,' they complained, 'they are not only wearying but ridiculous.' She had answered: 'You must understand that to them our customs seem coarse, which is perhaps worse than ridiculous. There is a saying: When you are in Rome you must do as the Romans do. I would say to you, the same applies to Spain.'

Yet she thought, if they cannot adapt themselves to Spanish ways they must go home. I, who am so happy, would not have them otherwise.

'Juan,' she said, 'I fancy I shocked the company a little tonight.'

'Shocked them?'

'Oh come, did you not notice raised eyebrows? My Flemish ways astonished them.'

'What does it matter as long as you pleased them?'

'Did I please them?'

'You pleased me – let us leave it at that.'

'But Juan, you are so easy to please. Perhaps I shall have to learn to be more solemn, more of a Spaniard, more like the Queen. I must try to model myself upon your mother, Juan.'

'Stay as you are,' he said, kissing her lips. 'That will please me best.'

She leaped up and began to dance a *pavana* with the utmost solemnity. Then suddenly her mood changed.

'This,' she said, 'is how we should dance it in Flanders.'

She performed such a wild travesty of the Spanish dance that Juan burst out laughing.

'Come, dance with me,' she said, and held out her hands to him. 'If you dance very nicely I will tell you a secret.'

As he stood beside her she noticed that he looked exhausted and that his face was unusually flushed.

'Juan,' she said, 'you are tired.'

'A little. It was hot in the ballroom.'

'Your hands are burning.'

'Are they?'

'Sit down. I shall help you to bed. Come, I will be your valet.'

He said, laughing: 'Margaret, what will your attendants think of your mad ways?'

'That I am Flemish . . . merely that. Did you not know that

the people of Flanders are people who love to joke and laugh rather than stand on ceremony? They'll forgive me my oddities simply because I'm Flemish. And when *they* know my news they'll be ready to forgive me everything.'

'What news is this?'

'Come, can you not guess?'

'Margot!'

She leaned towards him and kissed him gently on the forehead.

'Long life and happiness to you, little father,' she whispered.

❧

That was a never-to-be-forgotten night.

'I shall always love Salamanca,' said Margaret.

'We'll bring him to Salamanca as soon as he is old enough,' Juan told her.

'We will send him to the University here and we will tell the people that we love their town because there we spent some of the happiest days and nights of our honeymoon.'

'There I first knew that he existed.'

They laughed and made love again; they felt more serious, more responsible people. They were no longer merely lovers; they were almost parents, and felt awed at the prospect.

It was dawn when Margaret awoke. It was as though something had startled her. She did not know what. The city was wakening to life. The students were already in the streets.

Margaret had a feeling that something was wrong.

She sat up in bed. 'Juan!' she cried.

He did not answer her at once, and she bent over him calling him again.

The flush was still in his cheeks and as she laid her face against his she was struck by the heat of it.

'Juan,' she whispered, 'Juan, my dearest. Wake up.'

He opened his eyes and she felt that she wanted to sob with relief to see him smile at her.

'Oh Juan, for the moment I thought something was wrong.'

'What could be wrong?' he asked, taking her hand.

His fingers seemed to scorch her flesh.

'How hot you are!'

'Am I?' He began to raise himself but, even as he did so, he fell back on the pillows.

'What is wrong, Juan? What ails you?'

He put his hand to his head. 'It is a dizziness,' he said.

'You are sick,' she cried. She sprang from the bed and wrapped a robe about her trembling body. She ran to the door calling: 'Come quickly. The Prince is ill.'

❧❧

The physicians stood at his bedside.

His Highness had contracted a fever, they said. He would soon recover with their remedies.

All that day Margaret sat by his bedside. He watched her tenderly, trying hard to assure her with his glances that all was well.

But she was not deceived; and all through the next night she sat with him.

In the early morning he was delirious.

The physicians conferred together.

'Highness,' they said to her, 'we think that a message should be sent to the King and Queen without delay.'

'Let it be done with all speed,' said Margaret quietly.

While the messengers galloped to the frontier town of Valencia de Alcantara, Margaret sat at the bedside of her husband.

❧❦

Ferdinand received the messengers from Salamanca.

He read the letter from Margaret. Juan ill! But he had been perfectly well when he set out on his honeymoon. This was the hysterical fear of a young bride. Juan was a little exhausted; perhaps being married could be exhausting to a serious young man who, before his wedding, had lived an entirely virtuous life. Ferdinand's marriage had presented no such problems; but he was ready to concede that Juan was different from himself in that respect.

But there was another letter. This was signed by two physicians. The Prince's health was giving them cause for alarm. They believed he had contracted a malignant fever and that he was so ill that his parents should come immediately to his bedside.

Ferdinand looked grave. This was no hysteria; Juan must be really ill.

It was inconvenient. Emanuel and his daughter Isabella were still celebrating their marriage, and it would give rise to great anxiety if both he and the Queen left them abruptly to go to Juan's bedside.

Ferdinand went to Isabella's apartment, wondering how best he could break the news. She smiled as he entered, and he felt tenderness towards her. She looked a little older; the sorrow of parting with Juana, and now Isabella, had etched a few more lines on her face. When Ferdinand had his own way, as he had over this matter of Isabella's marriage, he had time to

112

feel affection for his Queen. She was a good, devoted mother, he reminded himself, and if she erred in her conduct towards her children it was on the side of over-indulgence.

He decided to suppress the physicians' letter and show her only that of Margaret. Thus he could avoid arousing too much anxiety at this moment.

'News,' he announced, 'from Salamanca.'

Her face lit up with pleasure.

'I heard,' she said, 'that the people have given them a welcome such as they have rarely given any before.'

'Yes, that is true,' answered Ferdinand, 'but . . .'

'But . . . ?' cried the Queen and the alarm shot up in her eyes.

'Juan is a little unwell. I have a letter here from Margaret. The poor child writes quite unlike the calm young lady she pretends to be.'

'Show me the letter.'

Ferdinand gave it to her, and put his arm about her shoulders while she read it.

'You see, it is the hysterical outburst of our little bride. If you ask me, our Juan finds being a husband to such a lively girl a little exhausting. He is in need of a rest.'

'A fever!' said the Queen. 'I wonder what that means . . . ?'

'Over-excitement. Isabella, you are getting anxious. I will go at once to Salamanca. You remain here to say your farewell to Isabella and Emanuel. I will write to reassure you from Salamanca.'

Isabella considered this.

'I know,' went on Ferdinand, 'that if I do not go you will continue anxious. And if we both go, we shall have all sorts of ridiculous rumours spreading throughout the country.'

'You are right, Ferdinand. Please go to Salamanca with all

speed. And write to me . . . as soon as you have seen him.'

Ferdinand kissed her with more tenderness than he had shown her for a long time. He was very fond of her when the submissive wife took the place of the Queen.

❦

As Ferdinand rode through the town of Salamanca he was greeted with silence. It was almost as though the University town was one of mourning.

The physicians were waiting for him, and he had but to look at them to sense their alarm.

'How is my son?' he asked brusquely.

'Highness, since we wrote to you his fever has not abated, but has in fact grown worse.'

'I will go to his bedside at once.'

He found Margaret there and noticed that several of the women in the room were weeping, and that the expressions on the faces of the men were so doleful that it appeared as though Juan were living through his last hours.

Ferdinand glowered at them, anger swamping his fear. How dared they presume that Juan was going to die. Juan must not die. He was the heir to united Spain, and there would be trouble in Aragon if there was not a male heir. He and Isabella had only daughters beside this one son. After all their hopes and plans Juan must not die.

Margaret's face was white and strained but she was composed, and Ferdinand felt a new affection for his daughter-in-law. But the sight of Juan's wan face on the pillow frightened him.

He knelt by the bed and took Juan's hand.

'My son, what is this bad news I hear?'

Juan smiled at him. 'Oh, Father, so you have come. Is my mother here?'

'Nay. Why should she come because you have a little indisposition? She is at the frontier, speeding your sister on her way to Portugal.'

'I should have liked to have seen her,' said Juan faintly.

'Well, you will see her soon enough.'

'She will have to come soon, I think, Father.'

Ferdinand's angry voice boomed out: 'But why so?'

'You must not be angry with me, Father, but I think I feel death close to me.'

'What nonsense! Margaret, it is nonsense, is it not?'

Margaret said stonily: 'I do not know.'

'Then I do!' cried Ferdinand. 'You are going to recover . . . and quickly. By God, are you not the heir to the throne . . . the only male heir? There would be a pretty state of affairs if you left us without a male heir.'

Juan smiled faintly. 'Oh, Father, there will be others. I am not so very important.'

'I never heard such nonsense. What of Aragon? Tell me that. They will not have a female sovereign, as you know. You must therefore consider your duty and not talk of dying and leaving us without a male heir. I will see your physicians at once. I will command them to cure you of this . . . honeymoon fever . . . at once.'

Ferdinand rose and stood glowering affectionately at his son. How he had changed! he thought uneasily. Juan had never been a strong boy as he himself had been, as young Alfonso was. Holy Mother, what a pity that boy was not his legitimate son. Action was needed here . . . drastic action.

Ferdinand stalked from the room, beckoning the physicians

to follow him; and in the ante-room before the bedchamber he shut the door and demanded: 'How sick is he?'

'Very sick, Highness.'

'What hope is there of his recovery?'

The physicians did not answer. They were afraid to tell Ferdinand what they really thought. As for Ferdinand, he was afraid to probe further. He had as much affection for his son as he was capable of, but mingled with it was the thought of the part that son had to play in his own ambitions. 'I think,' he said, 'that my son has overtaxed his strength. He has had his duty to do both day and night. He has had to be a good Prince to the people and a good husband to the Archduchess. It has been too much for him. We will nurse him back to health.'

'Highness, if this sickness has been brought on through his exhaustion perhaps it would be well to separate him from his bride. This would give him a chance to grow strong again.'

'Is that the only remedy you can suggest?'

'We have tried every other remedy, and the fever grips him the more firmly.'

Ferdinand was silent for a while. Then he said: 'Let us go back to the sickroom.'

He stood at the foot of Juan's bed and tried to speak jocularly.

'The doctors tell me that you have become exhausted. They propose keeping you very quiet, and even Margaret shall not visit you.'

'No,' said Margaret, 'I must stay with him.'

Juan put out a hand and gripped that of his wife. He held it tightly and, although he did not speak, it was clear that he wished her to remain with him.

Ferdinand stared at his son's hand and noticed how thin his

wrist had become. He must have lost a great deal of weight in a very short time. Ferdinand was realising at last that his son was very ill indeed.

Yes, he thought, he is very attached to Margaret. They must stay together, for ill as he is there might yet be time to beget an heir. A child conceived in the passion of fever was still a child. If Juan could give Margaret a child before he died, his death would not be such a tragedy.

'Have no fear,' he said. 'I could never find it in my heart to separate you.'

He turned and left them together. He was now more than uneasy; he was decidedly worried.

❧❧

He could not sleep that night. Juan's condition had worsened during the day and Ferdinand found that he was sharing the general opinion of all those about the Prince.

Juan was very seriously ill.

When he had said good night to him Juan had put his burning lips to his father's hand and had said: 'Do not grieve for me, Father. If I am to die, and I think I am, I shall go to a better world than this.'

'Do not say such things,' Ferdinand had answered gruffly. 'We need you here.'

'Break the news gently to my mother,' whispered Juan. 'She loves me well. Tell her that her Angel will watch over her if it is possible for him to do so. Tell her that I love her dearly and that she has been the best mother anyone ever had. Tell her this for me, Father.'

'You shall tell her such things yourself,' retorted Ferdinand.

'Father, you must not grieve for me. I shall be in the happier

117

place. Grieve more for those I leave. Comfort my mother and care for Margaret. She is so young and she does not always understand our ways. I love her very dearly. Take care of her . . . and our child.'

'Your child!'

'Margaret is with child, Father.'

Ferdinand could not hide the joy which illumined his face. Juan saw it and understood.

'You see, Father,' he said, 'if I go, I shall leave you consolation.'

A child! It made all the difference. Why had they not told him before? The situation was not so cruel as he had feared, since Margaret carried the heir to Spain and her Habsburg inheritance.

For the moment Ferdinand forgot to fear that his son might be dying.

But now that he was in his own room he thought of Juan, his gentle son, and how Isabella had doted on her 'angel'. Juan had never caused them anxiety except over his health. He had been a model son, clever, kindly and obedient.

Ferdinand found that even the thought of the heir whom Margaret carried could not compensate for the loss of his son.

What was he going to tell Isabella? He thought tenderly of his wife who had given such love and devotion to their family. How was he going to break the news to her? She had wept bitterly because she was losing Isabella; she suffered continual anxiety over Juana in Flanders. She was thinking now of the days when Maria and Catalina would be torn from her side. If Juan died . . . how could he break the news to Isabella?

There was a knock at his door. He started forward and flung it open.

He knew what this message meant even before the man spoke.

'The physicians think you should come to the Prince's bedside to say goodbye to him, Highness.'

Ferdinand nodded.

Juan lay back on his pillows, a faint smile on his lips. Margaret was kneeling by his bed, her face buried in her hands. Her body looked as still as that of her dead husband.

❧❦

Ferdinand faced his daughter-in-law. She seemed much older than the girl who only a few months before had married Juan. Her face was expressionless.

Ferdinand said gently: 'There is the child to live for, my dear.'

'Yes,' answered Margaret, 'I have the child.'

'We shall take great care of you, my dear daughter. Let us comfort each other. I have lost the best of sons; you have lost the best of husbands. Your fortitude wins my admiration. Margaret, I do not know how to send this terrible news to his mother.'

'She will wish to know the truth with all speed,' Margaret said quietly.

'The shock would kill her. She has no idea that he was suffering from anything but a mild fever. No, I must break this news gently. I am going to write to her now and tell her that Juan is ill and that you are with child. Two pieces of news, one good one bad. Then I will write again saying that Juan's condition is giving cause for anxiety. You see, I shall gradually break this terrible news to her. It is the only way she could bear it.'

'She will be heartbroken,' Margaret murmured, 'but I sometimes think she is stronger than any of us.'

'Nay. At heart she is only a woman . . . a wife and mother. She loves all her children dearly, but he was her favourite. He was her son, the heir to everything we have fought for.' Ferdinand suddenly buried his face in his hands. 'I do not know how she will survive this shock.'

Margaret did not seem to be listening. She felt numb, telling herself that this had not really happened and that she was living through some hideous nightmare. She would wake soon to find herself in Juan's arms and they would rise from their bed, go to the window and look out on the sunlit *patio*. They would ride again through the cheering crowds in the streets of Salamanca. She would laugh and say: 'Juan, last night I had a bad dream. I dreamed that the worst possible thing which could befall me happened to me. And now I am awake, in the sunshine, and I am so happy to be alive because I know how singularly my life has been blessed since I have you.'

❧❧

Ferdinand felt better when he was taking action. No sooner had he dispatched the two messengers than he called a secretary to him.

'Write this to Her Highness the Queen,' he commanded.

And the man began to write as the King dictated:

'A terrible calamity has occurred in Salamanca. His Highness the King has died of a fever.'

The man stopped writing and stared at Ferdinand.

'Ah, my good fellow, you look at me as though you think I am mad. No, this is not madness. It is good sense. The Queen will have to learn sooner or later of the death of the Prince. I have been considering how best I can break this news. I fear the effect it will have on her, and in this way I think I can soften the terrible blow. She will have had my two letters telling her of our son's indisposition. Now I will ride with all speed to her. I shall send a messenger on ahead of me with the news of my death. That would be the greatest blow she could sustain. While she is overcome with the horror of this news I will stride in and confront her. She will be so overjoyed to see me that the blow of her son's death will be less severe.'

The secretary bowed his head in melancholy understanding, but he doubted the wisdom of Ferdinand's conduct.

However, it was not for him to criticise the action of his King, so he wrote the letter and, shortly afterwards, left Salamanca.

≈≈≈

Isabella had said her last farewells to her daughter and Emanuel; the Infanta of Spain, now the Queen of Portugal, had set out with her husband and her retinue on the way to Lisbon.

How tired she was! She was becoming too old for long journeys, and taking leave of her daughter depressed her. She was extremely worried by the news of Juana which filtered through from Flanders. And now Juan was unwell.

The first of the messages arrived. Margaret was with child. The news filled her with joy; but the rest of the message said that Juan was unwell. The health of her children was a continual anxiety to her, and the two elder ones had always been delicate. Isabella's cough had caused her mother a great deal of misgiving; Juan had been almost too frail and fair for a young man. Perhaps she had been so concerned about Juana's mental condition that she had worried less about the physical health of the two elder children than she otherwise would have done. Maria and Catalina were much stronger; perhaps because they had been born in more settled times.

The second letter came almost immediately after the first. It appeared that Juan's condition was more serious than they had at first thought.

'I will go to him,' she said. 'I should be at his side at such a time.'

While she was giving orders to the servants to make ready for the journey to Salamanca another messenger arrived.

She was bewildered as she read the letter he brought. Ferdinand . . . dead! This could not be. Ferdinand was full of strength and vitality. It was Juan who was ill. She could not imagine Ferdinand anything but alive.

'Hasten,' she cried. 'There is not a moment to lose. I must go with all speed to Salamanca to see what is really happening there.'

Ferdinand! Her heart was filled with strangely mingling feelings. There were so many memories of a marriage which had lasted for nearly thirty years.

She was bewildered and found it difficult to collect her thoughts.

Was it possible that there had been some mistake? Should she read Juan for Ferdinand?

She was sick with anxiety. If Juan were dead she would no longer wish to live. He was her darling whom she wished to keep by her side for as long as she lived. He was her only son, her beloved Angel. He could not be dead. It would be too cruel.

She read the message again. It clearly said the King.

Juan . . . Ferdinand. If she had lost her husband she would

be sad indeed. She was devoted to him. If that great love which she had borne in the beginning had become a little battered by the years, he was still her husband and she could not imagine life without him.

But if Juan were spared to her she could rebuild her life. She would have her children, whose affairs would be entirely hers to manage as she would. She was experienced enough to rule alone.

'Not Juan . . .' she whispered.

And then Ferdinand strode into the room.

She stared at him as though he were a ghost. Then she ran to him and clasped his hands, pressing them in her own as though she wished to reassure herself that they were flesh and blood.

'It is I,' said Ferdinand.

'But this . . .' she stammered. 'Someone has played a cruel trick. This says . . .'

'Isabella, my dearest wife, tell me you are glad to know that paper lied.'

'I am so happy to see you well.'

'It is as I hoped. Oh, Isabella, fortunate we are indeed to be alive and together. We have had our differences, but what should we be without each other?'

She put her head against his chest and he embraced her. There were tears in his eyes.

'Isabella,' he continued. 'Now that you are happy to see me restored to you I have some sad news which I must break to you.'

She drew away from him. Her face had grown deathly pale and her eyes were wide and looked black with fear.

'Our son is dead,' he said.

Isabella did not speak. She shook her head from side to side.

'It is true, Isabella. He died of a malignant fever. The physicians could do nothing for him.'

'Then why . . . why . . . was I not told?'

'I thought to protect you. I have tried to prepare you for this shock. My dearest Isabella, I know how you suffer. Do I not suffer with you?'

'My son,' she whispered. 'My angel.'

'Our son,' he answered. 'But there will be a child.'

She did not seem to hear. She was thinking of that hot day in Seville when he had been born. She remembered holding him in her arms and the feeling of wild exultation which had come to her. Her son. The heir of Ferdinand and Isabella. She had been deeply concerned about the state of her country then; anarchy was in full spate, and there was the chaos which had followed on the disastrous reigns preceding her own; she had been setting up the Santa Hermandad in every town and village. And in her arms had lain that blessed child, so that at that time in spite of all her trials, she had been the happiest woman in Spain.

She could not believe that he was dead.

'Isabella,' said Ferdinand gently, 'you have forgotten. There is to be a child.'

'I have lost my son,' she said slowly. 'I have lost my angel child.'

'There will be grandsons to take his place.'

'No one will ever take his place.'

'Isabella, you and I have no time for looking backwards. We must look forward. This tragedy has overcome us. We must be brave. We must say: This was the will of God. But

God is merciful. He has taken our son, but not before he has left his fertile seed behind him.'

Isabella did not answer. She swayed a little and Ferdinand put his arm about her.

'You should rest for a while,' he said. 'This shock has been too much for you.'

'Rest!' she retorted. 'There is little rest left for me. He was my only son and I shall never see him smile again.'

She was fighting the impulse to rail against this cruel fate.

Is it not enough that two daughters have gone from me, and even my little Catalina will not long remain? she was demanding. Why should I suffer so? Juan was the one I thought to keep with me for ever.

Perhaps she should send for her confessor. Perhaps she was in need of prayer.

She sought to control herself. This cruel day had to be faced; life had to go on.

She lifted her face to Ferdinand and he saw that the wildness had gone from it.

She said in a clear voice which was as firm as ever: 'The Lord hath given, and the Lord hath taken away. Blessed be His Name.'

⮑ Chapter VI ⮐

JUANA AND PHILIP

All Spain was in mourning for the Prince of the Asturias. Sable banners were hung up in all the important towns. The streets of Salamanca were silent save for the tolling of bells.

The King and Queen had returned to Madrid. They shut themselves in their private apartments in the Alcazar and gave way to their grief.

Throughout the land the extraordinary qualities of the Prince were talked of in hushed voices.

'Spain,' said its people, 'has suffered one of the greatest losses she has ever been called upon to bear since she fell into the hands of the barbarians.'

But gradually the gloom lifted as the news spread. Before he died his child was conceived, and his widow, the young Archduchess from Flanders, carried this child in her womb.

When the child is born, it was said, Spain will smile again.

Catalina and Maria sat with their sister-in-law while they worked on their embroidery.

Margaret was more subdued than she had been before the death of Juan; she seemed even more gentle.

Catalina encouraged her to talk, but not of her life with Juan – that would be too painful. To talk of Flanders might also be an uneasy subject, for something was happening in Flanders, between Juana and her husband Philip, which was not pleasing to the Sovereigns. So the best subject was Margaret's life in France, of which neither Catalina nor Maria ever tired of hearing. As for Margaret, recalling it seemed to bring her some peace, for if she could project herself back into a past, in which she had never even heard of Juan, she could escape her anguish for a while and know some comfort.

She made the two young girls see the town of Amboise situated at that spot where the Loire and the Amasse met; they saw the château standing on its rocky plateau, imposing and as formidable as a fortress, and the surrounding country with its fields and undulating vineyards.

'And you thought,' said Catalina, 'that that would be your home for ever and that you would be Queen of France.'

'It shows, does it not,' said Margaret, 'that we can never be sure of what is in store for us.'

She looked a little sad and Maria put in: 'Were you unhappy to leave France?'

'Yes, I think I was. I thought it was a great insult, you see, and I knew that my father would be angry. It was not very pleasant to have been chosen to be the bride of the King of France and then find that he preferred someone else.'

'But you came to us instead,' whispered Catalina, and wished she had not said that because she saw the spasm of pain cross Margaret's face.

'Tell us more about Amboise,' she went on quickly.

Margaret was only too happy to do so. She told of Charles and his sister who had been her guardian, and their father Louis XI who delighted to wear the shabbiest clothes.

As she talked to the girls, Margaret felt the child moving within her and began to ask herself why she should wish to talk of the past. Juan was lost to her but she had his child.

She stopped and began to smile.

'What is it?' asked Catalina, and even Maria looked curious.

Margaret laid her hands on her body and said: 'I can feel the child . . . mine and Juan's . . . moving within me, and it is as though he kicks me. Perhaps he is angry that I talk of the past when he is about to come into the world, and is telling me that I should speak of the future.'

Maria looked a little startled and Catalina was shocked. Margaret's manners were often disconcerting, but they were both glad to see that look in her face. It was as though she had come alive again, as though she had realised that there was happiness waiting for her in this world.

After that she talked to them about Juan; she told them of how she had thought she was going to die when her ship had been almost wrecked. There was no more talk of Amboise. She went over everything that had happened since her arrival in Spain; she could not talk enough of the wedding, of the celebrations, of their triumphal journey across Spain to Salamanca.

Catalina rejoiced and Maria brightened; they looked forward to those times which they spent together.

'Whatever happens,' said Catalina to Maria, 'however evil our fate may seem, something good will come. Look at Margaret. Juan was taken from her; but she is to have Juan's child.'

That was a very comforting philosophy for Catalina; she cherished it.

～の～

Now there was less talk of Juan's death; everyone was awaiting the birth of Juan's son.

'It will be as though he lives again,' said the Queen. 'I shall feel fresh life within me when I hold my grandchild in my arms.'

Ferdinand talked of the child as though it were a boy.

'Please let it be a boy,' prayed Catalina. 'Then my mother will be happy again.'

It was an ordinary enough day. Margaret had sat with Catalina and Maria at their sewing and they had talked of the baby, as they did continually now.

'He will soon be with us,' Margaret told them. 'How I shall welcome him. I do assure you I do not greatly care to be seen in this condition.'

Maria looked shocked. She thought that it was tempting God and the saints to talk in such a way; but Catalina knew that it was only the Flemish manner and not to be taken seriously.

Margaret had put her hands on her bulging body and said: 'Oh, he is a sly one. He is very quiet today. Usually he kicks me to warn me that he will not long stay imprisoned in my body.'

Then she laughed and, although perhaps it was a shocking subject, Catalina rejoiced to see her so gay.

They chatted about the child and the clothes and the cradle which were being prepared for him; and the fêtes that would take place to celebrate his birth. They grew quite merry. It was an ordinary pleasant day.

Catalina did not know when she first became aware of the tension in the Palace. She, who loved her home perhaps more dearly than any of the others, was always conscious of its moods.

What was it? An unexpected quietness, followed by more activity than usual. Grave faces. Whisperings.

She went to the sewing room. Maria was there but Margaret was not.

'What has happened, Maria?'

'It is the baby.'

'But it is too soon. They said . . .'

'It has come nevertheless.'

Catalina's face broke into a smile. 'How glad I am. The waiting is over. I wonder when we shall see it, Maria.'

Maria said slowly: 'It is not good that it should come before its time.'

'What do you mean?'

'I don't quite know. But I think they are worried about it.'

The girls sat silently sewing, alert for every sound.

Then suddenly they heard a woman sobbing. Catalina ran to the door, and saw one of the attendants hurrying through the apartments.

'What has happened?' she cried.

But the woman did not answer; she stumbled blindly away. Terrible misgivings came to Catalina then. Was yet another tragedy to befall her family?

Catalina stood at the door of her mother's private apartment.

'The Queen is not to be disturbed,' said one of the two attendants who guarded the door.

Catalina stood desolate.

'I must see my mother,' she said firmly.

The attendants shook their heads.

'Is she alone?' asked Catalina.

'That is so.'

'She is mourning the dead baby, is she not? She will want me with her.'

The attendants looked at each other and, taking advantage of their momentary inattention, Catalina calmly opened the door and walked into her mother's apartment. The attendants were so astonished that the little Princess, who was usually so decorous in her behaviour, should do such a thing, that the door was closing on her before they realised what had happened.

Catalina sped across the room to that small antechamber where she knew her mother would be kneeling before her altar.

She went in and quietly knelt beside her.

The Queen looked at her small daughter, and the tears which before had remained unshed began to flow.

For a few minutes they wept in silence and prayed for strength to control their grief.

Then the Queen rose to her feet and held out her hand to Catalina.

'I had to come to you,' cried Catalina. 'It was not the fault of the attendants. They tried to stop me. But I was so frightened.'

'I am glad you came,' said the Queen. 'We should always be together in sorrow and in happiness, my darling.'

She led Catalina into the main apartment and sat on her bed, drawing her daughter down beside her. She smoothed the child's hair and said: 'You know that there is no baby.'

'Yes, Mother.'

'It never lived. It never suffered. It was born dead.'

'Oh, Mother, why . . . why when it meant so much to us all?'

'Perhaps because the shock of its father's death was too much for its mother to bear. In any case – because it was the will of God.'

'It was cruel . . . cruel.'

'Hush, my dearest. You must never question God's will. You must learn to accept with meekness and fortitude the trials He gives you to bear.'

'I will try to be as good and strong as you are, Mother.'

'My child, I fear I am not always strong. We must cease to grieve. We must think of comforting poor Margaret.'

'She will not die?'

'No, we think she will live. So you see it is not all tragedy. As for me, I have lost my son and my grandchild. But I have my daughters, have I not? I have my Isabella who may well give me a grandchild before long. I have my Juana who I am sure will have children. Then there is my Maria and my little Catalina. You see I am well blessed with many cherished possessions. They will bring me such happiness as will make up for this great tragedy I have suffered.'

'Oh, Mother, I hope they will.' Catalina thought of her sisters: Isabella who had dreamed she heard the voices cursing in her dreams, Juana, whose wildness had always caused the greatest anxiety. Maria? Herself? What would happen to them?

In the Brussels Palace Juana heard the news from Spain. It came in an affectionate letter from her mother. A terrible tragedy had befallen their House. The heir had died only a few months after his marriage, and all their hopes had been centred on a child of this union who was stillborn.

'Write me some good news of yourself,' Isabella begged her daughter. 'That will do more than anything to cheer me.'

The letter fluttered from Juana's hand. The troubles in Madrid seemed far away, and she had almost forgotten that she had ever lived there, so completely absorbed was she by the gay life of Brussels.

This was the way to live. Here balls, banquets, dancing, festivities were what mattered. Philip implied this and Philip was always right.

Juana could not think of her handsome husband without being overcome by many mingling emotions. Chief of these was her desire for him; she could scarcely bear to be absent from him and, when she was in his presence, she could not keep her eyes from watching him or her hands from reaching out to touch him.

This had amused him in the beginning. He had quickly initiated her into the erotic experiences which made up the greater part of his life, and she had followed eagerly, for everything that he did seemed wonderful and she was eager to share in it.

Some of her retinue who had come with her into Flanders warned her. 'Be a little more discreet, Highness. Do not be over eager for his embraces.'

But there was no restraint in Juana. There never had been; she could not begin learning, now that she was face to face with the greatest emotional experience of her life.

She wanted Philip with her every hour of the day and night. She could not hide the burning desire which was like a frenzy. Philip laughed at it. It had been very amusing at first.

Later she feared he was less amused and had begun to avoid her.

There were the mistresses. She could never be sure who was his mistress of the moment. It might be some little lace-maker whom he had seen on his journeys through the dominions, fancied and set up near the Palace that he might visit her. It might be – and so often was – one of the ladies of the Court.

When she saw these women Juana felt near to murder. She wanted to mutilate them in some way so that they would be hideous instead of desirable in his eyes.

There were nights when he did not visit her; when she knew that he was with some mistress. Then she would lie, biting her pillow, weeping passionate tears, giving vent to uncontrolled laughter, forgetting everything but her desire for Philip, the most handsome man in the world.

One of the Flemish women had whispered slyly: 'He takes his mistress. There are some who would say, if Your Highness took a lover, that you were provoked to it. Perhaps he would.'

'Take a lover!' cried Juana. 'You do not know Philip. What other man could ever satisfy or please me in the smallest way since I have known him!'

They were beginning to say in the Brussels Palace that Juana's wildness was alarming because it was not merely the fury of a jealous wife. It went deeper than that.

They avoided her eyes whenever possible.

Juana was now finding it difficult to think of her mother far away in Madrid, and this tragedy which had befallen her family. She stared into space trying to remember them all, those wearying days of sitting in the nursery stitching at some tiresome piece of needlework. She remembered being beaten because she had run away when it was time to go to confession.

She laughed aloud at the vague memory. All that was past. Philip would never beat her because she had failed to go to confession. Philip had not a great deal of respect for priests, and life in Brussels was very different from that in Madrid. There was not the same solemnity, the wearying religious services. The rule in Brussels was: Enjoy yourself. The Flemish people, lacking the dignity of the Spaniards, believed they had been put on this Earth to enjoy themselves. It was a doctrine which appealed to Juana.

Everything about Flanders appealed to Juana. It must be so, because Philip was in Flanders.

She was not sure now whether Philip would regard this news from Spain as a tragedy; and if he did not, how could she?

There was another side to Philip's nature besides his sensuality and his love of gaiety. He was not the son of Maximilian for nothing. He was proud of the possessions which were now his and those greater ones which he would inherit. He had wanted Juana for his bride, before he had seen her, because she was the daughter of Isabella and Ferdinand and great good could come to him through union with such an heiress.

Philip was ambitious.

He had been rather pleased, she knew, when he had heard of Juan's death, and not so pleased when he had heard that there was to be a child.

'By God, Juana,' he had cried, 'now that your brother is dead, who will be the Spanish heir? Tell me that. That sickly sister of yours? The Aragonese are a fierce people. They do not believe women should be their rulers. And quite right too, my love. Quite right too. Do you not agree with me?'

'Oh yes, Philip.'

He slapped her buttocks jauntily, because it amused him on occasions to treat the daughter of Ferdinand and Isabella as though she were a tavern girl.

'That's a good girl, Juana. Always agree with your husband. That makes him pleased with you.'

She held her face up to his and murmured his name.

'By God, woman,' said Philip, 'you are insatiable. Later perhaps . . . if you are a good girl. Listen carefully to what I have to say. If it had not been for this child your brother's wife is to have, you and I would be Prince and Princess of Castile.'

'Philip, you would be very pleased then?'

'I should be very pleased with my little Juana. But now I am not so pleased. If this child is a son . . . well, then, my little Juana does not bring the same gifts to her doting husband, does she?'

He had caressed her mildly and then had pushed her from him in order to go to one of his mistresses, she felt sure, because he was not pleased with her. A child had been conceived and therefore Philip was not pleased with his wife.

She had cursed Margaret for her fruitfulness. Such a short time married, and already to have conceived a child which Philip did not want! How tiresome of her.

But now there was this news and Philip would be delighted. She must go to him at once.

Before she could leave her apartment there was a knock on her door and a priest entered.

Juana frowned, but this man was Fray Matienzo, a confidential priest whom her mother had sent to Flanders to watch over her daughter; and although Juana was far from Isabella she still remembered the awe in which even she had held her mother.

So she stood impatiently waiting for what the priest had to say to her.

'Your Highness,' he began, 'I have received a letter from the Queen in which she tells me this tragic news which she also imparts to you. The Queen will be very sad.'

Juana said nothing; she was not even thinking of the priest nor of her mother. She was seeing Philip's fair flushed face, listening to her while she told him the news. She would throw herself into his arms, and he would be so pleased with her that he would forget all those big flaxen-haired women who seemed to give him so much pleasure. He would give all his attention to her.

'I thought,' said Fray Matienzo, 'that you might wish to pray with me for comfort.'

Juana looked bewildered. 'I do not wish to pray,' she said. 'I must go at once. I have something important to do.'

The priest laid a hand on her arm.

'The Queen, your mother, asks me questions about you.'

'Then pray answer them,' she retorted.

'I fear they might cause her pain if I told her the truth.'

'What's this?' said Juana half-heartedly.

'If I told her that you did not worship as frequently as you did in Spain, if I told her that you did not go to confession . . .'

'I do these things as frequently as my husband does.'

'That will not serve you as an excuse before God or your mother.'

Juana snapped her fingers; frenzied lights were beginning to show in her eyes. He was detaining her against her will; he was denying her her pleasure. What if Philip heard this news from others before she herself could impart it?

She threw off the priest's detaining hand.

'Go your way,' she said angrily, 'and let me go mine.'

'Highness, I implore you to dismiss the French priests who surround you now. Their ways are not ours.'

'I prefer them,' she answered.

'Unless you listen to me, unless you mind your ways, I shall have no alternative but to write to your mother and tell her that you have no true piety.'

Juana snarled at him between her teeth: 'Then do so. Do what you will, you interfering old fool. I am no longer of Spain. I belong to Flanders and Philip!'

She laughed wildly and ran from the room.

Those attendants who saw her looked at each other and shrugged their shoulders. There was little ceremony at the Flemish Court, but no one behaved in quite the same manner as the Infanta Juana. She was more than wild, she was strange, they said.

She found Philip in his apartments. He was sprawled on a sofa, his handsome face flushed. One golden-haired woman sat on a stool at his feet; she was lying back against him, embracing his leg. Another woman, also with brilliant flaxen hair, was fanning him. Someone was strumming on a lute, and men and women were dancing.

It was what Juana had seen many times before. If she could have had her way she would have taken one of those women by her flaxen hair, and have her bound and beaten. Then she would turn her attention to the other.

But she must calm herself. They might flaunt their long flaxen locks which fell over their big bare bosoms, but this was an occasion when she had something more to offer, and she was going to calm herself so thoroughly that she would not act foolishly this time.

She stood on the threshold of the room. No one took any notice of her. The dancers went on dancing and the women went on caressing Philip.

Juana screeched at the top of her voice: 'Silence!'

This had the desired effect. There was complete stillness in the room and, before Philip could command them all to go on as they were, Juana cried: 'I have important news from Spain.'

Philip rose to his feet without warning. The woman at his feet toppled off her stool and fell to the floor. Juana wanted to laugh exultantly as she watched her, but she controlled herself.

She waved the letter from her mother and, seeing it, Philip's eyes gleamed with interest.

'Leave me with my wife,' he ordered.

Juana stood aside, watching them file out. She did not look at the two women. She was determined not to lose control of her emotions. She was about to have him to herself and she was happy.

'What news?' he demanded. 'What news?'

She smiled at him with all the love she felt for him in her eyes. She knew that she was about to give him something which he greatly desired.

'The child is stillborn,' she said.

For a few seconds he did not speak. She watched the slow smile cross his face. Then he brought his clenched fist down on to his thigh. He took her cheek between his thumb and forefinger and pressed it so tightly that she wanted to scream with the joy of it. Whether it was pain or caresses he gave her she did not care. It was enough that his hands were upon her.

'Show me the letter,' he said gruffly, and snatched it from her.

She watched him reading it. It was all there, just as he wished it to be.

Then his hands fell to his sides and he began to laugh.

'You are pleased, Philip?' she said, as though to remind him that he owed this to her.

'Oh yes, my love, I am pleased. Are you?'

'I am always pleased when you are.'

'That's true, I know. Why Juana, do you see what this means?'

'That my sister Isabella is now the heir of Spain.'

'Your sister Isabella! They will not have a woman to rule them, I tell you.'

'But my parents have no more sons. And Isabella is the eldest.'

'I ought to beat you for not being born first, Juana.' She laughed wildly. The thought did not displease her. She only asked that she should have his undivided attention. Instead he went on: 'I will show you what an indulgent husband I am. You and I shall be Prince and Princess of Castile and, when your mother is no more, Castile will be ours.'

'Philip, it should be as you say. But they will remind me that I am not the eldest.'

'Do you think they will want the King of Portugal to rule Spain? Not they.'

'Not they!' she cried. And she wondered whether they would have the heir of Maximilian either. But this was not for her to say. Philip was pleased with her.

He took her in his arms and danced her round the room. She clung to him madly.

'You will stay with me for a while?' she pleaded. He put his head on one side and considered her. 'Please, Philip! Please, Philip!' she pleaded. 'The two of us . . . alone . . .'

He nodded slowly and drew her to the couch.

Her passion still had the power to amuse him.

He would not stay long with her though, and was soon calling back his friends.

He made Juana stand on the couch beside him.

'My friends,' he said, 'you have strangers among you, strangers of great importance. You must each come forward and pay homage to the Prince and Princess of Castile.'

It was a game similar to those they often played. Each person came to the couch and bowed low, kissing first the hand of Philip and then Juana's.

Juana was so happy. She suddenly remembered with unusual vividness her mother's apartment at Madrid, and she wondered what her parents and her sisters would say if they could see her and Philip now – clever Philip and his wife who had, without their consent, made themselves the heir and heiress of Castile.

She was so amused that she burst into laughter. The restraint of the last hour had been too much for her, and she could not stop laughing.

Philip looked at her coldly. He remembered her frenzied passion, her great desire for him – and he shuddered.

For the first time the thought occurred to him: I know why she is so strange. She is *mad*.

⮞ Chapter VII ⮜

THE QUEEN OF PORTUGAL

Ferdinand and Isabella were studying with dismay the letter they had received from Fray Matienzo. This was indeed disquieting news. Not only was Juana conducting herself in Flanders with the utmost impiety, but she had dared, with her husband, to assume the title of heir to Castile.

Isabella said bitterly: 'I wish I had never allowed her to leave me. She should never have been sent away from me. She is unstable.'

Ferdinand looked gloomy. He was wondering now whether it would not have been better to have sent Maria into Flanders. Maria had little spirit, it was true, but at least she would not have behaved with such abandon as Juana apparently did.

'There are times,' went on Isabella, 'when I say to myself, What blow will fall next? My son . . .'

Ferdinand laid his arm about her shoulders. 'My dear,' he murmured, 'you must not give way to your sorrow. It is true that our alliances with the Habsburgs are proving to be a mixed blessing. We have Margaret here on our hands . . . our daughter-in-law, who has failed to give us an heir. And now it seems that Philip is more our enemy than our friend.'

'You have written to Maximilian protesting against this wicked action of his son and our daughter?'

'I have.'

'But,' went on Isabella quickly, 'I do not blame Juana. She has been forced to do this. Oh, my poor child, I would to God I had never let her go.'

'Philip is a wild and ambitious young man. We must not take him too seriously. Have no fear. This is not as important as you think. You are upset because one of your daughters has so far forgotten her duty to us as to act in a manner certain to cause us pain. Juana was always half crazy. We should not take too much notice of what she does. There is only one answer to all this.'

'And that is?'

'Send for Isabella and Emanuel. Have them proclaimed as our heirs throughout Spain. Then it will avail Maximilian's son and our daughter very little what they *call* themselves. Isabella is our eldest daughter and she is the true heir to Castile. Her sons shall inherit our crowns.'

'How wise you are, Ferdinand. You are right. It is the only course. In my grief I could only mourn for the conduct of one of my children. It was foolish of me.'

Ferdinand smiled broadly. It was pleasant to have Isabella recognising his superiority.

'Leave these matters to me, Isabella. You will see that I know how to manage these erring children of ours.'

'Promise me not to feel too angry towards our Juana.'

'I'd like to lay my hands on her . . .' began Ferdinand.

'No, Ferdinand, no. Remember how unstable she is.'

Ferdinand looked at her shrewdly. 'There are times,' he said slowly, 'when she reminds me of your mother.'

At last those words had been spoken aloud, and Isabella felt as though she had received a blow. It was folly to be so cowardly. That idea was not new to her. But to hear it spoken aloud gave weight to it, brought her terrors into the daylight. They were no longer fancies, those fears; they had their roots in reality.

Ferdinand looked at her bowed head and, patting her shoulder reassuringly, he left her.

She was glad to be alone.

She whispered under her breath: 'What will become of her, what will become of my tragic child?'

And she knew at that moment that this was the greatest tragedy of her life; even now, with the poignant sorrow of loss upon her, she knew that the blow struck at her through the death of their beloved son was light compared with what she would suffer through the madness of her daughter.

Ferdinand on his way to his apartments met a messenger who brought him dispatches. He saw that these came from Maximilian, and it gave him pleasure to read them first, before taking them to Isabella.

She is distraught, he told himself. It is better for me to shield her from unpleasantness until she has recovered from these shocks; and as he read Maximilian's reply he told himself that he was glad he had done so. Maximilian made it quite clear that he was firmly behind his son's claim to the crown of Castile. He felt that the daughter-in-law of Maximilian had the right to come before the wife of the King of Portugal, even though she happened to be the younger.

This was a monstrous suggestion to make, even for such an

arrogant man. Maximilian also suggested that he had a right to the crown of Portugal through his mother, Doña Leoñor of Portugal; and that his claim was greater than that of Emanuel who was merely a nephew of the last King. There were sly hints that the King of France, Ferdinand's enemy and rival in the Italian project, was ready to stand beside Maximilian in this claim.

Ferdinand's fury was boundless. Was this what the Habsburg alliance had brought him?

He sat at his table and wrote furiously. Then he called his messengers.

'Leave at once,' he said, 'for Lisbon. Let there be no delay. This is a matter of the utmost importance.'

❧

Queen Isabella of Portugal had become reconciled to life. She was no longer tormented by nightmares. For this new peace which had come to her she was grateful to her husband. None could have been kinder than Emanuel. It was strange that here in Lisbon, where she had been so happy with her first husband Alonso, she was learning to forget him.

From her apartments in the Castelo she could look down on Lisbon, a city which she found entrancing to watch from this distance. She could see the Ashbouna where the Arabs lived, shut up in those walls which had long ago been erected by the Visigoths; she looked down past olive and fig trees to the Alcaçova which she and Emanuel sometimes inhabited. Along the narrow streets, which had been made hundreds of years before, the people congregated; there they bought and sold; gossiped, sang and danced. Some-times in the evenings the sound of a slave song would be heard, plaintive and infinitely sad with longing for a distant land.

The industrious Moors in the Mouraria turned clay on their wheels; they sat cross-legged making their pottery. Some sat weaving. They were adept at both arts and they grew rich.

It was a city of a hundred sights and beauties. Yet the Queen of Portugal did not care to mingle with her husband's people. She wished to remain in the castle looking on at them, as she wished to look on life, aloof, an onlooker rather than a participant.

In due course many of her and her husband's most industrious subjects would be driven from their country. Isabella could not forget the condition which had brought her into Portugal. The thought came back to torment her: One day they will curse me, those men and women.

But the time was not yet, and something had happened to bring her resignation.

Isabella was pregnant.

She prayed for a son. If she could give Emanuel and Portugal a son she felt she would in some small way have compensated them for the unhappiness their King's marriage was going to bring to numbers of his subjects.

When she had heard the news of her brother's death it had not been merely sorrow which had so stricken her that she had been kept to her bed for some days. That fear, which had been haunting her for so long, seemed to take a material shape, to become a tangible thing, something which would whisper in her ear: There is a curse on your House.

She had told Emanuel this and he had shaken his head. She was subject to strange fancies, he told her. Why, even though Juan was dead, Margaret was to have a child, and if that child were a son there would be an heir for Spain as surely as if Juan had lived.

She had begun to believe him.

And then came further news from Spain.

She had seen the messengers riding to the Castelo and she knew from their livery that they came from her parents. She put her hand to her heart which had begun to flutter uncomfortably.

Where was Emanuel? She would like him to be with her when she read what her parents had to say.

She called to one of her women, 'Go and see if the King is in his apartments. If he is, please tell him that I should be pleased if he would come to me here, or if he prefers it I will go to his apartment.'

There was only a short time to wait before Emanuel came hurrying to her.

She smiled and held out her hand. He was continually giving her proof of how she could rely on him.

When they were alone, she said: 'Emanuel, I have seen messengers riding up to the Castelo, and I know they come from my parents. I was afraid, so I asked you to come to me. Whenever I see my parents' seal I tremble and ask myself: What bad news now?'

'You must not, Isabella.' He kissed her cheek gently. She was looking a little better since her pregnancy and that delighted him; he had been alarmed by the thinness of her body when he remembered the young girl who had first come into Portugal to marry his cousin. Then she had not been strikingly healthy, but when he had seen her after the long absence he had noticed at once that she seemed more ethereal, her skin more transparent, her eyes larger because the fullness had disappeared from her cheeks. She was no less beautiful, but that look of not entirely belonging to this world faintly alarmed him.

It had been a great joy to discover that their marriage was to be fruitful. He was sure she had improved in health; and the effect on her spirits had been good.

'It seemed so strange to me that Juan should die. We had never thought of Juan's dying.'

'You are too fanciful, Isabella. Juan died because he caught a fever.'

'Why should a young and healthy man catch a fever on his honeymoon?'

'Men are not immune from fever merely because they are on their honeymoons, my dearest. It may well be that he was weakened by all the ceremonies. It is unwise to think of his death as an omen.' Emanuel laughed. 'Why, there was a time when you thought our union was to be ill-fated. Admit it. You thought, We want children, we *need* children, but we shall never have them. And you see, you are going to be proved wrong.'

'If it is a boy I carry,' cried Isabella with shining eyes, 'I shall say I have been foolish and I shall not talk of omens again.'

She looked over her shoulder almost furtively, as though she were speaking not to Emanuel, but to some unseen presence, as though she were pleading: Show me I was foolish to fear, by giving me a healthy son.

Emanuel smiled tenderly at her and at that moment the messengers arrived.

The letters were delivered to Isabella, who called attendants to take the messengers to where they could be refreshed after their journey.

When she was once more alone with Emanuel she held out the letters to him. Her face was white, her hands trembling.

'I pray you, Emanuel, read them for me.'

'They are meant for your eyes, my dear.'

'I know, but my hands shake so, and my eyes will not take in the words.'

As Emanuel broke the seal and read the letters, Isabella, watching him intently, saw his face whiten.

She said quickly: 'What is it, Emanuel? You must tell me quickly.'

'The child was stillborn,' he said.

Isabella gave a gasp and sank down on to a stool. The room appeared to swim round her, and she seemed to hear those malicious voices – the voices of a thousand tormented and persecuted people – whispering to her.

'But Margaret is well,' went on Emanuel.

There was silence and Isabella lifted her face to her husband's. 'There is something else?' she asked. 'I pray you keep nothing back.'

'Yes,' he said slowly, 'there is something else. Juana and Philip have proclaimed themselves heirs to Castile.'

'Juana! But that is impossible. She is younger than I.'

'That is what your parents say.'

'How could Juana do such a thing?'

'Because she has a very ambitious husband.'

'But this is terrible. This will break my mother's heart. This is like quarrelling within the family itself.'

'You need have no fear,' soothed Emanuel. 'Your parents will know how best to deal with such pretensions. They want us to prepare to leave Lisbon at once for Spain. They are going to have you publicly proclaimed heir of Castile.'

A weariness assailed Isabella. She put her hand to her aching head. In that moment she thought: I want none of these quarrels. I want to be left in peace to have my child.

Then she felt the child within her, and her mood changed. A Queen must not think of her own personal desires.

It occurred to her that the child in her womb might well be heir to the whole of Spain and all those dependencies of Spain, those lands of the New World.

There was no time in her busy life for lassitude. She had to fight for the rights of this child, even against her own sister.

Her voice was firm as she said: 'When could we be ready to leave for Spain?'

☙ Chapter VIII ❧

TORQUEMADA AND THE KING OF ENGLAND

omás de Torquemada lay on his pallet breathing heavily. His gout was a torture and he was finding it increasingly difficult to move about.

'So many things to do,' he murmured. 'So little time in which to do them.' Then because his words might have seemed like a reproach to the Almighty, he murmured: 'But Thy will be done.'

He thought often. of Ximenes, Archbishop of Toledo, who, he told himself, might one day wear the mantle of Torquemada. *There* was a man who he believed would one day overcome carnality to such an extent that he would, before his end, do as great a work as that which had been done by himself.

Torquemada could look back on the last thirty years with complacence. He could marvel now that it was not until he was fifty-eight years of age that he had emerged from the narrow life of the cloister and had begun to write his name in bold letters in the history of his country. His great achievements were the introduction of the Inquisition and the expulsion of the Jews.

He exulted when he remembered this. Alas, that his body was failing him. Alas, that he had his enemies. He wished that he had seen more of this man Ximenes. He believed that such a man could be trusted to guide the Sovereigns in the way they should go, that in his hands could safely be placed the destiny of Spain.

'I could have moulded him,' he murmured. 'I could have taught him much. Alas, so little time.'

He was weary because he had just taken his leave of the chief Inquisitors whom he had summoned to Avila that he might give them the new instructions, in the form of sixteen articles, which he had compiled for the use of the Inquisition. He was continually thinking of reforms, of strengthening the organization, making it more difficult for sinners to elude the *alguaʒils*.

He believed some eight thousand sinners against the Church had been burned at the stake since that glorious year of 1483, when he had established his Inquisition, until this day when he now lay on his painful pallet wondering how much longer was left to him.

'Eight thousand fires,' he mused. 'But there were many more brought to judgement. Somewhere in the region of one hundred thousand people were found guilty and suffered the minor penalties. A good record.'

He was astonished that a man such as himself should have enemies within the Church, and that perhaps the greatest of these should be the Pope himself.

How different it had been when the easy-going Innocent VIII had worn the Papal crown! Torquemada did not trust the Borgia Pope. There were hideous rumours in circulation regarding the life led by Roderigo Borgia, Pope Alexander VI.

He had his mistresses, it was said, and had a family of children of whom he was very proud and on whom he showered the highest honours.

To Torquemada, devotee of the hard pallet and the hair shirt, this was shocking; but more so was the fact that the sly and shrewd Borgia seemed to take an almost mischievous delight in frustrating Torquemada in every way possible.

'Perhaps it is inevitable that a whoremonger and evil liver should wish to bring down one who has always followed the holy life,' mused Torquemada. 'But pity of pities that such a one should be the Holy Father himself!'

Torquemada's eyes gleamed in his pale face. What pleasure it would give him to jostle for power against that man. Even at this moment he was expecting his messengers to return from England, whither he had sent them with a special message for King Henry VII, who might have cause to be grateful to Torquemada.

The wily King of England knew what power the Inquisitor wielded over the Sovereigns. His spies would let him know that Isabella and Ferdinand often visited him at Avila when he was too crippled by the gout to go to them. He would know that the body of Juan had been brought to him at Avila for burial – a mark of the respect the Sovereigns felt for him. It was comforting – particularly in view of the irritations he received from Rome – to know that England knew him for the influential man he was.

It was while he was lying on his pallet brooding on these matters that his messengers arrived from England, and as soon as he learned that they were in the monastery, he had them brought to him with all speed.

The messengers trembled in his presence; there was that in

this man to set others trembling. His cold accusing eyes might see some heresy of which a victim had been unaware; those thin lips might rap out a question, the answer to which might cost the one who made it the loss of his possessions, torture, or death.

To stand in the presence of Torquemada was to bring to the mind the gloomy dungeons of pain, the dismal ceremonies of the *auto de fe*; the smell of scorching human flesh.

'What news of the King of England?' demanded Torquemada.

'Your Excellency, the King of England sends his respects to you and wishes you to know that he desires to be your friend.'

'And you told him of my request?'

'Your Excellency, we told him and we had his answer from his own lips. The King of England will not allow in his Kingdom any man, woman or child who asks refuge from the Holy Office.'

'Did he say this lightly or did he swear it as an oath?'

'Excellency, he put his hands on his breast and swore it. He swore too that he would persecute any Jew or heretic who sought refuge in his Kingdom, should the Inquisition call attention to such a person.'

'And was there aught else?'

'The King of England said that, as he was your friend, he knew that you would be his.'

Torquemada smiled, well satisfied, and the relieved messengers were allowed to escape from his presence.

The King of England at least was his friend. He had given what Torquemada had asked, and he should be rewarded. This marriage between his eldest son and the Sovereigns' youngest daughter must not much longer be delayed. It was absurd sentimentality to talk of the child's being too young.

It was a matter which needed his attention and it should have it.

If only he were not so tired. But he must rouse himself. He had his duty to perform and, although the Queen was going to plead for her youngest daughter, Her Highness, as he had, must learn to subdue her desires; she must not let them stand in the way of her duty.

Chapter IX

ISABELLA RECEIVES CHRISTOBAL COLON

argaret went about the Palace like a sad, pale ghost. She had lost her Flemish gaiety; she seemed always to be looking back into the past.

Often Catalina would walk beside her in the gardens; neither would talk very much, but they had a certain comfort to give each other.

Catalina had a feeling that these walks were precious because they could not go on for long. Something was going to happen to her . . . or to Margaret. Margaret would not be allowed to stay here indefinitely, any more than she would. Maximilian would soon be wondering what new marriage could be arranged for his daughter; as for Catalina, her time of departure must be near.

Catalina said, one day as they walked together: 'Soon my sister Isabella will be coming home. Then there will be festivities to welcome her. Perhaps then the time of mourning will be over.'

'Festivities will not end my mourning,' Margaret answered.

Catalina slipped her arm through that of her sister-in-law. 'Will you stay here?' she asked.

'I do not know. My father may recall me. My attendants would be glad to return to Flanders. They say they can never learn your Spanish manners.'

'I should miss you sadly if you went.'

'Perhaps . . .' began Margaret and stopped short.

Catalina winced. 'You are thinking that I may be gone first.' She was silent for a moment, then she burst out: 'Margaret, I am so frightened when I think of it. I can tell you, because you are different from everyone else. You say what you think. I have a terror of England.'

'One country is not so very different from another,' Margaret comforted.

'I do not like what I hear of the King of England.'

'But it is his son with whom you will be concerned. There are other children, and perhaps they will not be like their father. Look how friendly I have become with you all.'

'Yes,' said Catalina slowly, 'perhaps I shall like Arthur and his brother and sisters.'

'Perhaps you will not go after all. Plans are often changed.'

'I used to think and hope that,' Catalina admitted. 'But since the ceremony has been performed by proxy, I feel there is little chance of escape for me.'

Catalina's brow was wrinkled; she was picturing that ceremony of which she had heard. It had had to be performed in secret because the King of England feared what the King of Scotland's reaction would be if he knew that England was making a marriage with Spain.

'In the Chapel of the Royal Manor of Bewdley . . .' she whispered. 'What strange names these English have. Perhaps in time they will not be strange to me. Oh, Margaret, when I think of that ceremony I feel I am already married. I feel there is no longer hope of escape.'

❧❧

Isabella watched her daughter from a window of her apartments. She was glad to see Margaret and Catalina together. Poor children, they could help each other.

Although she could not see the expression on her young daughter's face it seemed to her that there was desperation displayed in the droop of her head and the manner in which her hands hung at her sides.

She was probably talking of that marriage by proxy. The poor child would break her heart if she had to go to England. She was thirteen. Another year and the time would be ripe.

The Queen turned away from the window because she could no longer bear to look.

She went to her table and wrote to Torquemada.

'As yet my daughter is too young for marriage. There has been this proxy ceremony; that must suffice for a little longer. Catalina shall not go to England . . . yet.'

❧❧

Queen Isabella of Spain was often thankful that there was so much to demand her attention. If there had not been, she believed that she would not have been able to bear her grief for what had befallen her family. She had borne the terrible blow of Juan's death, and she had thought at that time that she had come as near to despair as any woman could come; and yet, when she thought of Juana in Flanders, something like terror would assail her.

The truth was that she dared not think too often of Juana.

Therefore she was glad of these continual matters of state to which it was her duty to attend. She would never forget that she was the Queen and that her duty to her country came before everything – yes, even the love which she, as an affectionate mother, bore her children.

Now she was concerned about her Admiral, Christobal Colon, who was on his way to see her. She had a great admiration for this man and never ceased to defend him when his enemies – and he had many – brought charges against him.

Now he wished to sail once more for the New World, and she knew that he would beg for the means to do so. This would mean money for equipment, men and women who would make good colonists.

She would always remember that occasion when he had come home, having discovered the New World and bringing proof of its riches with him. She remembered singing the Te Deum in the royal chapel, praising God for this great gift. Perhaps to some it had not fulfilled its promise. They had expected more riches, greater profit. But Isabella was a woman of vision and she could see that the new colony might have something more important to offer than gold and trinkets.

Men grew impatient. They did not wish to work for their riches. They wanted to grow rich effortlessly. As for Ferdinand, when he saw the spoils which were being brought from the New World, he regretted that they had promised Christobal Colon a share in them, and was continually seeking a way out of his bargain with the adventurer.

Many had desired to follow him on his return to the New World, but to found a colony one needed men of ideals. Isabella understood this as Ferdinand and so many others could not.

It had been a troublous tale of ambition and jealousies which had been brought to Spain from the new colony.

'Who is this Colon?' was a question on the lips of many. 'He is a foreigner. Why should he be put above us?'

Isabella understood that many of the would-be colonists had been adventurers, *hidalgos* who had no intention of submitting to any sort of discipline. Poor Colon! His difficulties were not over when he discovered the new land.

And now he was coming to see her again, and she wondered what comfort she would have to offer him.

When he arrived at the Palace she received him at once, and as he knelt before her she gave him a glance of affection. It grieved her that others did not share her faith in him.

She bade him rise and he stood before her, a broad man, long-legged, with deep blue eyes that held the dreams of an idealist in them; his thick hair, which had once been a reddish gold, was now touched with white. He was a man for whom a great dream had come true; but, energetic idealist that he was, one dream fulfilled was immediately superseded by another which seemed as elusive.

Perhaps, thought Isabella, it is easier to discover a New World than to found a peaceable colony.

'My dear Admiral,' she said, 'tell me your news.'

'Highness, the delay in leaving Spain for the colony alarms me. I fear what may be happening there.'

Isabella nodded. 'I would I could give you all you need. There has, as you realise, been a heavy drain on our purses during these sad months.'

Colon understood. The cost of the Prince's wedding must have been enormous. He could have fitted out his expedition on a quarter of it. He remembered how angry he had been during the celebrations, and how he had said to his dear Beatriz de Arana and their son, Ferdinand: What folly this is! To squander so much on a wedding when it could go towards enriching the colony and therefore Spain!

Beatriz and young Ferdinand agreed with him. They cared as passionately about his endeavours as he did himself, and he was a lucky man in his family. But what sad frustration he suffered everywhere else.

'The Marchioness of Moya has been telling me of your plight,' said the Queen.

'The Marchioness has ever been a good friend to me,' answered Colon.

It was true. Isabella's dearest friend, Beatriz de Bobadilla who was now the Marchioness of Moya, believed in Christobal Colon as few did. It was she who, in the days before he had made his discovery, had brought him to the notice of Isabella and given him her active support.

'I am deeply distressed for you and have been wondering how I can provide you with the colonists you need. I think it might be possible to find the money more easily than the men.'

'Highness,' said Christobal, 'an idea has come to me. It is imperative that I have men for the colony. I need them for mining, building and agricultural work. Previously I took with me men who were not primarily colonists. They did not wish to build the New World; they only wished to take from it and return to Spain with their spoils.'

Isabella smiled.

'They were disappointed,' she said. 'The climate did not agree with them, and it was said that they came back so sick and sallow that they had more gold in their faces than in their pockets.'

'It is true, Highness. And this is why I find it so difficult to find men who will sail with me. But there are some men who could be made to go. I refer to convicts. If they were offered freedom, in the colony, they would eagerly take it in preference to imprisonment here.'

'And,' said Isabella, 'it would not be a matter of choice. That should be their punishment.'

Christobal's sunburned, weather-scored face was alight with excitement. 'Out there,' he said, 'they will become new men. They will discover the delights of building a new world. How could they fail to do this?'

'All men are not as you are, Admiral,' Isabella reminded him.

But Christobal was certain that all men must prefer the adventure of the new world to incarceration in the old.

'Have I Your Highness's permission to go forward with this plan?'

'Yes,' said Isabella. 'Select your convicts, Admiral; and may good luck go with you.'

After he had gone she sent for the Marchioness of Moya. It was rarely that she had time to be with this dear friend; each had their duties, and it was not often enough that their paths crossed. Yet each remembered the friendship of their youth, and when they could be together they never lost the opportunity.

When Beatriz arrived Isabella told her of Christobal's plan to take convicts to the colony. Beatriz listened gravely and shook her head.

'That is going to mean trouble,' she said. 'Our dear Colon will find himself keeping the peace among a set of ruffians. How I wish we could send good colonists with him.'

'He must needs take what he can get,' Isabella answered.

'As we all must,' added Beatriz. 'What news of the Queen of Portugal?'

'They are setting out at once. They must. I would not have Isabella travel later, when she is far advanced in pregnancy.'

'Oh, how I hope . . .' began the impetuous Beatriz.

'Pray go on,' Isabella told her. 'You were going to say you hoped that this time I shall not be disappointed. This time I shall hold my grandchild in my arms.'

Beatriz went to Isabella and stooping over her kissed her. It was the familiar gesture of two friends who had been close to each other. Indeed, the forthright Beatriz, rather domineering as she was, was one of the few who treated the Queen at times as though she were a child. Isabella found it endearing. In the company of Beatriz she felt she could let down her defences and speak of her hopes and fears.

'Yes,' said Beatriz, 'you are anxious.'

'Isabella's health was never good. That cough of hers has persisted for years.'

'It is often the frail plants that live the longest,' Beatriz assured her. 'Isabella will have every care.'

'That is one reason why I can feel glad that it has been necessary to call her home. I shall be at the birth. I shall see that she has every possible care.'

'Then it is a good thing . . .'

'No,' answered Isabella sternly, 'it can never be a good thing when there is internal strife in families.'

'Strife! You call the strutting of this coxcomb, Philip, strife!'

'Remember who he is, Beatriz. He could make a great deal of trouble for us. And my poor Juana . . .'

'One day,' Beatriz said, 'you will find some reason to call *her* home. Then you will explain her duty to her.'

Isabella shook her head. It had never been easy to explain to Juana anything which she did not want to understand. She had a feeling that life in Flanders was changing Juana . . . and not for the better. Was it possible for such as Juana to grow more stable? Or would her mind, like her grandmother's, gradually grow more and more wayward?

'So many troubles,' mused Isabella. 'Our poor sad Margaret is like a ghost wandering about the Palace, looking for her happy past. And Juana . . . But do not let us talk of her. Then there is my frustrated Admiral with his convicts. I fear too there will be great trouble in Naples. Is there no end to our afflictions?'

'No end to our afflictions, and no end to our joys,' said Beatriz promptly. 'You will soon be holding your grandchild in your arms, my Queen. And when you do so you will forget all that has gone before. Isabella's son will mean as much to you as Juan's would have done.'

'You are my comforter, Beatriz, as you ever were. I trust we can spend more time together before we must part.'

❧ Chapter X ❦

THE BIRTH OF MIGUEL

oledo lay before them. Neither Isabella nor Ferdinand, riding at the head of the cavalcade, could help feeling pride in this city. There it stood perched on a lofty granite plateau which from this distance looked as though it had been moulded to the shape of a horseshoe among the mountains above the Tagus. A perfect fortress city, for it could only be reached on the north side by way of the plain of Castile. At every other point the steep rock would prevent entry.

There was little that was Spanish in its architecture, for the Moors seemed to have left their mark on every tower, on every street.

But Isabella was not concerned with her city of Toledo; her thoughts were of the meeting which would shortly take place.

I shall be happy, she told herself, when I see Isabella and assure myself that this pregnancy has not weakened her.

'You grow impatient,' Ferdinand whispered, a smile on his lips.

'And you too?'

He nodded. He was impatient for the birth of the child. If it were a son, the unhappy deaths of Juan and his offspring would be of little significance. The people would be glad to accept the son of Isabella and Emanuel as the heir.

'If it is a boy,' he said, 'he must stay with us in Spain.'

'Perhaps,' ventured Isabella, 'our daughter should stay with us also.'

'What! You would separate husband and wife!'

'I see,' said Isabella, 'that you are thinking there should be more children; and how could Isabella and Emanuel beget children if they were not together!'

'That is true,' replied Ferdinand. His eyes strayed to those three girls in the party – Margaret, Maria and Catalina. If his daughters had but been boys . . . But never mind, if Isabella had a male heir, this would be some solution of their troubles.

They were entering the town. How could she ever do so, Isabella asked herself, without remembering that it was the birthplace of Juana? That memorable event had occurred on a November day when the city looked different from the way it did this day in springtime. When she had first heard the cry of her little daughter she had not guessed what anxieties were to come because of her. Perhaps it would have been better if the child, to which she had given birth here in Toledo in the year 1479, had been stillborn as poor Margaret's child had been. She felt an impulse to call Margaret to her and tell her of this. How foolish of her! Her grief was nowadays often weakening her sense of propriety.

They were at the gates of the city and the Toledans were coming out of their homes to welcome them. Here were the goldsmiths and silversmiths, the blacksmiths, the weavers and embroiderers, the armourers and the curriers, all members of the guilds of this city which was one of the most prosperous in Spain.

Thus it had been at that time when she and Ferdinand had come here to inspect the work on San Juan de los Reyes which they had given to the city. She remembered well the day they had seen the chains of the captives whom they had liberated when they conquered Malaga. These chains had been hung outside the walls of the church for significant decoration; they rested there today and they should remain there for ever – a reminder to the people that their Sovereigns had freed Spain from Moorish domination.

They would go to the church, or perhaps that of Santa Maria la Blanca, and give thanks for the safe arrival of the King and Queen of Portugal.

She would be happy among those horseshoe arches, among those graceful arabesques; there she would ask to be purged of all resentment against the sorrows of the last year. She would be cleansed of self-pity, and ready for the miracle of birth, the recompense which was to be the son her dearest Isabella would give to her and Spain.

It was meet that the Archbishop of Toledo should be in the city to greet them – gaunt, emaciated Ximenes de Cisneros, his robes of state hanging uneasily on his spare figure.

Isabella felt a lifting of her spirits as she greeted him. She would tell her old confessor of her weakness; she would listen to his astringent comments; he would scorn her mother-love as unworthy of the Queen; he would deplore her weakness in questioning the will of God.

Ferdinand's greeting of the Archbishop was cool. He could never look at him without recalling that the office with all its pomp and grandeur might have gone to his son.

'It does me good to see my Archbishop,' murmured Isabella graciously.

Ximenes bowed before her, but even his bow had arrogance. He set the Church above the State.

Ximenes rode beside the Queen through the streets of Toledo.

∽∾∾

With what great joy the Queen embraced her daughter Isabella!

This was when they were alone after the ceremonial greeting which had been watched by thousands. Then they had done all that was required of them, this mother and daughter, bowing graciously, kissing hands, as though they were not yearning to embrace and ask a thousand questions.

The Queen would not allow herself to look too closely at her daughter; she was afraid that she might see that which had made her anxious and betray her anxiety.

But now they were alone and the Queen had dismissed all her attendants and those of her daughter, for she told herself they must have this short time together.

'My dearest,' cried the Queen, 'let me look at you. Why, you are a little pale. And how is your health? Tell me exactly when the little one is expected.'

'In August, Mother.'

'Well, that is not long to wait. You have not told me how you are.'

'I feel a little tired, and rather listless.'

'It is natural.'

'I wonder.'

'What do you mean? You wonder! A pregnant woman has

a child to carry. Naturally she does not feel as other women do.'

'I have seen some women seem perfectly healthy in pregnancy.'

'Nonsense. It differs from woman to woman and from birth to birth. I know. Remember I have had five children of my own.'

'Then perhaps this tiredness is nothing.'

'And your cough?'

'It is no worse, Mother.'

'You think I am foolish with all my questions?'

'Mother, it is good to hear those questions.' Isabella suddenly flung herself into her mother's arms and, to the Queen's dismay, she saw tears on her daughter's cheeks.

'Emanuel is good to you?'

'No husband could be better.'

'I noticed his tenderness towards you. It pleased me.'

'He does everything to please me.'

'Then why these tears?'

'Perhaps . . . I am frightened.'

'Frightened of childbirth! It is natural. The first time can be alarming. But it is the task of all women, you know. A Queen's task as well as a peasant's. Nay, more so. It is more important for a Queen to bear children than for a peasant to do so.'

'Mother, there are times when I wish I were a peasant.'

'What nonsense you talk.'

Isabella realised then that there were matters she could not discuss even with her mother. She could not depress her by telling her that she had a strange foreboding of evil.

She wanted to cry out: Our House is cursed. The persecuted Jews have cursed us. I feel their curses all about me.

Her mother would be shocked at such childishness.

But is it childishness? Isabella asked herself. In the night I feel certain that this evil is all about me. And Emanuel feels it too.

How could that be? Such thoughts were foolish superstition.

She fervently wished that she had not to face the ordeal of childbirth.

❧

How tiring it was to stand before the Cortes, to hear them proclaim her the heiress of Castile.

These worthy citizens were pleased with her, because none who looked at her could be in any doubt of her pregnancy. They were all hoping for a boy. But if she did not give birth to a boy, still the child she carried would, in the eyes of the Toledans, be the heir of Spain.

She listened to their loyal shouts and smiled her thanks. How glad she was that she had been brought up to hide her feelings.

After the ceremony with the Cortes, she must be carried through the streets to show herself to the people. Then she was received in the Cathedral and blessed by the Archbishop.

The atmosphere inside the massive Gothic building seemed overpowering. She stared at the treasures which hung on the walls and thought of the rich citizens of Toledo who had reason to be grateful to her mother for restoring order throughout Spain where once there had been anarchy. In this town lived the finest goldsmiths and silversmiths in the world; and the results of their labours were here in the cathedral for all to see.

She looked at the stern face of Ximenes and, as she studied the rich robes of his office, the brocade and damask studded with precious jewels, she thought of the hair shirt which she knew would be worn beneath those fine garments, and shivered.

She tried to pray then to the Virgin, the patron saint of Toledo, and she found that she could only repeat: 'Help me, Holy Mother. Help me.'

When they had returned to the Palace, Emanuel said she must rest; the ceremony had tired her.

'There are too many ceremonies,' he said.

'I do not believe it is the ceremony which tires me, Emanuel,' she said. 'I think I should be equally tired if I lay on my bed all the day. Perhaps I am not really tired.'

'What then, my dearest?'

She looked at him frankly and answered: 'I am afraid.'

'Afraid! But, my love, you shall have the very best attention in Spain.'

'Do you think that will avail me anything?'

'But indeed I do. How I long for September! Then you will be delighting in your child. You will laugh at these fears . . . if you remember them.'

'Emanuel, I do not think I shall be here in September.'

'But, my darling, what is it you are saying . . . ?'

'Dear Emanuel, I know you love me. I know you will be unhappy if I die. But it is better for you to be prepared.'

'Prepared! I am prepared for birth, not for death.'

'But if death should come . . .'

'You are overwrought.'

'I am fatigued, but I think at such times I see the future more clearly. I have a very strong feeling that I shall not get well after the child is born. It is our punishment, Emanuel. For me death, for you bereavement. Why do you look so shocked? It is a small payment for the misery we shall bring to thousands.'

Emanuel threw himself down by the bed. 'Isabella, you must not talk so. You must not.'

She stroked his hair with her thin white hand.

'No,' she said, 'I must not. But I had to warn you of this feeling I have. It is so strong. Well, I have done so. Now let us forget it. I shall pray that my child will be a boy. That I think will make you very happy.'

'And you will be happy too.'

She only smiled at him. Then she said quickly: 'Toledo is a beautiful town, is it not? I think my father loves it. It is so prosperous. It is so Moorish. There is everything here to remind my parents of the reconquest; there are more than the chains from Malaga on the walls of San Juan de los Reyes. But my mother, while she exults in the prosperity and beauty of Toledo, feels a certain sadness.'

'There must be no sadness,' said Emanuel.

'But there must always be sadness, it seems, sadness to mingle with pride, with laughter, with joy. Is it not beautiful here? I love to watch the Tagus dashing against the stones far below. Where in Spain is there such a fertile *vega* as that around Toledo? The fruit is so luscious here, the corn so plentiful. But did you notice how the flies pestered us as we came in? I saw the Rock too. The Rock of Toledo from which criminals are hurled down . . . down into the ravine. So much beauty and so much sorrow. That is what my mother feels when she rides into Toledo. In this rich and lovely city my sister Juana was born.'

'That should make your mother love it all the more.'

Isabella took her husband's hand in hers and cried out: 'Emanuel, let there be complete trust between us. Let us not pretend to one another. Can you not see it? It is like the writing on the wall. I see it clearly. As I come nearer and nearer to my confinement I seem to acquire a new sensitivity. I feel I am not entirely of this world but have not yet reached the next. Therefore I sometimes see what is hidden from most human eyes.'

'Isabella, you must be calm, my dearest.'

'I am calm, Emanuel. But I distress you. I do not want my passing to be the shock to you that my brother's death was to my mother. Emanuel, my dear husband, it is always better to be prepared. Shall I tell you what is in my mind, or shall I pretend that I am a woman who looks into the future and sees her child playing beside her? Shall I lie to you, Emanuel?'

He kissed her hands. 'There must be truth between us.'

'That is what I thought. So I would tell you. Emanuel, my House has brought greatness to Spain, great prosperity and great sorrow. Is it never possible to have one without the other? On our journey to Toledo we passed through a town where, in the Plaza Mayor, I saw the ashes and I smelt the fires which had recently burned there. It was human flesh which burned, Emanuel.'

'Those who died were condemned by the Holy Office.'

'I know. They were heretics. They had denied their faith. But they have hearts in which to harbour hatred, lips with which to curse. They would curse our House, Emanuel, even as those who were driven from Spain would curse us. And their curses have not gone unheeded.'

'Should we suffer for pleasing God and all the saints?'

'I do not understand, Emanuel; and I am too tired to try to.

We are told that this is a Christian country. It is our great desire to bring our people to the Christian faith. We do it by persuasion. We do it by force. It is God's work. But what of the devil?'

'These are strange thoughts, Isabella.'

'They come unbidden. See what has happened to us. My parents had five children – four daughters and one son. Their son and heir died suddenly, and his heir was stillborn. My sister Juana is strange, so wild that I have heard it whispered that she is half-way to madness. Already she has caused trouble to our parents by allowing herself to be proclaimed Princess of Castile. You see, Emanuel, it is like a pattern, an evil pattern built up by curses.'

'You are distraught, Isabella.'

'No. I think I see clearly . . . more clearly than the rest of you. I am to have a child. Childbearing can be dangerous. I am the daughter of a cursed House. I wonder what will happen next.'

'This is a morbid fancy due to your condition.'

'Is it, Emanuel? Oh, tell me it is. Tell me that I can be happy. Juan caught a fever, did he not? It might have happened to anybody. And the child was stillborn because of Margaret's grief. Juana is not mad, is she? She is merely high-spirited, and she has fallen completely under the spell of that handsome rogue who is her husband. Is that not natural? And I . . . I was never very strong, so I have morbid fancies . . . It is merely because of my condition.'

'That is so, Isabella. Of course that is so. Now there will be no more morbidity. Now you will rest.'

'I will sleep if you will sit beside me and hold my hand, Emanuel. Then I shall feel at peace.'

'I shall remain with you, but you must rest. You have forgotten that we have to start on our travels tomorrow.'

'Now we must go to Saragossa. The Cortes there must proclaim me the Heiress as the Cortes here at Toledo have done.'

'That is right. Now rest.'

She closed her eyes, and Emanuel stroked back the hair from her hot forehead.

He was worried. He did not like this talk of premonitions. He had an idea that the ceremony in Saragossa would not be such a pleasant one as that of Toledo. Castile was ready to accept a woman as heir to the crown. But Saragossa, the capital of Aragon, did not recognise the right of women to rule.

He did not mention this. Let her rest. They would overcome their troubles the better by taking them singly.

❧❧

Into Saragossa came Isabella, Princess of Castile, with Emanuel her husband.

The people watched them with calm calculating gaze. This was the eldest daughter and heiress of their own Ferdinand, but she was a woman, and the Aragonese did not recognise the right of women to reign in Aragon. Let the Castilians make their own laws; they would never be accepted as the laws of Aragon. The Aragonese were a determined people; they were ready to fight for what they considered to be their rights.

So as Isabella rode into their city they were silent.

How different, thought Isabella, from the welcome they had received in Toledo. She did not like this city of bell turrets and sullen people. She had felt the vague resentment as soon as she passed into Aragon; she had been nervous as she rode along the banks of the Ebro past those caves which seemed to have been formed in this part of the country among the sierras as well as along the banks of the river. The yellow water of the Ebro was turbulent; and the very houses seemed too much like fortresses, reminding her that here was a people who would be determined to demand and fight for its dues.

On her arrival in this faintly hostile city she went to pray to the statue of the Virgin which, it was said, had been carved by the angels fourteen hundred years before. Precious jewels glittered in her cloak and crown which seemed to smother her; and it occurred to Isabella that she must have looked very different when, as the legend had it, she appeared to St James all those years ago.

From the Virgin she went to the Cathedral close by, and there she prayed anew for strength to bear whatever lay before her.

The people watched her and whispered together.

'The crown of Aragon was promised to the *male* heirs of Ferdinand.'

'And this is but a woman.'

'She is our Ferdinand's daughter nevertheless, and he has no legitimate sons.'

'But the crown should go to the next male heir.'

'Castile and Aragon are as one now that Ferdinand and Isabella rule them.'

There was going to be resistance in Aragon to the female succession. Isabella of Castile had remained Queen in her own right, but it was well known that she had greater power than Ferdinand. In the eyes of the Aragonese, it was their Ferdinand who should have ruled Spain with Isabella merely as his consort.

'Nay,' they said, 'we'll not have women on the throne of Spain. Aragon will support the male heir.'

'But wait a moment . . . the Princess is pregnant, is she not? If she were to have a son . . .'

'Ah, that would be a different matter. That would offend none. The Aragonese crown goes to the male descendants of Ferdinand, and his grandson would be the rightful heir.'

'Then, we must wait until the birth. That's the simple answer.'

It *was* the simple answer, and the Cortes confirmed it. They would not give their allegiance to Isabella of Portugal because she was a woman; but if she bore a son, then they would accept that son as the heir to the crown of Aragon and all Spain.

It was a wearying occasion for Isabella.

She had been alarmed by the hostile looks of the members of the Cortes. She had disliked their arrogant manner of implying that unless she produced a son they would have none of her.

She lay on her bed while her women soothed her; and when Emanuel came to her they hurried away and left them together.

'I feel a great responsibility rests upon me,' she said. 'I almost wish I were a humble woman waiting the birth of her child.'

◦◦◦

The Queen faced Ferdinand in anger.

'How dare they!' she demanded. 'In every town of Castile our daughter has been received with honours. But in Saragossa, the capital of Aragon, she is submitted to insult.'

Ferdinand could scarcely suppress a wry smile. There had been so many occasions when he had been forced to take second place, when he had been reminded that Aragon was of secondary importance to Castile and that the Queen of Castile was therefore senior to the King of Aragon.

'They but state their rights,' he answered.

'Their rights – to reject our daughter!'

'We know well that Aragon accepts only the male line as heirs to the crown.'

A faint smile played about his lips. He was reminding her that in Aragon the King was looked upon as the ruler and the Queen as his consort.

Isabella was not concerned with his private feelings. She thought only of the humiliation to her daughter.

'I picture them,' she said, 'quizzing her as though she were some fishwife. How far advanced in pregnancy is she? She will give birth in August. Then we will wait until August and, if she gives birth to a male child, we will accept that child as heir to the throne. I tell you, our daughter Isabella, being our eldest, is our heir.'

'They will not accept her, because they will not accept a woman.'

'They have accepted me.'

'As my wife,' Ferdinand reminded her.

'Rather than endure this insolence of the Saragossa Cortes I would subdue them by sending an armed force to deal with them. I would force them to accept our Isabella as the heir of Spain.'

'You cannot mean that.'

'But I do,' insisted Isabella.

Ferdinand left her and returned shortly with a statesman whose integrity he knew Isabella trusted. This was Antonio de Fonesca, a brother of the Bishop who bore the same name; this man Ferdinand had once sent as envoy to Charles VII of

France, and the bold conduct of Fonesca had so impressed both the Sovereigns that they often consulted him with confidence and respect.

'The Queen's Highness is incensed by the behaviour of the Cortes at Saragossa,' said Ferdinand. 'She is thinking of sending soldiers to subdue them over this matter of accepting our daughter as heir to the throne.'

'Would Your Highness care to hear my opinion?' asked Fonesca of the Queen.

Isabella told him that she would.

'Then, Highness, I would say that the Aragonese have only acted as good and loyal subjects. You must excuse them if they move with caution in an affair which they find difficult to justify by precedent in their history.'

Ferdinand was watching his wife closely. He knew that her love of justice would always overcome every other emotion.

She was silent, considering the statesman's remarks.

Then she said: 'I see that you are right. There is nothing to be done but hope – and pray – that my grandchild will be a boy.'

❧❧

Isabella, Queen of Portugal, lay on her bed. Her pains had started and she knew that her time had come.

There was a cold sweat on her brow and she was unconscious of all the people who stood about her bed. She was praying: 'A son. Let it be a son.'

If she produced a healthy son she would begin to forget this legend of a curse which had grown up in her mind. A son could make so much difference to her family and her country.

The little boy would be heir not only to the crown of Spain

but to that of Portugal. The countries would be united; the hostile people of Saragossa would be satisfied; and she and Emanuel would be the proudest parents in the world.

Why should it not be so? Could her family go on receiving blow after blow? They had had their share of tragedy. Let this be different.

'A boy,' she murmured, 'a healthy boy to make the sullen people of Saragossa cheer, to unite Spain and Portugal.' What an important little person this was who was now so impatient to be born!

The pains were coming regularly now. If she did not feel so weak she could have borne them more easily. She lay moaning while the women crowded about her. She drifted from consciousness into unconsciousness and back again.

The pain still persisted; it was more violent now.

She tried not to think of it; she tried to pray, to ask forgiveness of her sins, but her lips continued to form the words: 'A boy. Let it be a boy.'

❧❧

There were voices in the bedchamber.

'A boy! A bonny boy!'

'Is it indeed so?'

'No mistake!'

'Ah, this is a happy day.'

Isabella, lying on her bed, heard the cry of a child. She lay listening to the voices, too exhausted to move.

Someone was standing by her bed. Someone else knelt and was taking her hand and kissing it. Emanuel was standing, and it was her mother who knelt.

'Emanuel,' she whispered. 'Mother . . .'

'My dearest . . .' began Emanuel.

But her mother cried out in a voice loud with triumph: 'It is over, my darling. The best possible news for you. You have given birth to a fine baby boy.'

Isabella smiled. 'Then everyone is happy.'

Emanuel was bending over her, his eyes anxious. 'Including you?' he said.

'But yes.'

His eyes were faintly teasing: No more talk of curses, they were telling her. You see, all your premonitions were wrong. The ordeal is over and you have a beautiful son. 'Can you hear the bells ringing?' her mother asked the young Queen.

'I . . . I am not sure.'

'All over Spain the bells shall ring. Everyone will be rejoicing. They shall all know that their Sovereigns have a grandson, a male heir, at last.'

'Then I am happy.'

'We will leave her to rest,' said the Queen.

Emanuel nodded. 'She is exhausted – no wonder.'

'But first . . .' whispered Isabella.

'I understand,' laughed her mother. She stood up and called to the nurse.

She took the baby from her and placed it in its mother's arms.

❧

Ferdinand said: 'He shall be called Miguel, after the saint on whose day he was born.'

'God bless our little Miguel,' answered the Queen. 'He's a lively little fellow, but I wish his mother did not look so exhausted.'

Ferdinand bent over the cradle, exulting in the infant; he found it hard to take his hands from the child who meant so much to him.

'We must have a triumphant pilgrimage as soon as Isabella is well enough to leave her bed,' went on Ferdinand. 'The people will want to see their heir. We should do this without delay.'

Isabella agreed as to the desirability of this, but it should not be, she assured herself, until Miguel's mother had recovered from her ordeal.

One of the women of the bedchamber was coming quickly towards them.

'Your Highnesses, Her Highness of Portugal . . .'

'Yes?' said Isabella sharply.

'She seems to find breathing difficult. Her condition is changing . . .'

Isabella did not wait for more. With Ferdinand following she hurried to her daughter's bedside.

Emanuel was already there.

The sight of her daughter's wan face, her blue-encircled eyes, her fight for her breath, made Isabella's heart turn over with fear.

'My darling child,' she cried, and there was a note of anguish in her voice which was a piteous appeal.

'Mother . . .'

'It is I, my darling. Mother is with you.'

'I feel so strange.'

'You are tired, my love. You have given birth to a beautiful boy. No wonder you are exhausted.'

'I . . . cannot . . . breathe,' she gasped.

'Where are the physicians?' demanded Ferdinand.

Emanuel shook his head as though to imply they had admitted their ignorance. There was nothing they could do.

Ferdinand walked to a corner of the room, and the doctors followed him.

'What is wrong with her?'

'It is a malaise which sometimes follows childbirth.'

'Then what is to be done?'

'Highness, it must take its course.'

'But this is . . .'

The doctors did not answer. They dared not tell the King that in their opinion the Queen of Portugal was on her death-bed.

Ferdinand stood wretchedly looking at the group round the bed. He was afraid to join them. It can't happen, he told himself. Isabella, his wife, could never endure this in addition to all she had suffered. This would be too much.

Isabella's eyes seemed to rest on her mother.

'Do we disturb you here, my darling?' asked the elder Isabella.

'No, Mother. You . . . never disturb me. I am too tired to talk, but . . . I want you here. You too, Emanuel.'

'You are going to stay with us for months . . . you and Emanuel and little Miguel. We are going to show the baby to the people. They will love their little heir. This is a happy day, my daughter.'

'Yes . . . a happy day.'

Emanuel was looking appealingly at his mother-in-law as though imploring her to tell him that his wife would recover.

'Mother,' said the sick woman, 'and Emanuel . . . come near to me.'

They sat on the bed and each held a hand.

'Now,' she said, 'I am happy. I am . . . going, I think.'

'No!' cried Emanuel.

But the younger Isabella saw the anguish in the eyes of the elder and she knew; they both knew.

Neither spoke, but they looked at each other and the great love they bore for one another was in their eyes.

'I . . . I gave you the boy,' whispered Isabella.

'And you are going to get well,' insisted Emanuel.

But the two Isabellas did not answer him, because they knew that a lie could give them no comfort.

'I am so tired,' murmured the Queen of Portugal. 'I . . . will go now. Goodbye.'

The Queen of Spain signed for the priests to come to her daughter's bedside. She knew that the moment had come for the last rites.

She listened to their words; she saw her daughter's attempts to repeat the necessary prayers; and she thought: This is not true. I am dreaming. It cannot be true. Not Juan *and* Isabella. Not both. That would be too cruel.

But she knew it was true.

Isabella was growing weaker with every moment; and only an hour after she had given them little Miguel, she was dead.

❧ Chapter XI ❧

THE COURT AT GRANADA

The bells were tolling for the death of the Queen of Portugal. Throughout Spain the people were beginning to ask themselves: 'What blight is this on our royal House?'

The Queen lay sick with grief in her darkened bedchamber. It was the first time any of her people had known her to succumb to misery.

About the Palace people moved in their garments of sackcloth, which had taken the place of white serge for mourning at the time of Juan's death. What next? they asked themselves. The little Miguel was not the healthy baby they had hoped he might be. He was fretful; perhaps he was crying for his mother who had died that he might come into the world.

Catalina sat with Maria and Margaret; they were sewing shirts for the poor; and, thought Margaret, it was almost as if they hoped that by this good deed they might avert further disaster, as though they might placate that Providence which seemed determined to chastise them.

The rough material hurt Margaret's hands. She recalled the

gaiety of Flanders and she knew that there would never be any happiness for her in Spain.

She looked at little Catalina, her head bent over her work. Catalina suffered more deeply than Maria would ever suffer. The poor child was now thinking of her mother's grief; she was longing to be with her and comfort her.

'It will pass,' said Margaret. 'People cannot go on grieving for ever.'

'Do you believe that?' asked Catalina.

'I know it; I have proved it.'

'You mean you no longer mourn Juan and your baby?'

'I shall mourn them for the rest of my life, but at first I mourned every waking hour. Now there are times when I forget them for a while. It is inevitable. Life is like that. So it will be with your mother. She will smile again.'

'There are so many disasters,' murmured Catalina.

Maria lifted her head from her work. 'You will find that we have many good things happening all together later on. That is how life goes on.'

'She is right,' said Margaret.

Catalina turned to her sewing but she did not see the coarse material; she was thinking of herself as a wife and mother. The joys of motherhood might after all be worth all that she had to suffer to achieve it. Perhaps she would have a child — a daughter who would love her as she loved her mother.

They sat sewing in silence, and at length Margaret rose and left them.

In her apartments she found two of her Flemish attendants staring gloomily out of the window.

They started up as Margaret came in, but she noticed that the expressions on their faces did not change.

'I know,' said Margaret. 'You are weary of Spain.'

'Ugh!' cried the younger of the women. 'All these dreary sierras, these dismal plains . . . and worst of all these dismal people!'

'Much has happened to make them dismal.'

'They were born dismal, Your Highness. They seem afraid to laugh or dance as people were meant to. They cling too firmly to their dignity.'

'If we went home . . .' began Margaret.

The two women's faces were alight with pleasure suddenly. Margaret caught at that pleasure. She told herself then: There will never be happiness for me here. Only if I leave Spain can I begin to forget.

'If we went home,' she repeated, 'that might be the best thing we could do.'

❧❧

Ferdinand stood by his wife's bedside looking down at her.

'You must rouse yourself, Isabella,' he said. 'The people are getting restive.'

Isabella looked at him, her eyes blank with misery.

'A ridiculous legend is being spread throughout the land. I hear it is said that we are cursed, and that God has turned His face away from us.'

'I was beginning to ask myself if that were so,' whispered the Queen.

She raised herself, and Ferdinand was shocked to see the change in her. Isabella had aged by at least ten years. Ferdinand asked himself in that moment whether the next blow his family would have to suffer would be the death of the Queen herself.

'My son,' she went on, 'and now my daughter. Oh, God in Heaven, how can You so forget me?'

'Hush! You are not yourself. I have never before seen you thus.'

'You have never before seen me smitten by such sorrow.'

Ferdinand beat his right fist into the palm of his left hand.

'We must not allow these foolish stories to persist. We are inviting disaster if we do. Isabella, we must not sit and mourn; we must not brood on our losses. I do not trust the new French King. I think I preferred Charles VIII to this Louis XII. He is a wily fellow and he is already making treaties with the Italians – we know well to what purpose. The Pope is sly. I do not trust the Borgia. Alexander VI is more statesman than Pope, and who can guess what tricks he will be up to? Isabella, we are Sovereigns first, parents second.'

'You speak truth,' answered Isabella sadly. 'But I must have a little time in which to bury my dead.'

Ferdinand made an impatient gesture. 'Maximilian, who might have helped to halt these French ambitions, is now engaged in war against the Swiss, and Louis has secured our neutrality by means of the new treaty of Marcoussis. But I don't trust Louis. We must be watchful.'

'You are right, of course.'

'We must keep a watchful eye on Louis, on Alexander, on Maximilian, as well as on our own son-in-law Philip and our daughter Juana, who seem to have ranged themselves against us. Yes, we must be watchful. But most important is it that all should be well in our own dominions. We cannot have our subjects telling each other that our House is cursed. I have heard it whispered that Miguel is a weakling, that he will not live more than a few months, that it is a miracle that he was not born as was our other grandchild, poor Juan's child. These rumours must be stopped.'

'We must stop them with all speed.'

'Ah then, my Queen, we are in agreement. As soon as you are ready to leave your bed, Miguel must be presented to the Cortes of Saragossa as the heir of Spain. And this ceremony must not be long delayed.'

'It shall not be long delayed,' Isabella assured him, and he was delighted to see the old determination in her face. He knew he could trust his Isabella. No matter what joy was hers, or what sorrow, she would never forget that she was the Queen.

The news of the Queen of Portugal's death was brought to Tomás de Torquemada in the monastery of Avila.

He lay on his pallet, unable to move, so crippled was he by the gout.

'Such trials are sent for our own good,' he murmured to his sub-prior. 'I trust the Sovereigns did not forget this.'

'The news is, Excellency, that the Queen is mightily stricken and has had to take to her bed.'

'I deplore her weakness and it surprises me,' said Torquemada. 'Her great sin lies in her vulnerability where her family is concerned. It is high time the youngest was sent to England. And so would she be, but for the Queen's constant excuses. Learn from her faults, my friend. See how even a good woman can fail in her duty when she allows her emotions regarding her children to come between her and God.'

'It is so, Excellency. But all have not your strength.'

Torquemada dismissed the man.

It was true. Few men on Earth possessed the strength of will to discipline themselves as he had done. But he had great hopes of Ximenes de Cisneros. There was one who, it would seem, might be worthy to tread in his, Torquemada's, footsteps.

'If I were but a younger man,' sighed Torquemada. 'If I might throw off this accursed sickness, this feebleness of my body! My mind is as clear as it ever was. Then I would still rule Spain.'

But when the body failed a man, however great he was, his end was near. Even Torquemada could not subdue his flesh so completely that he could ignore it.

He lay back complacently. It was possible that his death would probably be the next one which would be talked of in the towns and villages of Spain. There was death in the air.

But people were constantly dying. He himself had fed thousands of them to the flames. He had done right, he assured himself. It was only in his helplessness that he was afraid.

'Not,' he said aloud, 'of the pain I might suffer, not of death – for what fear should I have of facing my Maker? – but of the loss to the world which my passing must mean.

'Oh, Holy Mother of God,' he prayed, 'give this man Ximenes the power to take my place. Give Ximenes strength to guide the Sovereigns as I have done. Then I shall die happy.'

The faggots in the *quemaderos* all over the country were well alight. In the dungeons of the Inquisition men, women and children awaited trial through ordeal. In the gloomy chambers of the damned the torturers were busy.

'I trust, O Lord,' murmured Torquemada, 'that I have done my work well and shall find favour in Your sight. I trust You have noted the number of souls I have brought to You, the numbers I have saved, as well as those I have sent from this world to hell by means of the fiery death. Remember, O Lord, the zeal of Your servant, Tomás de Torquemada. Remember his love of the Faith.'

When he thought over his past life he had no qualms about death. He was certain that he would be received into Heaven with great glory.

His sub-prior came to him, as he lay there, with news from Rome.

He read the dispatch, and his anger burned so fiercely that it set his swollen limbs throbbing.

He and Alexander were two men who were born to be enemies. The Borgia had schemed to become Pope not through love of the Faith but because it was the highest office in the Church. His greatest desire was to shower honours on his sons and daughter, whom, as a man of the Church, he had no right to have begotten. This Borgia, it seemed, could be a merry man, a flouter of conventions. There were evil rumours about his incestuous relationship with his own daughter, Lucrezia, and it was well known that he exercised nepotism and that his sons, Cesare and Giovanni, swaggered through the towns of Italy boasting of their relationship to the Holy Father.

What could a man such as Torquemada – whose life had been spent in subduing the flesh – have in common with such as Roderigo Borgia, Pope Alexander VI? Very little.

Alexander knew this and, because he was a mischievous man, he had continually obstructed Torquemada in his endeavours.

Torquemada remembered early conflicts.

As far back as four years ago he had received a letter from the Pope; he could remember the words clearly now.

Alexander cherished him in 'the very bowels of affection for his great labours in raising the glory of the Faith'. But Alexander was concerned because from the Vatican he considered the many tasks which Torquemada had taken upon himself, and he remembered the great age of Torquemada and he was not going to allow him to put too great a strain upon himself. Therefore he, Alexander, out of love for Torquemada, was going to appoint four assistants to be at his side in this mighty work of establishing and maintaining the Inquisition throughout Spain.

There could not have been a greater blow to his power. The new Inquisitors, appointed by the Pope, shared the power of Torquemada and the title Inquisitor General lost its significance.

There was no doubt that Alexander in the Vatican was the enemy of Torquemada in the monastery of Avila. It may have been that the Pope considered the Inquisitor General wielded too much power; but Torquemada suspected that the enmity between them grew from their differences – the desire of a man of great carnal appetites, which he made no effort to subdue, to denigrate one who had lived his life in the utmost abstention from all worldly pursuits.

And now, when Torquemada was near to death, Alexander had yet another snub to offer.

The Pope had held an *auto de fe* in the square before St Peter's, and at this had appeared many of those Jews who had been expelled from Spain. If the Pope had wished to do the smallest honour to Torquemada he would have sent those Jews to the flames or inflicted some other severe punishment.

But Alexander was laughing down his nose at the monk of Avila. Sometimes Torquemada wondered whether he was laughing at the Church itself which he used so shamefully to his advantage.

Alexander had ordered that a service should be read in the square, and the one hundred and eighty Judaizers, and fugitives from Torquemada's wrath were dismissed. No penalties. No wearing of the *sanbenito*. No imprisonment. No confiscation of property.

Alexander dismissed them all to go about their business like good citizens of Rome.

Torquemada clenched his fists tightly together as he thought of it. It was a direct insult, not only to himself but to the Spanish Inquisition; and he believed that the Pope was fully aware of this and it was his main reason for acting as he had.

'And here I lie,' he mused, 'in this my seventy-eighth year of life, my body crippled, unable to protest.'

His heart began to beat violently, shaking his spare frame. The walls of the cell seemed to close in upon him.

'My life's work is done,' he whispered and sent for his sub-prior.

'I feel my end is near,' he told the man. 'Nay, do not look concerned. I have had a long life and in it I think I have served God well. I would not have you bury me with pomp. Put me to rest in the common burial ground among the friars of my monastery. There I would lie happiest.'

The sub-prior said quickly: 'You are old in years, Excellency, but your spirit is strong. There are years ahead of you.'

'Leave me,' Torquemada commanded; 'I would make my peace with God.'

He waved the man away, but he did not believe it was necessary to make his peace with God. He believed that there would be a place in Heaven for him as there had been on Earth.

He lay quietly on his pallet while the strength slowly ebbed from him.

He thought continually of his past life, and as the days went on his condition grew weaker.

It was known throughout the monastery that Torquemada was dying.

On the 16th of September, one month after the death of the Queen of Portugal, Torquemada opened his eyes and was not sure where he lay.

He dreamed he was ascending into Heaven to the sound of music – music which was composed of the cries of heretics as the flames licked their limbs, the murmurs of a band of exiles who trudged wearily, from the land which had been their home for centuries, to what grim horrors they could not know but only fear.

'All this in Thy name . . .' murmured Torquemada and, because he was too weak to control his feelings, a smile of assurance and satisfaction touched his lips.

The sub-prior came to him a little later, and he knew that it was time for the last rites to be administered.

Isabella roused herself from her bed of sickness and grief. She had her duty to perform.

The little Prince Miguel must be shown to the citizens and accepted by the Cortes as heir to the throne. So the processions began.

The people of Saragossa, who had declined to accept his mother, assembled to greet little Miguel as their future King.

Ferdinand and Isabella swore that they would be his faithful guardians, and that before he was allowed to assume any rights as Sovereign he should be made to swear to respect those liberties to which the proud people of Aragon were determined to cling.

'Long live the lawful heir and successor to the crown of Aragon!' cried the Saragossa Cortes.

This ceremony was repeated not only throughout Aragon and Castile but in Portugal, for this frail child would, if he came to the throne, unite those countries.

Isabella took her leave of the sorrowing Emanuel.

'Leave the child with me,' she said. 'You know how deeply affected I have been by the loss of my daughter. I have brought up many children. Give me this little one who will be our heir, that he may help to assuage my grief.'

Emanuel was stricken with pity for his stoical mother-in-law. He knew that she was thinking it could not be long before her remaining daughters were taken from her. Moreover, his Spanish inheritance would be of greater importance to little Miguel than that which would come from his father.

'Take the child,' he said. 'Bring him up as you will. I trust he will never give you cause for anxiety.'

Isabella held the child against her and, as she did so, she felt a stirring of that pleasure which only her own beloved family could give her.

It was true that the Lord took away, but He also gave.

She said: 'I will take him to my city of Granada. There he shall have the greatest care that it is possible for any child to have. Thank you, Emanuel.'

So Emanuel left the child with her, and Ferdinand was

195

delighted that they would be in a position to supervise his upbringing.

Isabella gently kissed the baby's face, and Ferdinand came to stand beside her.

If I could only be as he is, thought Isabella, and feel as he does that the death of our daughter Isabella was not such a great tragedy, since their child lives.

'Emanuel will need a new wife,' Ferdinand mused.

'It will be a long time yet. He dearly loved our Isabella.'

'Kings have little time for mourning,' answered Ferdinand. 'He said nothing of this matter to you?'

'Taking a new wife! Indeed he did not. I am sure the thought has not occurred to him.'

'Nevertheless it has occurred to me,' retorted Ferdinand. 'A King in need of a wife. Have you forgotten that we have a daughter as yet not spoken for?'

Isabella gave him a startled look.

'Why should not our Maria be Queen of Portugal?' demanded Ferdinand. 'Thus we should regain that which we have lost by the death of Isabella.'

❧❧

'Farewell,' said Margaret. 'It grieves me to leave you, but I know that I must go'

Catalina embraced her sister-in-law. 'How I wish that you would stay with us.'

'For how long?' asked Margaret. 'My father will be making plans for a new marriage for me. It is better that I go.'

'You have not been very happy here,' said Maria quietly.

'It was not the fault of the King and Queen, nor of any of

you. You have done everything possible to make me happy. Farewell, my sisters. I shall think of you often.'

Catalina shivered. 'How life changes!' she said. 'How can we know where any of us will be this time next year . . . or even this time next month?'

Catalina was terrified every time envoys came from England. She knew that her mother was putting off the day when her youngest daughter would leave her home; but it could not be long delayed. Catalina was too fatalistic to believe that was possible.

'Farewell, farewell,' said Margaret.

And that day she was on her way to the coast, to board the ship which would take her back to Flanders.

❧

Isabella's great delight was her little grandson. He was too young as yet to accompany her on all her journeys throughout the country so, after his acceptance by the Cortes of Castile and Aragon, he was left with his nurses in the Alhambra at Granada. Isabella often discussed his future with Ferdinand, and it was her desire that as soon as he was old enough he should always be with them.

'He cannot learn his state duties too early,' she said; but what she really meant was that she was not going to be separated from the child more than she could possibly help.

Ferdinand smiled indulgently. He was ready to pass over Isabella's little weaknesses as long as they did not interfere with his plans.

The Court was on its way to Seville, and naturally Isabella would call first at Granada to see her little Miguel.

Catalina, who was with the party, was delighted to note her

mother's recovery from despair, and she herself thought as tenderly of Miguel as Isabella did. Miguel was the means of making the Queen happy again; therefore Catalina loved him dearly.

Leisurely the Court moved southwards, and with them travelled the Archbishop of Toledo.

Ximenes had been deeply affected by the death of Tomás de Torquemada. There was a man who had written his name large across a page of Spanish history. He had clearly in his heyday been the most important man in his country, for he had guided the King and Queen and in the days of his strength had had his will.

It was due to him that the Inquisition was now a power in the land and that there was not a man, woman or child who did not dread the knock on the door in the dead of night, the entry of the *alguazils* and the dungeons of torture.

That was well, thought Ximenes, for only through torture could man come to God. And for those who had denied God the greatest torture man could devise was not bad enough. If these people burned at the stake, it was but a foretaste of the punishment which God would give them. What were twenty minutes at the stake compared with an eternity in Hell?

Riding south towards Granada, Ximenes was conscious of a great desire: to do, for Spain and the Faith, work which could be compared with that of Torquemada.

He thought of those who were in this retinue, and it seemed to him that the conduct of so many left much to be desired.

Ferdinand was ever reaching for material gain; Isabella's weakness was her children. Even now she had Catalina beside her. The girl was nearly fifteen years old and still she remained in Spain. She was marriageable, and the King of England grew impatient. But for her own gratification – and perhaps because the girl pleaded with her – Isabella kept her in Spain.

Ximenes thought grimly that her affection for the new heir, young Miguel, must approach almost idolatry. The Queen should keep a sharp curb on her affections. They over-shadowed her devotion to God and duty.

Catalina had withdrawn herself as far as possible from the stern-faced Archbishop. She read his thoughts and they terrified her. She hoped he would not accompany them to Seville; she was sure that, if he did, he would do his utmost to persuade her mother to send her with all speed to England.

Granada, which some had called the most beautiful city in Spain, was before them. There it lay, a fairy-tale city against the background of the snow-tipped peaks of the Sierra Nevada. High above the town was the Alhambra, that Moorish Palace, touched by a rosy glow, a miracle of architecture, strong as a fortress, yet so daintily and so delicately fashioned and carved, as Catalina knew.

There was a saying that God gives His chosen people the means to live in Granada; and Catalina could believe that was so.

She hoped that Granada would bring happiness to them all, that the Queen would be so delighted with her little grandson that she would forget to mourn, that there would be no news from England; and that, for the sunny days ahead, her life and that of her family would be as peacefully serene as this scene of snowy mountains, of rippling streams, the water of which sparkled like diamonds and was as clear as crystals.

She caught the eye of the Archbishop fixed upon her and felt a tremor of alarm.

She need not have worried. He was not thinking of her.

He was saying to himself: It is indeed our most beautiful city. It is not surprising that the Moors clung to it until the last. But what a tragedy that so many of its inhabitants should be those who deny the true faith. What sin that we should allow these Moors to practise their pagan rites under that blue sky, in the most beautiful city in Spain.

It seemed to Ximenes that the ghost of Torquemada rode beside him. Torquemada could not rest while such blatant sin existed in this fair city of Spain.

Ximenes was certain, as he rode with the Court into Granada, that the mantle of Torquemada was being placed about his shoulders.

⁓⁓

While Isabella was happy in the nursery of her grandson, Ximenes lost no time in examining the conditions which existed in Granada.

The two most influential men in the city were Iñigo Lopez de Mendoza, the Count of Tendilla, and Fray Fernando de Talavera, Archbishop of Granada; and one of Ximenes's first acts was to summon these men to his presence.

He surveyed them with a little impatience. They were, he believed, inclined to be complacent. They were delighted at the peaceful conditions prevailing in this city, which, they congratulated themselves, was in itself near the miraculous. This was a conquered city; a great part of its population consisted of Moors who followed their own faith; yet these Moors lived side by side with Christians and there was no strife between them.

Who would have thought, Ximenes demanded of himself, that this could possibly be a conquered city!

'I confess,' he told his visitors, 'that the conditions here in Granada give me some concern.'

Tendilla showed his surprise. 'I am sure, my lord Archbishop,' he said, 'that when you have seen more of the affairs in this city you will change your mind.'

Tendilla, one of the illustrious Mendoza family, could not help but be conscious of the comparatively humble origins of the Archbishop of Toledo. Tendilla lived graciously and it disturbed him to have about him those who did not. Talavera, who had been a Hieronymite monk and whose piety was indisputable, was yet a man of impeccable manners. Tendilla considered Talavera something of a bigot but it seemed to him that such an attitude was essential in a man of the Church; and in his tolerance Tendilla had not found it difficult to overlook that in Talavera which did not fit in with his own views. They had worked well together since the conquest of Granada, and the city of Granada was a prosperous and happy city under their rule.

Both resented the tone of Ximenes, but they had to remember that as Archbishop of Toledo he held the highest post in Spain under the Sovereigns.

'I could not change my mind,' went on Ximenes coldly, 'while I see this city dominated by that which is heathen.'

Tendilla put in: 'We obey the rules of their Highnesses' agreement with Boabdil at the time of the reconquest. As Alcayde and Captain-General of the Kingdom of Granada it is my duty to see that this agreement is adhered to.'

Ximenes shook his head. 'I know well the terms of that agreement, and pity it is that it was ever made.'

'Yet,' said Talavera, 'these conditions *were* made and the

Sovereigns could not so dishonour themselves and Spain by not observing them.'

'What conditions!' cried Ximenes scornfully. 'The Moors to retain possession of their mosques with freedom to practise their heathen rites! What sort of a city is this over which to fly the flag of the Sovereigns?'

'Nevertheless these were the terms of surrender,' Tendilla reminded him.

'Unmolested in their style of dress, in their manners and ancient usages; to speak their own language, to have the right to dispose of their own property! A fine treaty.'

'Yet, my lord Archbishop, these were the terms Boabdil asked for surrender. Had we not accepted them there would have been months – perhaps years – of slaughter, and no doubt the destruction of much that is beautiful in Granada.'

Ximenes turned accusingly to these two men. 'You, Tendilla, are the Alcayde; you, Talavera, are the Archbishop. And you content yourselves with looking on at these practices which cannot but anger our God and are enough to make the saints weep. Are you surprised that we suffer the ill fortune we do? Our heir dead. His child stillborn. The Sovereigns' eldest daughter dead in childbirth. What next, I ask you? What next?'

'My lord Archbishop cannot suggest that these tragedies are the result of what happens here in Granada!' murmured Tendilla.

'I say,' thundered Ximenes, 'that we have witnessed the disfavour of God, and that it behoves us to look about and ask ourselves in what manner we are displeasing Him.'

Talavera spoke then. 'My lord, you do not realise what efforts we have made to convert these people to Christianity.'

Ximenes turned to the Archbishop. It was from a man of the

Church that he might expect good sense, rather than from a soldier. Talavera had at one time been Prior of the Monastery of Santa Maria del Prado, not far from Valladolid; he had also been confessor to the Queen. He was a man of courage. Ximenes had heard that when Isabella's confessor had listened to the Queen's confession he had insisted on her kneeling while he sat, and when Isabella had protested Talavera had remarked that the confessional was God's tribunal and that, as he acted as God's minister, it was fitting that he should remain seated while the Queen knelt. Isabella had approved of such courage; so did Ximenes.

It was known also that this man, who had previously been the Bishop of Avila, refused to accept a larger income when he became Archbishop of Granada; he lived simply and spent a great deal of his income on charity.

This was all very well, thought Ximenes; but what good was it to appease the hunger of the poor, to give them sensuous warmth, when their souls were in peril? What had this dreamer done to bring the heathen Moor into the Christian fold?

'Tell me of these efforts,' said Ximenes curtly.

'I have learned Arabic,' said Talavera, 'in order that I may understand these people and speak with them in their own tongue. I have commanded my clergy to do the same. Once we speak their language we can show them the great advantages of holding to the true Faith. I have had selections from the Gospels translated into Arabic.'

'And what conversions have you to report?' demanded Ximenes.

'Ah,' put in Tendilla, 'this is an ancient people. They have their own literature, their own professions. My lord Archbishop, look at our Alhambra itself. Is it not a marvel of architecture? This is a symbol of the culture of these people.'

'Culture!' cried Ximenes, his eyes suddenly blazing. 'What culture could there be without Christianity? I see that in this Kingdom of Granada the Christian Faith is considered of little importance. That shall not continue, I tell you. That shall not continue.'

Talavera looked distressed. Tendilla raised his eyebrows. He was annoyed, but only slightly so. He understood the ardour of people such as Ximenes. Here was another Torquemada. Torquemada had set up the Inquisition, and men such as Ximenes would keep the fires burning. Tendilla was irritated. He hated unpleasantness. His beloved Granada delighted him with its beauty and prosperity. His Moors were the most industrious people in Spain now that they had rid themselves of the Jews. He wanted nothing to break the peaceful prosperity of his city.

He smiled. Let this fanatical monk rave. It was true he was Primate of Spain – what a pity that the office had not been given to a civilised nobleman – but Tendilla was very well aware of the agreement which Isabella and Ferdinand had made with Boabdil, and he believed that Isabella at least would honour her agreement.

Therefore he smiled without much concern while Ximenes ranted.

Granada was safe from the fury of the fanatic.

❧❧

Isabella held the baby in her arms. The lightness of the little bundle worried her.

Some children are small, she comforted herself. I have had so much trouble that I look for it where it does not exist.

She questioned his nurses.

His little Highness was a good child, a contented child. He took his food and scarcely cried at all.

Isabella thought, Would it not be better if he kicked and cried lustily? Then she remembered her daughter Juana who had done these things.

I must not build up fears where they do not exist, she admonished herself.

There was his wet nurse – a lusty girl, her plump breasts bursting out of her bodice, smelling faintly of *olla podrida* in a manner which slightly offended the Queen's nostrils. But the girl was healthy and she had the affection which such girls did have for their foster children.

It was useless to question the girl. How does he suck? Greedily? Is he eager for his feed?

She would give the answers which she thought would best please the Queen, rather than what might be the truth.

Catalina begged to be allowed to hold the baby, and Isabella laid the child in her daughter's arms.

'Here, sit beside me. Hold our precious little Miguel tightly.'

Isabella watched her daughter with the baby. Perhaps it would not be long before she held a child of her own in such a manner.

The thought made her uneasy. How could she bear to part with Catalina? And she would have to part with her soon. The King of England was indicating that he was growing impatient. He was asking for more concessions. Since the death of Juan and his child the bargaining position had not been so favourable for Spain. It was very likely that Margaret would be married soon, and her share of the Habsburg inheritance was lost.

Ferdinand had said to her during their journey to Granada: 'The English alliance is more important to us now than ever.'

So it would not be long.

Ferdinand came into the nursery. He too took a delight in the child. Isabella, watching him peering into the small face, realised that he suffered from none of those fears which beset her.

'How like his father Miguel begins to grow,' he said, beaming. 'Ah, my daughter, I trust it will not be long before you hold a child of your own in your arms. A Prince of England, eh, a Prince who will one day be a King.'

He had shattered the peace of the nursery for Catalina. It was no use being annoyed with him. He could never understand Catalina's fears as her mother could.

Ferdinand turned to Isabella: 'Your Archbishop is in a fine mood,' he said with an ironical smile. 'He begs audience. I did not think you would wish to receive him in the nursery.'

Isabella felt relieved to leave Catalina and Miguel, for poor Catalina's face was creased in pitiable anxiety.

'I will receive the Archbishop now,' she said. 'Does he ask to see us both?'

'Both,' echoed Ferdinand.

He held out his hand to Isabella and led her from the room.

In a small ante-chamber Ximenes was pacing up and down; he turned as the Sovereigns entered. He did not greet them with the homage etiquette demanded. Ferdinand noticed this and raised his eyebrows slightly in an expression which clearly said to Isabella: *Your* Archbishop – what manners he has!

'You have bad news, Archbishop?' asked Isabella.

'Your Highness, bad news indeed. Since I entered this city I have received shock after shock. Who could believe, as one walks these streets, that one was in a Christian land!'

'It is a prosperous and happy city,' Isabella reminded him.

'If it is prosperous, it is the prosperity of the devil!' cried Ximenes. 'Happy! You can call people happy – you a Christian – when they wallow in darkness!'

'They are an industrious people,' Ferdinand put in, and he spoke coldly as he always did to Ximenes. 'They bring great wealth to the place.'

'They bring great wealth!' repeated Ximenes. 'They worship in a heathen way. They pollute our country. How can we call Spain all-Christian when it harbours such people?'

'They have their own faith,' said Isabella gently, 'and we are doing our best to bring them to the true faith. My Archbishop of Granada has been telling me that he has learned Arabic and has had the catechism and part of the Gospels translated into Arabic. What more could we do?'

'I could think of much that we could do.'

'What?' demanded Ferdinand.

'We could force them to baptism.'

'You forget,' Isabella put in quickly, 'that in the agreement we made with Boabdil these people were to continue in their own way of life.'

'It was a monstrous agreement.'

'I think,' Ferdinand interrupted, 'that it would be well if the men of the Church confined their attention to Church matters and left the governing of the country to its rulers.'

'When an Archbishop is also Primate of Spain, matters of State are his concern,' retorted Ximenes.

Ferdinand was astonished at the arrogance of this man, but he could see that Isabella immediately forgave him his insolence on the grounds that all he said was either for the good of the Church or State. She had often defended him to Ferdinand, by reminding him that Ximenes was one of the few men about them who did not seek personal advantage, and that he seemed brusque in his manners because he said what he meant, without thought of any damage this might do to himself.

But she was adamant on this matter of the Moors. She had given her word to Boabdil, and she intended to keep it.

She said in that cool, somewhat curt voice of hers which she reserved for such occasions: 'The treaty we made with the Moors must stand. Let us hope that in time, under the guidance of our good Talavera, they will see the light. Now you will retire, my lord, for there are matters which the King and I must discuss, since shortly we must continue our journey.'

Ximenes, his mind simmering with plans which he had no intention of laying before the Sovereigns, retired.

'The monk over-reaches even his rank,' said Ferdinand lightly. 'Do you know, it would not surprise me if Master Ximenes became so arrogant that in time even you would be unable to endure him.'

'Oh, he is a good man; he is the best to fill the position. We must perforce put up with his manners.'

'I do not relish the thought of his company in Seville. The man irritates me with his hair shirt and his ostentatious saintliness.'

Isabella sighed. 'In time you will appreciate him . . . even as I do.'

'Never,' said Ferdinand, and his tone was harsh because he was thinking of young Alfonso and how grand he would have looked in the fine vestments of the Archbishop of Toledo.

Ferdinand was glad when they left for Seville and Ximenes did not accompany them.

Chapter XII

THE FATE OF THE MOORS

Ximenes was excited. He looked almost human as he waited to receive his guests. He had planned this meeting so carefully and it was to be the first step in a mighty campaign. He had not asked the Sovereigns' permission to act as he did; he was very glad that they were on their way to Seville. They would be delighted when they saw the results of his work; they would also know that, well as he served them, he served God and the Faith better.

He had had some difficulty with those two old fools, Tendilla and Talavera. They had assured him that his proposed methods would not work. The Moors were courteous by nature; they would listen to what he had to say; they would not contradict his word that the most fortunate people in the world were those who called themselves Christians; but they would remain Mohammedans.

He must understand that these were not savages; they were not as little children to be taught a catechism which they could repeat parrot fashion.

'Not savages!' Ximenes had cried. 'All those who are not Christians are savages.'

He was not going to diverge from his plan in any way. He was the Primate of Spain and as such was in complete authority under the Sovereigns; as for the Sovereigns, they were on their way to Seville and none could appeal to them.

He ordered that bales of silk and a quantity of scarlet hats should be brought to him. He now studied these with a wry smile on his lips. They were the bait and he believed the expenditure on the articles would be well worth while.

When his guests arrived he received them graciously. They were *alfaquis* of Granada, the learned Moorish priests whose word was law to the Mussulmans of Granada. Once he had seduced these men from their faith, the simple people would be ready to follow their leaders.

The *alfaquis* bowed low. They knew that they were in the presence of the greatest Archbishop in Spain, and their eyes lighted when they saw the bales of rich silk and the scarlet hats which they greatly admired, for they guessed these were gifts.

'I am delighted that you should have accepted my invitation,' said Ximenes, and his face showed none of the contempt that he felt for these people. 'I wish to talk to you. I think it would be of great interest to us all if we compared our respective religions.'

The *alfaquis* smiled and bowed again. And eventually they sat cross-legged around the chair of Ximenes while he talked to them of the Christian Faith and the joys of Heaven which awaited those who embraced it; also of the torments of Hell which were reserved for those who refused it. He spoke of baptism, a simple ceremony which enabled all those who partook of it to enter the Kingdom of Heaven.

He then took one of the bales and unfurled the crimson silk.

There was a murmur of admiration among his guests.

He wished to make presents, he told them, to all those who would undergo baptism.

Black eyes sparkled as they rested on the bales of coloured silks, and those delightful red hats were irresistible.

Several of the *alfaquis* agreed to be baptised, a ceremony which Ximenes was prepared to perform on the spot; and they went away with their silks and scarlet hats.

There was talk in the streets of Granada.

A great man had come among them. He gave rich presents, and to receive these presents all that was required was to take part in a strange little ceremony.

Each day little companies of Moors would present themselves before Ximenes, to receive baptism, a bale of silk and a scarlet hat.

Ximenes felt such delight that he had to curb it. It seemed sinful to be so happy. He was anxious that Talavera and Tendilla should not know what was happening, for he was sure they would endeavour to let the innocent Moors know what they were undertaking when they submitted to baptism.

What did it matter how they were brought into the Church, Ximenes asked himself, as long as they came?

So he continued with his baptisms and his presents. The costliness of the silk and hats was disturbing, but Ximenes had always been ready to dig deep into the coffers of Toledo for the sake of the Faith.

❦

News of what was happening came to the ears of one of the most learned of the *alfaquis* in Granada; this was Zegri, who, quietly studious, had not known what was taking place in the city.

One of his fellows called on him wearing a magnificent red hat, and he said: 'But you are extravagant. You have become rich, my friend.'

'This is not all,' he was told. 'I have a silk robe, and both were presents from the great Archbishop who is now in Granada.'

'Costly presents are often given that costlier presents may be received.'

'Ah, but all I did to earn these was to take part in some little Christian game called baptism.'

'Baptism! But that is the ceremony which is performed when one accepts the Christian Faith.'

'Oh, I was a Christian for a day . . . and for this I received my silk and hat.'

'What is this you say?' cried Zegri. 'You cannot be a Christian for a day!'

'It is what the Archbishop told us. "Be baptised," he said, "and these gifts are yours." Our fellows are crowding to his Palace each day. We play this little game and come away with our gifts.'

'Allah preserve us!' cried Zegri. 'Do you not know that once you have been baptised you are a Christian, and do you not know what these Christians do to those whom they call heretics?'

'What do they do?'

Zegri seized his robe as though he would rend it apart. He said: 'Here in Granada we live in peace. In other parts of Spain, there is that which is called the Inquisition. Those who do not practise Christianity – and Christianity in a particular manner – are called heretics. They are tortured and burned at the stake.' His visitor had turned pale.

'It would seem,' said Zegri impatiently, 'that our country-men have been lulled into stupidity by the beauty of the flowers that grow about our city, by the prosperity of our merchants, by the continued brilliance of our sunshine.'

'But . . . they are going in their hundreds!'

'We must call a meeting at once without delay. Send out messages to all. Tell them that I have a stern warning to give. Bring here to me as many of the *alfaquis* as you can muster. I must stop this at once.'

❧❧

Ximenes waited for more visitors. They did not come. There were his bales of silk, his scarlet hats, but it seemed that now nobody wanted them.

Ximenes, enraged, sent for Talavera and Tendilla.

They came immediately. Tendilla had discovered what had been happening and was very angry. Talavera also knew, but he was less disturbed; as a Churchman he admired the zeal of Ximenes; never had he seen such rapid proselytism.

'Perhaps,' said Ximenes, 'you can tell me what is happening in this city.'

'It would seem,' replied Tendilla lightly, 'that certain simple men have become Christians without understanding what this means.'

'You sound regretful,' accused Ximenes.

'Because,' Tendilla answered, 'these men have accepted baptism without understanding. They have accepted your gifts and in return they wished to give you what you asked — baptism into the Christian Faith for a bale of silk and a red hat. I should be glad to hear they had accepted our Faith without the bribe.'

'Yet there are more conversions in this city since the Archbishop of Toledo came here,' Talavera reminded him.

'I do not call this true conversion to Christianity,' retorted Tendilla. 'These simple souls have no knowledge of what they are undertaking.'

'We need not discuss your views on this matter,' Ximenes put in coldly. 'For the last two days there have been no conversions. There must be a reason. These savages cannot have taken a dislike to bales of silk and scarlet hats.'

'They have become wary of baptism,' said Tendilla.

'You two go among them as though you were of the same race. You doubtless know the reason for this sudden absence. I command you to tell me.'

Tendilla was silent, but Talavera, as an Archbishop himself, although of junior rank, answered his superior's command: 'It is due to the warnings of Zegri.'

'Zegri? Who is this man Zegri?'

Tendilla spoke then. 'He is the leading *alfaquis*, and not such a simple fellow as some. He understands a little of what baptism into the Christian Faith means. He has heard what has been going on and has warned his fellow Moors that baptism demands more of men and women than the acceptance of gifts.'

'I see,' said Ximenes. 'So it is this man Zegri. Thank you for your information.'

When they had left him he sent for one of his servants, a man named Leon, and he said to him:' I wish you to take a message from me to the house of the *alfaquis*, Zegri.'

❧❧

Zegri stood before Ximenes, while Ximenes showed him two

bales of silk. 'You may take as many of the hats as you wish,' he told his guest.

'No,' said Zegri.' I know of this baptism. I know what it means. Here in Granada we have not known the Inquisition, but I have heard what it does to Jews who have accepted baptism and go back to their own Faith.'

'Once you were a Christian you would not wish to go back to your own Faith. Each day you would become more and more aware of the advantages which Christianity has to offer.'

'I am a Mohammedan. I do not look for advantages.'

'You are a man stumbling in darkness.'

'I live very well, I am a happy man . . . with the love of Allah.'

'There is only one true Faith,' said Ximenes. 'That is the Christian Faith.'

'Allah forgive you. You know not what you say.'

'You will go to eternal torment when you die.'

'Allah will be good to me and mine.'

'If you become a Christian you will go to Heaven when you die. Allow me to give you baptism and eternal joy shall be yours.'

Zegri smiled and said simply: 'I am a Mohammedan. I do not change my religion for a bale of silk and a red hat.' His eyes flashed defiance as he stood there, and Ximenes realised that argument would never convince such a man. Yet it was necessary that he should be convinced. This was a powerful man, a man who would sway a multitude. One word from him and the conversions had ceased.

It was not to be tolerated, and in Ximenes's eyes all that was done in the service of the Faith was well done.

'I see,' he said, 'that I cannot make you a good Christian.'

'I do not believe that I could make you a good Mussulman,' retorted Zegri, smiling widely.

Ximenes crossed himself in horror.

'Here in Granada we shall continue in our own Faith,' said Zegri quietly.

But you shall not! thought Ximenes. I have sworn to convert this place to Christianity, and I will do it.

'I will take my leave of you,' said Zegri, 'and I will thank you for receiving me in your Palace, oh mighty Archbishop.'

Ximenes bowed his head and called to his servant Leon.

'Leon,' he said, 'show my guest the way out. He will come and talk with me again, for I have yet to persuade him.'

Leon, a tall man with broad shoulders answered: 'So shall it be, Your Excellency.' He led the way, and Zegri followed. They went through chambers which he did not remember seeing before, down some stairs to more apartments.

This was not the way he had come in, Zegri was thinking as Leon opened a door and stood aside for him to enter.

Unthinking, Zegri stepped forward. Then he stopped. But he was too late. Leon gave him a little push from behind and he stumbled down a few dark steps. He heard the door shut behind him and a key turned in the lock.

He was not outside the Archbishop's Palace. He was in a dark dungeon.

❧≈

Zegri lay on the floor of his dungeon. He was weak, for it must have been long since food had passed his lips. When the door had been locked on him he had beaten on it until his hands had bled; he had shouted to be let out, but no one answered him.

The floor was damp and cold and his limbs were numb.

'They have tricked me,' he said aloud, 'as they have tricked my friends.'

He thought that they would leave him here until he died, but this was not their intention.

Exhausted, he was lying on the floor, when he was aware of a blinding light flashed into his face. It was only a man with a lantern, but Zegri had been so long in the dark that it seemed as brilliant as the sun at noon.

This man was Leon, and with him was another. He pulled Zegri to his feet and slipped an iron ring about his neck; to this was attached a chain which he fixed to a staple in the wall.

'What do you plan to do with me?' demanded Zegri. 'What right have you to make me your prisoner? I have done no wrong. I must have a fair trial. In Granada all men must have fair trials.'

But Leon only laughed. And after a while the Archbishop of Toledo came into the dungeon.

Zegri cried out: 'What is this you would do to me?'

'Make a good Christian of you,' Ximenes told him.

'You cannot make me a Christian by torturing me.'

A gleam came into Ximenes's eyes, but he said: 'You have nothing to fear if you accept baptism.'

'And if I will not?'

'I do not despair easily. You will stay here in the darkness until you see the light of truth. You shall be without food for the body until you are prepared to accept food for the soul. Will you accept baptism?'

'Baptism is for Christians,' answered Zegri. 'I am a Mussulman.'

Ximenes inclined his head and walked from the dungeon. Leon followed him, and Zegri was in the cold darkness again.

He waited for these visits. There were several of them. Always he hoped that they would bring him food and drink. It was long since he had eaten and his body was growing weak. There were gnawing pains in his stomach and it cried out for nourishment. Always the words were the same. He would stay here in cold and hunger until he accepted baptism.

At the end of a few days and nights Zegri's discomfort was intense. He knew that if he continued thus he could not live very long. Zegri had spent all his life in the prosperous city of Granada. He had never known hardship before.

What good can I do by remaining here? he asked himself. I should only die.

He thought of his fellow Moors who had been deceived by the bales of silk and the red hats. They had been lured to baptism by bribes; he was being forced to it by this torture.

He knew there was only one way out of his dungeon.

❧❧

The blinding light was flashed into his face. There was the big man with the cruel eyes – Leon, the servant of the even more terrifying one with the face of a dead man and the eyes of a fiend.

'Bring him a chair, Leon,' said Ximenes. 'He is too weak to stand.'

The chair was brought and Zegri sat in it.

'Have you anything to say to me?' asked Ximenes.

'Yes, my lord Archbishop, I have something to say. Last night Allah came to my prison.'

Ximenes's face in the light from the lantern looked very stern.

'And he told me,' went on Zegri, 'that I must accept Christian baptism without delay.'

'Ah!' It was a long drawn out cry of triumph from the Archbishop of Toledo. For a second his lips were drawn back from his teeth in what was meant to be a smile. 'I see your stay with us has been fruitful, very fruitful. Leon, release him from his fetters. We will feed him and clothe him in silk. We will put a red hat on his head and we will baptise him in the name of Our Lord Jesus Christ. I thank God this victory is won.'

It was a great relief to have the heavy iron removed from his neck, but even so Zegri was too weak to walk.

Ximenes signed to the big man, Leon, who slung Zegri over his shoulder and carried him out of the damp dark dungeon.

He was put on a couch; his limbs were rubbed; savoury broth was put into his mouth. Ximenes was impatient for the baptism. He had rarely been as excited as when he scattered the consecrated drops from a hyssop over the head of this difficult convert.

So Zegri had now received Christian baptism.

'You should give thanks for your good fortune,' Ximenes told him. 'Now I trust many of your countrymen will follow your example.'

'If you and your servant do to my countrymen as you have done to me,' said Zegri, 'you will make so many Christians that there will not be a Mussulman left within the walls of Granada.'

Ximenes kept Zegri in his Palace until he had recovered from the effects of his incarceration, but he let the news be carried through the city: 'Zegri has become a Christian.'

The result satisfied even Ximenes. Hundreds of Moors were now arriving at the Archbishop's Palace to receive baptism and what went with it — bales of silk and scarlet hats.

Ximenes was not satisfied for long. The more learned of the Moorish population held back and exhorted their friends to do the same. They stressed what had happened to Jews who had received baptism and had been accused of returning to the faith of their fathers; they talked of the dreary *autos de fe* which were becoming regular spectacles in many of the towns of Spain. This must not be so in Granada. And those foolish people whose desire for silk and red hats had overcome their good sense were making trouble for themselves.

The people of Granada could not believe in any such trouble. This was Granada, where living had been easy for years; and even after their defeat at the hands of the Christians and the end of the reign of Boabdil, they had gone on as before. They would always go on in that way. Many of them remembered the day when the great Sovereigns, Ferdinand and Isabella, had come to take possession of the Alhambra. Then they had been promised freedom of thought, freedom of action, freedom to follow their own faith.

Ximenes knew that those who were preventing his work from succeeding as he wished it to, were the scholars, and he decided to strike a blow at them. They had declared that they had no need of this Christian culture because they had a greater culture of their own.

'Culture!' cried Ximenes. 'What is this culture? Their books, is it?'

It was true that they produced manuscripts of such beauty that they were spoken of throughout the world. Their binding and illuminations were exquisite and unequalled.

'I will have an *auto de fe* in Granada,' he told Talavera. 'It shall be the first. They shall see the flames rising to their beautiful blue sky.'

'But the agreement with the Sovereigns . . .' began Talavera.

'This *auto de fe* shall be one in which not bodies burn but manuscripts. This shall be a foretaste of what shall come if they forget their baptismal oaths. Let them see the flames rising to the sky. Let them see their evil words writhing in the heat. It would be wise to say nothing of this to Tendilla as yet. There is a man who doubtless would wish to preserve these manuscripts because the bindings are good. I fear our friend Tendilla is a man given to outward show.'

'My lord,' said Talavera, 'if you destroy these people's literature they may seek revenge on us. They are quiet people only among their friends.'

'They will find they never had a better friend than myself,' said Ximenes. 'Look how many of them I have brought to baptism!'

He was determined to continue with his project and would have no interference. Only when he saw those works reduced to ashes would he feel he was making some headway. He would make sure that none of the children should suffer from contamination with those heathen words.

The decree went out. Every manuscript in every Moorish house was to be brought out. They were to be put in heaps in the squares of the town. Severest penalties would be inflicted on those who sought to hide any work in Arabic.

Stunned, the Moors watched their literature passing from their hands into that of the man whom they now knew to be their enemy. Zegri had returned from his visit to the Archbishop's Palace a changed man. He was thin and ill; and he seemed deeply humiliated; it was as though all his spirit had gone from him.

Ximenes had ordered that works dealing with religion were

to be piled in the squares; but those dealing with medicine were to be brought to him. The Moors were noted for their medical knowledge and it occurred to Ximenes that there could be no profanity in profiting from it. He therefore selected some two or three hundred medical works, examined them and had them sent to Alcalá to be placed in the University he was building there.

Then he gave himself up to the task of what he called service to the Faith.

In all the open places of the town the fires were burning.

The Moors sullenly watched their beautiful works of art turned to ashes. Over the city there hung a pall of smoke, dark and lowering.

In the Albaycin, that part of the city which was inhabited entirely by the Moors, people were getting together behind shutters and even in the streets.

❧❧

Tendilla came to see Ximenes. He was not alone; he brought with him several leading Castilians who had lived for years in Granada.

'This is dangerous,' Tendilla blurted out.

'I do not understand you,' retorted Ximenes haughtily.

'We have lived in Granada for a long time,' pointed out Tendilla. 'We know these people. Am I not right?' He turned to his companions, who assured Ximenes that they were in complete agreement with Tendilla.

'You should rejoice with me,' cried Ximenes contemptuously, 'that there is no longer an Arabic literature. If these people have no books, their foolish ideas cannot be passed on to their young. Our next plan shall be to educate their children in the true Faith. In a generation we shall have everyone, man, woman and child, a Christian.'

Tendilla interrupted boldly: 'I must remind you of the conditions of the treaty.'

'Treaty indeed!' snapped Ximenes. 'It is time that was forgotten.'

'It will never be forgotten. The Moors remember it. They have respected the Sovereigns because ever since '92 that treaty has been observed . . . and now you would disregard it.'

'I ask the forgiveness of God because I have not attempted to do so before.'

'My lord Archbishop, may I implore you to show more forbearance. If you do not there will be bloodshed in our fair city of Granada.'

'I am not concerned with the shedding of blood. I am only concerned with the shedding of sin.'

'To follow their own religion is not to sin.'

'My lord, have a care. You come close to heresy.'

Tendilla flushed an angry red. 'Take the advice of a man who knows these people, my lord Archbishop. If you must make Christians of them, I implore you, if you value your life . . .'

'Which I do not,' Ximenes interjected.

'Then the lives of others. If you value them, I pray you take a tamer policy towards these people.'

'A tamer policy might suit temporal matters, but not those in which the soul is at stake. If the unbeliever cannot be drawn to salvation, he must be driven there. This is not the time to stay our hands, when Mohammedanism is tottering.'

Tendilla looked helplessly at those citizens whom he had brought with him to argue with Ximenes.

'I can see,' he said curtly, 'that it is useless to attempt to influence you.'

'Quite useless.'

'Then we can only hope that we shall be ready to defend ourselves when the time comes.'

Tendilla and his friends took their leave of Ximenes, who laughed aloud when he was alone.

Tendilla! A soldier! The Queen had been mistaken to appoint such a man as Alcayde. He had no true spirit. He was a lover of comfort. The souls of Infidels meant nothing to him as long as these people worked and grew rich and so made the town rich.

They thought he did not understand these Moors. They were mistaken. He was fully aware of the growing surliness of the Infidels. He would not be in the least surprised if they were making some plot to attack him. They might attempt to assassinate him. What a glorious death that would be – to die in the service of the Faith. But he had no wish to die yet, for unlike Torquemada he knew no one who would be worthy to wear *his* mantle.

This very day he had sent three of his servants into the Albaycin. Their task was to pause at the stalls and buy some of the goods displayed there, and to listen, of course. To spy on the Infidel. To discover what was being said about the new conditions which Ximenes had brought into their city.

He began to pray, asking for success for his project, promising more converts in exchange for Divine help. He was working out new plans for further forays against the Moors. Their literature was destroyed. What next? He was going to forbid them to follow their ridiculous customs. They were constantly taking baths or staining themselves with henna. He was going to stamp out these barbarous practices.

He noticed that the day was drawing to its close. It was time his servants returned. He went to the window and looked out. Only a little daylight left, he mused.

He went back to his table and his work, but he was wondering what had detained his servants.

When he heard the sound of cries below, he went swiftly down to the hall and there he saw one of those servants whom he had sent into the Albaycin; he was staggering into the hall surrounded by others who cried out in horror at the sight of him. His clothes were torn and he was bleeding from a wound in his side.

'My lord . . .' he was moaning. 'Take me to my lord.'

Ximenes hurried forward. 'My good man, what is this? What has happened to you? Where are your companions?'

'They are dead. Murdered, my lord. In the Albaycin. We were set upon . . . known as your servants. They are coming here. They have long knives. They have sworn to murder you. My lord . . . they are coming. There is little time left . . .'

The man fell swooning at the feet of the Archbishop.

Ximenes ordered: 'Make fast all doors. See that they are guarded. Take this man and call my physician to attend to him. The Infidel comes against us. The Lord is with us. But the Devil is a formidable enemy. Do not stand there. Obey my orders. We must prepare.'

❧≈

There followed hours of terror for all those in the Palace with the exception of Ximenes. From an upper chamber he watched those glowering faces in the light of their torches. He heard their shouts of anger.

He thought: Only these frail walls between myself and the Infidel. 'Lord,' he prayed, 'if it be Thy will to take me into Heaven, then so be it.'

They were throwing stones. They had tried to storm the gates but the Palace had stood many a siege and would doubtless stand many more.

They shouted curses on this man who had come among them and destroyed their peace; but Ximenes smiled blandly, for the cursings of the Infidel, he told himself, could be counted as blessings.

How long could the Palace hold out against the mob? And what would happen when those dark-skinned men broke through?

There was a lull outside, but Ximenes guessed that soon the tumult would break out again. They would storm the walls; they would find some way in, and then . . .

'Let them come, if it be Thy will,' he cried aloud.

He stood erect, waiting. He would be the one they sought. He wondered if they would inflict torture on him before they killed him. He was not afraid. His body had been schooled to suffer.

He heard a shout from without and in the light of the torches he saw a man on horseback riding up to the leader of the Moors.

It was Tendilla.

Ximenes could not hear what was said, but Tendilla was clearly arguing with the Moors. There he stood among them all, and Ximenes felt a momentary admiration for the soldier who could be as careless of his safety as Ximenes was of his.

He was now addressing the Moors, waving his hands and shouting, placating them no doubt, perhaps making promises which Ximenes had no intention of keeping.

But the Moors were listening. They had ceased to shout and it was quiet out there. Then Ximenes saw them turn and move away.

Tendilla was alone outside the Palace walls.

Tendilla was let into the Palace. His eyes were flashing with anger and that anger was directed not against the Moors but against Ximenes.

'So my lord,' he said, 'perhaps now you begin to understand.'

'I understand that your docile Moors are docile no longer.'

'They believe they have suffered great provocation. They are a very angry people. Do you realise that in a very short time they would have forced an entry into this place? Then it would have gone hard with you.'

'You are telling me that I owe you my life.'

Tendilla made an impatient gesture. 'I would not have you imagine that the danger is past. I persuaded them to return to their homes, and they agreed to do this ... tonight. But this will not be an end to this matter. A proud people does not see its literature burned to ashes and murmur, Thank you, my lord. You are unsafe in this place. Your life is not worth much while you stay here. Make ready at once and accompany me back to the Alhambra. There I can give you adequate protection.'

Ximenes stood still as a statue.

'I shall not cower behind the walls of the Alhambra, my good Tendilla. I shall stay here, and if these barbarians come against me, I shall trust in God. If it be His will that I become a martyr to their barbarism, then I say, Thy will be done.'

'They believe that they have been victims of your barbarism,' retorted Tendilla. 'They seek revenge. They will go back to the Albaycin and prepare for a real attack on your Palace. They will come again . . . this time in cold blood, fully armed. Do you realise, my lord Archbishop, that a major revolt is about to break out?'

For the first time Ximenes felt a twinge of uneasiness. He had believed he could successfully proselytise without trouble of this nature. If he were setting in motion warfare between Moors and Christians the Sovereigns would not be pleased. Their great aim had been to preserve peace within their own country so that they might conserve their strength for enemies beyond their borders.

But he held his head high and told himself that what he had done had been for the glory of God; and what was the will of the Sovereigns compared with that!

Tendilla said: 'I will ask one thing of you. If you will not come to the Alhambra, then stay here, as well guarded as possible, and leave me to deal with this insurrection.'

He bowed briefly and left the Archbishop.

❧❦

Tendilla rode back to the Alhambra. His wife, who was waiting for him, betrayed her relief when she saw him.

'I was afraid, Iñigo,' she said.

He smiled tenderly. 'You need have no fear. The Moors are my friends. They know that I have always been fair to them. They are a people who respect justice. It is not I who am in danger but that fool of an Archbishop of ours.'

'How I wish he had never come to Granada.'

'There are many who would echo those words, my dear.'

'Iñigo, what are you going to do now?'

'I am going into the Albaycin. I'm going to talk to them and ask them not to arm themselves for a revolt. Ximenes is responsible for this trouble, but if they kill the Archbishop of Toledo they will find the might of Spain raised against them. I must make them understand this.'

'But they are in a dangerous mood.'

'It is for this reason that I must not delay.'

'But, Iñigo, think. They are rising against the Christians, and you are a Christian.'

He smiled at her. 'Have no fear. This is something which must be done and I am the one to do it. If things should not go as I believe they will, be ready to leave Granada with the children and lose no time.'

'Iñigo! Do not go. This is the Archbishop's affair. Let them storm his Palace. Let them torture him . . . kill him if they will. He has brought this trouble to Granada. Let him take the consequences.'

Tendilla smiled gently. 'You have not understood,' he said. 'I am the Alcayde. I am responsible for this zealous reformer of ours. I have to protect him against the results of his own folly.'

'So you are determined?'

'I am.'

'Go well armed, Iñigo.'

Tendilla did not answer.

❧❧

Meanwhile Talavera had heard what was happening in the Albaycin. Something must be done quickly to calm the Moors.

They had always respected him. They had listened gravely when he had preached to them of the virtues of Christianity. They knew him for a good man.

Talavera was certain that he, more than any man in Granada, could help to restore order to the Albaycin.

He called for his chaplain and said: 'We are going into the Albaycin.'

'Yes, my lord,' was the answer.

'You and I alone,' went on Talavera, watching the expression on the face of the chaplain.

He saw the man's alarm. The whole of Granada must know, thought Talavera, of the trouble which was brewing in the Moorish quarter.

'There is trouble there,' went on the Archbishop of Granada. 'The Moors are in an ugly mood. They may well set upon us and murder us in their anger. I do not think they will. I think they will listen to me as they have always done. They are a fierce people but only when their anger is aroused, and I do not think we – you and I, my dear chaplain – have done anything to arouse their anger.'

'My lord, if we took soldiers with us to protect us . . .'

'I have never gone among them with a bodyguard. To do so now would make it appear that I do not trust them.'

'Do you trust them, my lord?'

'I trust in my Lord,' was the answer. 'And I would not ask you to accompany me if you would not do so of your own free will.'

The chaplain hesitated for a few moments, then he said: 'Where you go, my lord, there will I go.'

'Then prepare, for there is little time.'

So with only his chaplain to accompany him the Archbishop

of Granada rode into the Albaycin. The chaplain rode before him carrying the crucifix, and the Moors stared at these men in sullen silence for a few moments.

The Archbishop rode right into their midst and said to them: 'My friends, I hear that you are arming yourselves, and I come among you unarmed. If you desire to kill me, then you must do so. If you will listen to me, I will give you my advice.'

A faint murmuring broke out. The chaplain trembled; many of the Moors carried long knives. He thought of death which might not come quickly; then he looked into the calm face of his Archbishop and felt comforted.

'Will you do me the honour of listening to me?' asked the Archbishop.

There was a short silence. Then one of the *alfaquis* cried out: 'Speak, oh Christian lord.'

'You are an angry people, and you seek vengeance which, my friend, is not good for those who plan it nor for those who bear the brunt of it. It is a two-edged weapon, to harm those whom it strikes and those who strike. Do nothing rash. Pause and consider the inevitable result of your actions. Pray for guidance. Do not resort to violence.'

'We have seen our beautiful manuscripts destroyed before our eyes, oh Talavera,' cried one voice. 'We have seen the flames rising in the squares of Granada. What next will be burned? Our mosques? Our bodies?'

'Be calm. Pray for guidance.'

'Death to the Christian dogs!' cried a wild voice in the crowd.

There was a move forward and the *alfaquis* who had first spoken cried: 'Wait! This is our friend. This is not that other. This man is not guilty. In all the years he has been with us he has been just and although he has tried to persuade us he has never sought to force us to that which we did not want.'

'It is true,' someone called out.

'Yes,' cried several voices then. 'It is true. We have no quarrel with this man.'

'Allah preserve him.'

'He is not our enemy.'

Many remembered instances of his goodness. He had always helped the poor, Moor or Christian. They had no quarrel with this man.

One woman came forward and knelt at the side of Talavera's horse and said: 'You have been good to me and mine. I pray you, oh lord, give me your benediction.'

And Talavera placed his hands on this woman's head and said: 'Go in peace.'

Others came forward to ask his blessing, and when Tendilla rode into the Albaycin this was the scene he witnessed.

Tendilla came with half a dozen soldiers, and when the Moors saw his guards many hands tightened about their knives. But Tendilla's first action was to take his bonnet from his head and throw it into their midst.

'I give you my sign,' he cried, 'that I come in peace. Many of you are armed. Look at us. We have come among you unarmed.'

The Moors then saw that it was so, and they remembered too that from this man they had received nothing but justice and tolerance. He had come among them unarmed. They could have slain him and his few men together with the Archbishop and his chaplain without any loss to themselves.

This was certainly a sign of friendship.

'Long life to the Alcayde!' cried one, and the others took up this cry.

Tendilla lifted a hand.

'My friends,' he said, 'I pray you listen to me. You are armed and plan violence. If you carry out this plan you might have some initial success here in Granada. And what then? Beyond Granada the whole might of Spain would be assembled and come against you. If you gave way to your feelings now you would bring certain disaster and death upon yourselves and your families.'

The leading *alfaquis* came to Tendilla and said: 'We thank you, oh lord Alcayde, for coming to us this night. We have in your coming proof of the friendship of yourself and the Archbishop of Granada towards us. But we have suffered great wrongs. The burning of our works of art has caused us great distress.'

'You have your grievances,' Tendilla replied. 'If you will go back to your homes and put all thoughts of rebellion from your minds I will bring your case before the Sovereigns.'

'You yourself will do this?'

'I will,' said Tendilla. 'Their Highnesses are now in Seville. As soon as I can put my affairs in order I will ride there and explain to them.'

Zegri, who had learned at first hand of what he had come to think of as Christian perfidy, elbowed his way to the side of their leader.

'How can we know,' he said, 'that the Alcayde does not speak thus to gain time? How do we know that he will not become our enemy and bring the Christians against us?'

'I give you my word,' said Tendilla.

'Oh lord Alcayde, I was invited to the house of the

Archbishop of Toledo as a guest, and I found myself his prisoner. He changed towards me in the space of an hour. What if you should so change?'

There was a murmuring in the crowd. They were all remembering the experiences of Zegri.

Tendilla saw that the angry mood was returning, the fury which the conduct of Ximenes had aroused was bursting out again.

Tendilla made a decision. 'I shall go to Seville,' he said. 'You well know the love I bear my wife and two children. I will leave them here with you as hostages. That will be a token of my good intentions.'

There was silence in the crowd.

Then the leading *alfaquis* said: 'You have spoken, oh lord Alcayde.'

The crowd began to cheer. They did not love violence. They trusted Tendilla and Talavera to rid them of the trouble-making Ximenes that all might be peace once more in their beautiful city of Granada.

❧❧

News of what had happened in the Albaycin was brought to Ximenes. He was now alarmed. He had hoped to continue with his proselytising unimpeded; he realised now that he must be wary.

Tendilla had come storming into his Palace and had not hesitated to say what he meant. He blamed Ximenes for the first trouble that had occurred in the city since the reconquest, adding that within the next few days he was leaving for Seville, and there he would lay the matter before the Sovereigns.

Ximenes coldly retorted that he would do all that he had

done, over again, should the need arise, and the need was sore in Granada.

'You will do nothing,' retorted Tendilla, 'until this matter has been laid before their Highnesses.'

And Ximenes had of course agreed to the wisdom of that.

As soon as Tendilla had left, Ximenes fell on his knees in prayer. This was a very important moment in his life. He knew that the version of this affair which Tendilla would carry to the Sovereigns would differ from the tale he had to tell; and it was all-important that Ferdinand and Isabella should hear Ximenes's account first.

It might well be that on the following day Tendilla would set out for Seville. Ximenes must therefore forestall him.

He rose from his knees and sent for one of his Negro servants, a tall long-limbed athlete who could run faster than any other known in the district.

'I shall want you to leave for Seville within half an hour,' he said. 'Prepare yourself.'

The slave bowed, and when he was alone Ximenes sat down to write his account of what had happened in Granada. The need to save souls was imperative. He wanted more power and, when he had it, he would guarantee to bring the Moors of Granada into the Christian fold. He had been unable to stand calmly aside and watch the heathenish habits which were practised in that community. He had acted under guidance from God, and he was now praying that his Sovereigns would not shut their eyes to God's will.

He sent for the slave.

'With all speed to Seville,' he commanded.

And he smiled, well satisfied, believing that Isabella and Ferdinand would receive the news from him hours before they could possibly see Tendilla. By that time they would have read his version of the revolt, and all Tendilla's eloquence would not be able to persuade them that Ximenes had been wrong in what he had done.

~~~

The Negro slave ran the first few miles. As he sped onwards there passed him on the road a Moor who was riding on a grey horse; and the Negro wished that he had a horse on which to ride, but he quickly forgot it and gave himself up to the pleasure of exercise.

He was noted for his fleetness of foot and proud of it. Anyone could ride a horse. None could match him for running speed.

But the way was long and even the fleetest of foot grew tired; the throat became parched, and there on the road between Granada and Seville the slave saw a tavern. Tied to a post was the horse which had passed him on the way, and standing close to the horse was the rider.

The man called to the Negro: 'Good day to you. I saw you running on the road.'

'I envied you your horse,' said the Negro, pausing.

''Tis thirsty work, running as you run.'

'You speak truth there.'

'Well, here is an inn and the wine is good. Why do you not fortify yourself with some of this good wine?'

'Oh . . . I am on a mission. I have to reach Seville with all speed.'

'You'll go the quicker for the wine.'

The Negro considered this. It might be true.

'Come,' said the Moor. 'Drink with me. Let me be your host.'

'You are generous,' said the Negro, smiling.

'Come inside and wine shall be brought for us.'

They sat together drinking the wine. The Moor encouraged the Negro to talk of his triumphs: how he had won many a race and had not in recent years met the man who could outrun him.

The Moor replenished his glass, and the Negro did not notice how much he was drinking, and forgot that he was unused to such wine.

His speech became slower; he had forgotten where he was; he slumped forward and, smiling, the Moor rose and taking him by the hair jerked his face upwards. The Negro was too intoxicated to protest; he did not even know who the man was.

The Moor called to the innkeeper.

'Let your servants take this man to a bed,' he said. 'He has drunk much wine and he will not be sober until morning. Give him food then and more wine . . . a great deal of it. It is necessary that he should stay here for another day and night.'

The innkeeper took the money which was given him, and assured his honoured customer that his wishes should be carried out.

The Moor smiled pleasantly, went out to his horse and began the journey back to Granada.

Later that night the Count of Tendilla set out for Seville with his retinue. There was rejoicing in the Albaycin. The cunning of Ximenes would be foiled. Isabella and Ferdinand would first hear the story of the Moorish revolt from their friend, not from their enemy.

❧

When Ferdinand heard from Tendilla what had happened in Granada his first feeling was of anger, then dismay, but these were later tinged with a faint satisfaction.

He lost no time in confronting Isabella.

'Here is a fine state of affairs,' he cried. 'Revolt in Granada. All brought about through this man Ximenes. So we are to pay dear for the conduct of *your* Archbishop. That for which we fought for years has been endangered in a few hours by the rashness of this man whom you took from his humble station to make Archbishop of Toledo and Primate of Spain.'

Isabella was astounded by the news. She had taken great pride in maintaining the treaty. She had always been delighted to hear of the prosperity of her city of Granada, of the industry of the Moorish population and the manner in which they lived peaceably side by side with the Christians. She was overjoyed when she heard of the few conversions to Christianity which Talavera had brought about. But revolt in Granada! And Ximenes, *her* Archbishop – as Ferdinand always called him – was apparently at the very root of it.

'We have not heard his side of the story . . .' she began.

'And why not?' demanded Ferdinand. 'Does your Archbishop think he may act without our sanction? He has not thought fit to inform us. Who are we? Merely the Sovereigns. It is Ximenes who rules Spain.'

'I confess I am both alarmed and astonished,' admitted Isabella.

'I should think so, Madam. This is what comes of giving high office to those who are unable to fill it with dignity and responsibility.'

'I shall write to him at once,' said the Queen, 'informing him of my displeasure and summoning him to our presence without delay.'

'It would certainly be wise to recall him from Granada before we have a war on our hands.'

Isabella went to her table and began to write in the most severe terms, expressing her deep concern and anger that the Archbishop of Toledo should have so far forgotten his duty to his Sovereigns and his office as to have acted against the treaty of Granada and, having brought about such dire results, had not thought fit to tell his Sovereigns.

Ferdinand watched her, a slow smile curving his mouth. He was anxious as to the state of Granada, but he could not help feeling this pleasure. It was very gratifying to see his prophecies, concerning that upstart, coming true. How different it would have been if his own dear son Alfonso had graced the highest office in Spain.

※ ❧ ※

Ximenes stood before the Sovereigns. His face was pale but he was as arrogant as ever.

There was no contrition at all, Ferdinand noticed in amazement. What sort of man was this? He had no fear whatsoever. He could be stripped of office and possessions and he would still flaunt his self-righteousness. He could be beaten, tortured, taken to the stake – still he would preserve that air of arrogance.

Even Ferdinand was slightly shaken as he looked at this man. As for Isabella, from the moment he had stood before her she was ready to listen sympathetically and to believe that what she had heard before had not been an accurate account.

'I do not understand,' began Isabella, 'on what authority you have acted as you did in Granada.'

'On that of God,' was the answer.

Ferdinand made an impatient gesture but Isabella went on gently: 'My lord Archbishop, did you not know that the Treaty of Granada lays down that the Moorish population should continue to worship as it wished?'

'I did know this, Highness, but I thought it an evil treaty.'

'Was that your concern?' demanded Ferdinand with sarcasm.

'It is always my concern to fight evil, Highness.'

Isabella asked: 'If you wished to take these measures would it not have been wiser to have consulted us, to ask our permission to do so?'

'It would have been most unwise,' retorted Ximenes. 'Your Highnesses would never have given that permission.'

'This is monstrous!' cried Ferdinand.

'Wait, I beg of you,' pleaded Isabella. 'Let the Archbishop tell us his side of the story.'

'It was necessary,' continued Ximenes, 'that action should be taken against these Infidels. Your Highness did not see fit to do so. In the name of the Faith I was forced to do it for you.'

'And,' fumed Ferdinand, 'having done it, you did not even take the trouble to inform us.'

'There you wrong me. I dispatched a messenger to you in all haste. He should have reached you before you received the news from any other. Unhappily my enemies waylaid him and intoxicated him so that he did not reach you . . . and then, having failed in his duty, was afraid to present himself either to you or to me.'

Isabella looked relieved. 'I knew I could trust you to keep us informed, and the failure of your messenger to arrive was certainly no fault of yours.'

'There is still this astonishing conduct, which led to revolt in Granada, to be explained,' Ferdinand reminded them.

Then Ximenes turned to him and delivered one of those

sermons of invective for which he was famous. He reminded them of the manner in which he had served God, the state, and themselves. He told them how much of the revenues of Toledo had gone into the work of proselytising. He hinted that both had been guilty of indifference to the Faith – Ferdinand in his desire for aggrandisement, Isabella in her affection for her family. Here he touched them both where they were most vulnerable. He made them feel guilty; slowly, with infinite cunning he turned the argument in his favour so that it was as though they were under an obligation to explain themselves to him, not he to them.

Ferdinand was saying to himself: I have found the need always to fight, to protect what is mine and to seek to make it safe; I have seen that only by adding to my possessions can I make Aragon safe.

And Isabella: Perhaps it is sin for a mother to love her children as I have done, to evade her duty in the desire to keep them with her.

Ximenes then came to the point up to which he was leading them.

'It is true,' he said, 'that there was this Treaty of Granada. But the Moors in Granada have been in revolt against Your Highnesses. By so doing they have broken the treaty, the core of which was that both sides were to live in amity. It was they who rose against us. Therefore, since they have broken their word, there is no need for us to have any compunction in changing our attitude towards them.'

Subtly Ximenes reminded the Sovereigns of the expulsion of the Jews. Much of the property of these unfortunate Jews had enriched the state. The thought of that made Ferdinand's eyes gleam. For Isabella's sake he spoke of the great work that could be done in bringing these Infidels into the Christian fold.

Then he cried: 'They have broken the treaty. You are under no obligation. Any means should be used to bring these poor lost souls to Christianity.'

Ximenes had won his battle. The Treaty of Granada was no more.

An almost benevolent expression was on Ximenes's face. He was already making plans to bring the Moors of Granada to baptism. In a short time there should be what he called a truly Christian Granada.

⊜ Chapter XIII ⊜

THE DEPARTURES OF MIGUEL AND
CATALINA

Maria and her sister Catalina were at the window watching the comings and goings to and from the Madrid Alcazar. The expression of each was intent; and in both cases their thoughts were on marriage.

Catalina could immediately recognise the English messengers, and on those occasions when she saw these men with their letters from their King to her parents she felt sick with anxiety. The Queen had told her that in each dispatch the King of England grew more and more impatient.

Then Catalina would cling to her mother wildly for a few seconds, holding back her tears; and although the Queen reproved her, there was, Catalina knew, a rough note in her voice which betrayed her own nearness to tears.

It cannot be long now, Catalina said to herself every morning. And each day which could be lived through without word from England was something for which she thanked the saints in her prayers at night.

Maria was different. She was as nearly excited as Catalina had ever seen her.

Now she chattered: 'Catalina, can you see the Naples livery? Tell me if you do.'

Doesn't she care that she will have to leave her home? wondered Catalina. But perhaps Naples did not seem so far away as England.

There was gossip throughout the Alcazar that the next marriage would either be that of Maria to the Duke of Calabria who was the heir of the King of Naples, or that of Catalina to the Prince of Wales.

Maria actually enjoyed talking of her prospective marriage.

'I was afraid I was going to be forgotten,' she explained. 'There were husbands for everybody else and none for me. It seemed unfair.'

'I should rejoice if they had found no husband for me,' Catalina reminded her.

'That is because you are so young. You cannot imagine anything but staying at home here with Mother all your life. That is quite impossible.'

'I fear you are right.'

'When you are as old as I am you will feel differently,' Maria comforted her sister.

'In three years' time I shall be as old as you are now. I wonder what I shall be doing by then? Three years from now. That will be the year 1503. It's a long way ahead. Look. There is a messenger. He comes from Flanders, I am sure.'

'Then it will be news from our sister.'

'Oh,' said Catalina and fell silent. That which she feared next to news from England was news from Flanders, because news which came from that country had the power to make her mother so unhappy.

❧❧

The girls were summoned to their parents' presence. This was a ceremonial occasion. They were not the only ones in the big apartment. Their parents stood side by side, and Catalina knew immediately that some important announcement was about to be made.

In the Queen's hand were the dispatches from Flanders.

It must concern Juana, thought Catalina; but there was no need to worry. Something had happened which made her mother very happy. As for her father, there was an air of jubilance about him.

Into the apartment came all the officers of state who were at that time resident in the Alcazar, and when they were all assembled a trumpeter who stood close to the King and Queen sounded a few notes.

There was silence throughout the room. Then Isabella spoke.

'My friends, this day I have great news for you. My daughter Juana has given birth to a son.'

These words were followed by fanfares of triumph.

And then everyone in the room cried: 'Long life to the Prince!'

❧❧

Isabella and Ferdinand were alone at last.

Ferdinand's face was flushed with pleasure. Isabella's eyes were shining.

'This, I trust,' she said, 'will have a sobering effect on our daughter.'

'A son!' cried Ferdinand. 'What joy! The first born and a son.'

'It will be good for her to be a mother,' mused Isabella. 'She will discover new responsibilities. It will steady her.'

Then she thought of her own mother and those uncanny

scenes in the Castle of Arevalo when she had raved about the rights of her children. Isabella remembered that she had been at her most strange when she had feared that her children might not gain what she considered to be their rights.

But she would not think such thoughts. Juana was fertile. She had her son. That was a matter for the utmost rejoicing.

'They are calling him Charles,' murmured Isabella.

Ferdinand frowned. 'A foreign name. There has never been a Charles in Spain.'

'If this child became Emperor of the Austrians he would be their Charles the Fifth,' said Isabella. 'There have been other Charleses in Austria.'

'I like not the name,' insisted Ferdinand.' It would have been a pleasant gesture if they had named their first, Ferdinand.'

'It would indeed. But I expect we shall become accustomed to the name.'

'Charles the Fifth of Austria,' mused Ferdinand, 'and Charles the First of Spain.'

'He cannot be Charles the First of Spain while Miguel lives,' Isabella reminded him.

'Not . . . while Miguel lives,' repeated Ferdinand.

He looked at Isabella with that blank expression which, during the early years of their marriage, she had begun to understand. He believed Miguel would not live, and that this which had caused him great anxiety before the letter from Juana had arrived, no longer did so. For if Miguel died now there was still a male heir to please the people of Aragon: there was Juana's son, Charles.

'From all reports,' said Ferdinand, 'our grandson with this odd name appears to be a lusty young person.'

'They tell us so.'

'I have had it from several sources,' answered Ferdinand. 'Sources which are warned not to feed me with lies.'

'So Charles is big for his age and strong and lusty. Charles will live.'

Isabella's lips trembled slightly; she was thinking of that wan child in his nursery in the troubled town of Granada, where the Moorish population had now been called upon to choose between baptism and exile.

Miguel was such a good child. He scarcely ever cried. He coughed a little though, in the same way as his mother had done just before she died.

'Ferdinand,' Isabella had turned to her husband, 'this child which has been born to our Juana will one day inherit all the riches of Spain.'

Ferdinand did not answer. But he agreed with her.

It was the first time that Isabella had given voice to the great anxiety which Miguel had brought to her since his birth.

But all was well now, thought Ferdinand. One heir might be taken from them, but there was another to fill his place.

Isabella once again read Ferdinand's thoughts. She must try to emulate her husband's calm practical common sense. She must not grieve too long for Juan, for Isabella. They had little Miguel. And if little Miguel should follow his mother to the grave, they had lusty little Habsburg Charles to call their heir.

❦

Ferdinand at this time was deeply concerned over Naples. When Charles VIII of France had been succeeded by Louis XII it had become clear that Louis had his eyes on Europe, for he immediately laid claim to Naples and Milan. Ferdinand himself had for long cast covetous eyes on Naples which was occupied by his cousin, Frederick. Frederick belonged to an illegitimate line of the House of Aragon, and it was for this reason that Ferdinand itched to take the crown for himself.

Frederick, who might have expected help from his cousin against the King of France, had received a blow when his effort to marry his son, the Duke of Calabria, to Ferdinand's daughter Maria, was thwarted.

Frederick's great hope had been to bind himself closer to his cousin Ferdinand by this marriage; and Ferdinand might have considered the alliance, but for the fact that the King of Portugal was a widower.

Of all his potential enemies Ferdinand most feared the King of France who, by the conquest of Milan, was now a power in Italy. The situation was further aggravated by the conduct of the Borgia Pope, who quite clearly was determined to win wealth, honour and power for himself and his family. The Pope was no friend to Ferdinand. Isabella had been profoundly shocked by the conduct of the Holy Father, whose latest scandalous behaviour had concerned transferring his son Cesare, whom he had previously made a Cardinal, from the Church to the army, simply because that ambitious young man, whose reputation was as evil as that of his father, felt that he could gain more power outside the Church. Ferdinand, believing that nothing could be gained by ranging himself on the side of the Borgias, joined Isabella in accusing the Pope of his crimes.

Alexander had been furious, had torn up the letter in which these complaints were made and had retaliated by referring to the Sovereigns of Spain with some indecency.

Therefore an alliance between the Vatican and Spain was out of the question. Maximilian was heavily engaged, and in any case had not the means of helping Ferdinand. Meanwhile the French, triumphant in Milan, were now preparing to annex Naples.

Frederick of Naples, a gentle peace-loving person, awaited with trepidation the storm which was about to break over his little Kingdom. He feared the French and he knew that he could not expect help from his cousin Ferdinand who wanted Naples for himself. There seemed no way out of his dilemma except by calling in the help of the Turkish Sultan, Bajazet.

When Ferdinand heard this he was gleeful.

'This is monstrous,' he declared to Isabella. 'My foolish cousin – I must say my wicked cousin – has asked for help from the greatest enemy of Christianity. Now we need have no qualms about stepping in and taking Naples from him.'

Isabella, who previously had been less eager for the Neapolitan campaign, was quickly won over by Ferdinand's arguments when she heard that Frederick had called for help from Bajazet.

But Ferdinand was in as great a dilemma as his cousin Frederick. If he allied himself with the powerful Louis, and victory was theirs, it was certain that Louis would eventually oust Ferdinand from Naples. To help Frederick against Louis was not to be thought of, because he would be fighting for Frederick and that would bring him no gain.

Ferdinand was a wily strategist where his own advancement was concerned. His sharp acquisitive eyes took in every salient point.

When Bajazet ignored Frederick's cry for help, Ferdinand set in motion negotiations between France and Spain, and the result was a new treaty of Granada.

This document was a somewhat sanctimonious one. In it was stated that war was evil and it was the duty of all Christians to preserve peace. Only the Kings of France and Aragon could pretend to the throne of Naples, and as the present King had called in the help of the enemy of all Christians, Bajazet, the Turkish Sultan, there was no alternative left to the Kings of France and Aragon, but that they should take possession of the Kingdom of Naples and divide it between them. The north would be French, the south Spanish.

This was a secret treaty; and so it should remain while the Spaniards and the French prepared to take what the treaty made theirs.

'This should not be difficult,' Ferdinand explained to Isabella. 'Pope Alexander will support us against Frederick. Frederick was a fool to refuse his daughter Carlotta to Cesare Borgia. Alexander will never forgive this slight to a son on whom he dotes; and the hatred of the Borgias is implacable.'

Isabella was delighted by the cunning strategy of her husband.

She said to him on the signing of the treaty: 'I do not know what would have become of us but for you.'

These words gave Ferdinand pleasure. He often thought what an ideal wife Isabella would have been if she had not been also Queen of Castile, so determined to do her duty that she subdued everything else to that; yet it was precisely because she was Queen of Castile that he had wanted her to be his wife.

His busy mind was looking ahead. There would have to be a campaign against Naples. It was important that the friendship with England should not be broken. He would be glad when he could marry Maria into Portugal.

It would be wise to discuss the matter of England with Isabella while she was in this humble mood.

He laid his hand on Isabella's shoulder and looked serenely into her eyes.

'Isabella, my dear,' he said, 'I have been patient with you because I know of the love you bear our youngest. The time is passing. She should now begin to prepare for her journey to England.'

He saw the fear leap into Isabella's eyes.

'I dread to tell her this,' she said.

'Oh come, come, what is this folly? Our Catalina is going to be Queen of England.'

'She is so close to me, Ferdinand, more close than any of the others. There are going to be many sad tears when we are parted. She is so alarmed by the thought of this journey that sometimes I fear she has a premonition of evil.'

'Is this my wise Isabella talking?'

'Yes, Ferdinand, it is. Our eldest daughter believed she was going to die in childbed, and she did. In the same way our youngest has this horror of England.'

'It is time I was firm with you all,' said Ferdinand. 'There is one way to stop our Catalina's fancies. Let her go to England, let her see for herself what a fine thing it is to be the wife of the heir to the English throne. I'll swear that in a few months' time we shall be having glowing letters about England. She will have forgotten Spain and us.'

'I have a feeling that Catalina will never forget us.'

'Break the news to her then.'

'Oh, Ferdinand, so soon?'

'It has been years. I marvel at the patience of the King of England. We dare not lose this match, Isabella. It is important to my schemes.'

Isabella sighed. 'I shall give her a few more days of pleasure,' she said. 'Let her enjoy another week in Spain. There will not be many weeks left to her in which to enjoy her home.'

Isabella knew now that she could no longer put off the date of departure.

⁖⁖⁖

There was an urgent call to Granada, where little Miguel was suffering from a fever. The Queen rode into the city with Ferdinand and her two daughters. The news of Miguel's illness had had one good result, for because of it Isabella had put off giving Catalina instructions to prepare to leave Spain.

How different the city looked on this day. There were the towers of the Alhambra, rosy in the sunlight; there were the sparkling streams; but Granada had lost its gaiety. It was a sad city since Ximenes had ridden into it and had decided that only Christians should enjoy it.

Everywhere there was evidence of those days when it had been the Moorish capital, so that it was impossible to ride through those streets without thinking of the work which was steadily going forward under the instructions of the Archbishop of Toledo.

Isabella's heart was heavy. She was wondering now what she would find when she reached the Palace. How bad was the little boy? She read between the lines of the messages she had received and she guessed that he was very bad indeed.

She felt numbed by this news. Was it, she asked herself, that when blow followed blow, one was prepared for the next?

Ferdinand would not mourn. He would tell her that she must be grateful because they had Charles.

But she would not think of Miguel's dying. She herself would nurse him. She would keep him with her; she would not allow even her State duties to separate her from the child. He was the son of her darling daughter Isabella who had left him to her mother when she died. No matter how many grandsons her children should give her, she would always cherish Miguel, as the first grandson, the heir, the best loved.

She reached that part of this magnificent building which had been erected about the Court of Myrtles and made her way to the apartments which opened on to the Courtyard of Lions.

Her little Miguel could not have lived his short life in more beautiful surroundings. What did he think of the gilded domes and exquisite loveliness of the stucco work? He would be too young as yet to understand the praises which were set out on the walls, praises to the Prophet.

When she went to the apartment which was his nursery, she noticed at once that his nurses wore that grave look which she had become accustomed to see on the faces of those who waited at the sick-beds of the members of her family.

'How fares the Prince?' she asked.

'Highness, he is quiet today.'

Quiet today! She was filled with anguish as she leaned over his bed. There he lay, her grandson who was so like his mother, with the same patient resignation in his gentle little face.

'Not Miguel,' prayed Isabella. 'Have I not suffered enough? Take Charles . . . if you must take from me, but leave me my little Miguel. Leave me Isabella's son.'

What arrogance was this? Was she presuming to instruct Providence?

She crossed herself hastily: 'Not my will but Thine.'

She sat by the bed through the day and night; she knew that Miguel was dying, that only by a miracle could he throw off this fever and grow up to inherit his grandparents' kingdom.

He will die, she thought wearily; and on the day he dies, our heir is Juana. And the people of Aragon will not accept a woman. But they will accept that woman's son. They will accept Charles. Charles is strong and lusty, though his mother grows wilder every day. Juana inherits her wildness from my mother. Is it possible that Charles might inherit wildness from his?

What trouble lay in store for Spain? Was there no end to the ills which could befall them? Was there some truth in the rumours that theirs was an accursed House?

She was aware of the short gurgling breaths for which the child was struggling.

She sent for the doctors, but there was nothing they could do.

This frail little life was slowly slipping away.

'Oh God, what next? What next?' murmured Isabella.

Then the child lay still, and silent, and the doctors nodded one to another.

'So he has gone, my grandson?' asked the Queen.

'That we fear is so, Your Highness.'

'Then leave me with him awhile,' said Isabella. 'I will pray for him. We will all pray for him. But first leave me with him awhile.'

When she was alone she lifted the child from his bed and sat holding him in her arms while the tears slowly ran down her cheeks.

≈≈≈

There was little time to grieve. There was the invasion of Naples to be planned; there was the affair of Christobal Colon to demand Isabella's attention.

Her feelings towards the adventurer were now mixed. He had incurred her wrath by using the Indians as slaves, a practice which she deplored. She did not follow the reasoning of most Catholics that, as these savages were doomed to perdition in any case, it mattered little what happened to their bodies on Earth. Isabella's great desire for colonization had been not so much to add to the wealth of Spain as to bring those souls to Christianity which had never been in a position to receive it before. Colon needed workmen for his new colony and he was not over-scrupulous as to how he obtained them. But Isabella at home in Spain asked: 'By what authority does Christobal Colon venture to dispose of my subjects?' She ordered that all those men and women who had been taken into slavery should immediately be returned to their own country.

This was the first time she had felt angered by the behaviour of Christobal Colon.

As for Ferdinand he had always regarded the adventurer with some irritation. Since the discovery of the pearl fisheries of Paria he had thought with growing irritation of the agreement he had made – that Colon should have a share of the treasures he discovered. Ferdinand itched to divert more and more of that treasure into his coffers.

There were complaints from the colony, and Isabella had at last been persuaded to send out a kinsman of her friend Beatriz de Bobadilla, a certain Don Francisco de Bobadilla, to discover what was really happening.

Bobadilla had been given great powers. He was to take possession of all fortresses, vessels and property, and to have the right to send back to Spain any man who he thought was not working for the good of the community, that such person should then be made to answer to the Sovereigns for his conduct.

Isabella had at first been pleased to give Bobadilla this important post because he was a distant kinsman of her beloved friend; now she deeply regretted her action, as the only resemblance that Don Francisco bore to his kinswoman Beatriz was in his name.

It was while they were at Granada, mourning the death of little Miguel, that Ferdinand brought Isabella the news that Colon had arrived in Spain.

'Colon!' cried Isabella.

'Sent home for trial by Bobadilla,' Ferdinand explained.

'But this is incredible,' declared Isabella. 'When we gave Bobadilla such powers we did not think he would use them against the Admiral!'

Ferdinand shrugged his shoulders. 'It was for Bobadilla to use his power where he thought it would do the most good.'

'But to send Colon home!'

'Why not, if he thinks he is incompetent?'

Isabella forgot the disagreement she had had with the Admiral over the sale of slaves. She was immediately ready to spring to his defence because she remembered that day in 1493 when he had come home triumphant, the discoverer of the new land, when he had laid the riches of the New World at the feet of the Sovereigns.

And now to be sent home by Francisco de Bobadilla! It was too humiliating.

'Ferdinand,' she cried, 'do you realise that this man is the greatest explorer the world has known? You think it is right that he should be sent home in disgrace?'

Ferdinand interrupted. 'In more than disgrace. He has come in fetters. He is now being kept in fetters at Cadiz.'

'This is intolerable,' cried Isabella. She did not wait to discuss the matter further with Ferdinand. She immediately wrote an order. Christobal Colon was to be released at once from his fetters and was to come with all speed to Granada.

'I am sending a thousand ducats to cover his expenses,' she told Ferdinand; 'and he shall come in the style befitting a great man who has been wronged.'

༄༅

So, the people cheering as he came, Christobal Colon rode into Granada. He was thin, even gaunt, and they remembered that this great man had come across the ocean in fetters.

When she heard that he was in Granada, Isabella immediately sent for him and, when he arrived before her and Ferdinand, she would not let him kneel. She embraced him warmly, and Ferdinand did the same.

'My dear friend,' cried the Queen, 'how can I tell you of my distress that you have been so treated?'

Colon held his head high, and said: 'I have crossed the ocean in fetters as a criminal. I understand I am to answer charges which have been brought against me, the charges of having discovered a New World and given it to Your Highnesses.'

'This is unforgivable,' the Queen declared.

But Ferdinand was thinking: You did not give it entirely to your Sovereigns, Christobal Colon. You kept something for yourself.

He was calculating how much richer he would be if Christobal Colon did not have his share of the riches of the New World.

'I have suffered great humiliation,' Colon told them; and Isabella knew that to him humiliation would be the sharpest pain. He was a proud man, a man who for many years of his life had worked to make a dream come true. He had been a man with a vision of a New World and, by his skill in navigation and his extreme patience and refusal to be diverted from his project, he had made that New World a reality.

'Your wrongs shall be put right,' Isabella promised. 'Bobadilla shall be brought home. He shall be made to answer for his treatment of you. We must ask you to try to forget all that you have suffered. You need have no fear; your honours will be restored to you.'

When the proud Colon fell on his knees before the Queen and began to sob like a child, Isabella was shaken out of her serenity.

What he has suffered! she thought. And I, who have suffered in my own way, can understand his feelings.

She laid a hand on his shoulder.

'Weep, my dear friend,' she said, 'weep, for there is great healing in tears.'

So there, at the feet of the Queen, Christobal Colon continued to weep and Isabella thought of her own sorrows as she remembered suddenly the handsome boys she had seen with Colon . . . his son Ferdinand by Beatriz de Arana, and his son Diego by his first marriage. He had two sons, yet he had suffered deeply. His great love was the New World which he had discovered.

She wanted to say to him: I have no sons. Take comfort, my friend, that you have two.

But how could she, the Queen, talk of her sorrows with this adventurer?

She could only lay her hand on his heaving shoulders and seek to offer some comfort.

Ferdinand also was ready to comfort this man. He was thinking that the people would not be pleased to know that the hero of the New World had been sent home like a common criminal in fetters. He was also wondering how he could avoid allowing Christobal Colon such a large share of the riches of the New World and direct them into his own coffers.

⚜

It was a brilliant May day in that year 1501 when Catalina said goodbye to the Alhambra.

She would carry the memory of that most beautiful of buildings in her mind for ever. She told herself that in the misty, sunless land to which she was going she would, when she closed her eyes, see it often standing high on the red rock with the sparkling Darro below. She would remember always the sweet-smelling flowers, the views from the Hall of the Ambassadors, the twelve stone lions supporting the basin of the fountain in the Courtyard of the Lions. And there would be a pain in her heart whenever she thought of this beautiful Palace which had been her home.

There was no longer hope of delay. The day had come. She was to begin the journey to Corunna and there embark for England.

She would embrace her mother for the last time, for although the Queen talked continually of their reunion Catalina felt that there was something final about this parting.

The Queen was pale; she looked as though she had slept little.

Is life to be all such bitter partings for those of us who wear the badge of royalty? Isabella asked herself.

One last look back at the red towers, the rosy walls.

'Farewell, my beloved home,' whispered Catalina. 'Farewell for ever.' Then she turned her face resolutely away, and the journey had begun . . . to Corunna . . . to England.

⪼ Chapter XIV ⪻

THE WISE WOMAN OF GRANADA

iguel was dead and Catalina had gone to England. The Queen roused herself from her sorrow. There was a duty to perform and it was a duty which should be a pleasure.

'Now that Miguel is dead,' she said to Ferdinand, 'we should lose no time in calling Juana and Philip to Spain. Juana is now our heir. She must come here to be accepted as such.'

'I have already sent to her telling her she must come,' Ferdinand answered. 'I had thought to hear news by now that they would have set out on their journey.'

'Philip is ambitious. He will come soon.'

'He is also pleasure-loving.'

Isabella was clearly anxious, and Ferdinand, mindful of her sufferings over her recent losses, remembered to be tender towards her.

My poor Isabella, he thought, she is growing frail. She would seem to be more than a year older than myself. She has brooded too much on the deaths in our family; they have aged her.

He said gently: 'I'll swear you are longing to see your grandson.'

'Little Charles,' she mused; but somehow his very name seemed foreign to her. The child of wild Juana and selfish Philip. What manner of man would he grow up to be?

'When I see him,' she replied, 'I know I shall love him.'

'It might be,' said Ferdinand, 'that we could persuade them to leave Charles here with us to be brought up. After all he will be the heir to our dominions.'

Isabella allowed herself to be comforted, but she bore in mind that Philip and Juana were not like Isabella and Emanuel; and she did not believe that Charles could ever mean as much to her as Miguel had.

Still she looked forward to the visit of her daughter and son-in-law; yet there was no news of their coming, and the months were passing.

❧

In his apartments in the Alhambra Ximenes, while working zealously for the Christianisation of Granada, was suddenly smitten with a fever. With his usual stoicism he ignored his weakness and sought to cast it aside, but it persisted.

The Queen sent her doctors to Granada that they might attend her Archbishop. She had now persuaded herself that what Ximenes was doing in Granada should have been started at the time when the city had been taken from the Moors. She told Ferdinand that they should never have agreed to the arrangement with Boabdil for the sake of peaceful surrender. Now she was firmly behind Ximenes in all that he was doing.

She was disturbed to hear that Ximenes was not recovering, that his fever was accompanied by a languor which confined him to his bed; she ordered that he should take up his residence in that summer Palace, the Generalife, where he would only be a stone's throw from the Alhambra, but in quieter surroundings.

Ximenes availed himself of this offer, but his health did not improve and the fever and the languor continued.

He lay in his apartment in that most delicately beautiful of summer palaces. From his window he looked out on the terraced gardens in which the myrtles and cypresses grew; he longed to leave his bed that he might wander through the tiny courtyards and meditate beside the sparkling fountains.

But even the peace of the Generalife did not bring a return to good health; and he thought often of Tomás de Torquemada who had lain thus in the Monastery of Avila and waited for the end.

Torquemada had lived his life; Ximenes had the feeling that he had only just begun. He had not completed his work in Granada, and that he believed to be only a beginning. He admitted now that he had seen himself as the power behind the throne, as head of this great country, with Ferdinand and Isabella in leading strings.

The Queen's health was failing. He had been aware of that when he had last seen her. If she were to die and Ferdinand were left, he would need a strong guiding hand. The fact that Ferdinand did not like him and would always be resentful of him, did not disturb him. He knew Ferdinand well – an ambitious man, an avaricious man – one who needed the guiding hand of a man of God.

I must not die, Ximenes told himself. My work is not yet completed.

Yet each day he felt weaker.

One day as he lay in his bed, a Moorish servant of the Generalife came to his bedside and stood watching him.

For a moment he thought she had come to do him some injury, and he remembered that day when his brother Bernardín had tried to suffocate him by holding a pillow over his face. He had not seen Bernardín since that day.

These Moors might feel the need for vengeance on one who had disrupted the peace of their lives. He knew many of them had accepted baptism because they preferred it to the exile which was to be imposed on those who did not come into the Christian Faith. They were not such an emotional people as the Jews. He believed many of them had said to each other: 'Be a Mussulman in private and a Christian in public. Why not, if that is the only way to live in Granada?'

There would be the Inquisition, of course, to deal with those who were guilty of such perfidy. The Inquisitors would have to watch these people with the utmost care. They would have to be taught what would happen to them if they thought to mock baptism and the Christian Faith.

All these thoughts passed through Ximenes's mind as the woman stood by his bedside.

'What is it, woman?' he asked.

'Oh, lord Archbishop, you are sick unto death. I have seen this fever and the languor often. It has a meaning. With the passing of each day and night the fever burns more hot, the languor grows.'

'Then,' said Ximenes, 'if that is so, it is the will of God and I shall rejoice in it.'

'Oh, lord Archbishop, a voice has whispered to me to come to you; to tell you that I know of one who could cure your sickness.'

'One of your people?'

The woman nodded. 'A woman, oh lord. She is a very old woman. Eighty years she has lived in Granada. Often I have seen her cure those of whom the learned doctors despaired. She has herbs and medicines known only to our people.'

'Why do you wish to save me? There are many of your people who would rejoice to see me die.'

'I have served you, oh lord. I know you for a good man, a man who believes that all he does is in the service of God.'

'You are a Christian?'

A glazed look came into the woman's eyes. 'I have received baptism, oh lord.'

Ximenes thought: Ay, and practise Mohammedanism in private doubtless. But he did not voice these thoughts. He was a little excited. He wanted to live. He knew now that he wanted it desperately. A little while before he had prayed for a miracle. Was this God's answer? God often worked in a mysterious way. Was he going to cure Ximenes through the Moors whom he had worked so hard to bring to God?

The Moors were skilled in medicine. Ximenes himself had preserved their medical books when he had committed the rest of their literature to the flames.

'Do you propose bringing this wise woman to me?' asked Ximenes.

'I do, oh lord. But she could only come at midnight and in secret.'

'Why so?'

'Because, my lord, there are some of my people who would wish you dead for all that has happened since you came to Granada, and they would not be pleased with this wise woman who will cure you.'

'I understand,' said Ximenes. 'And what does this woman want for her reward should she cure me?'

'She cures for the love of the cure, oh lord. You are sick unto death, she says, and the Queen's own doctors cannot cure you. She would like to show you that we Moors have a medicine which excels yours. That is all.'

Ximenes was silent for a few seconds. It might be that this woman would attempt to avenge her people. It might be that she had some poison to offer him.

He thought again of Bernardín, his own brother, who had hated him so much that he had attempted to murder him.

There were many people in the world who hated a righteous man.

He made a quick decision. His condition was growing daily weaker. He would die in any case unless some miracle were performed. He would trust in God, and if it were God's will that he should live to govern Spain – by means of the Sovereigns – he would rejoice. If he must die he would accept death with resignation.

He believed that this was an answer to his prayers.

'I will see your woman,' he said.

❧

She came to him at midnight, smuggled into the apartment, an old Moorish woman whose black eyes were scarcely visible through the folds of flesh which encircled them.

She laid her hands on him and felt his fever; she examined his tongue and his eyes and his starved body.

'I can cure you in eight days,' she told him. 'Do you believe me?'

'Yes,' answered Ximenes, 'I do.'

'Then you will live. But you must tell none that I am treating you, and you must take only the medicines I shall give you. None must know that I come to you. I shall come in stealth at midnight eight times. At the end of that time your fever will have left you. You will begin to be well. You must then abandon your rigorous diet until you are recovered. You must eat rich meat and broths. If you will do this I can cure you.'

'It shall be done. What reward do you ask if you cure me?'

She came close to the bed and the folds of flesh divided a little so that he saw the black eyes. There was a look in them which matched his own. She believed in the work she did, even as he believed in his. To her he was not the man who had brought misery to Granada; he was a malignant fever which the doctors of his own race could not cure.

'You seek to save souls,' she said. 'I seek to save bodies: If my people knew that I had saved yours they would not understand.'

'It is a pity that you do not burn with the same zeal to save souls as you do to save bodies.'

'Then, my lord Archbishop, it might well be that eight days from now you would be dead.'

She gave him a potion to drink and she left more with the woman who had brought her. Then she was stealthily taken away.

When she had gone Ximenes lay still thinking about her. He wondered whether the herbs she had given him had been poisoned, but he did not wonder for long. Had he not seen that look in her eyes?

Why had she, a Moorish woman, risked perhaps her life in coming to him – for he knew he had many enemies in the Albaycin and any friend of his would be their enemy. Did she hope that if she saved his life he would relent towards the people of Granada, would restore the old order in payment for his life? If she thought that, she would be mistaken.

He lay between sleeping and waking, wondering about that woman, and in the morning he knew, before his doctors told him, that his fever had abated a little.

He refused their medicines and lay contemplating this strange situation until midnight, when the old woman came to him again. She had brought oils with her and these she rubbed into his body. She gave him more herbal drinks and she left him, promising to come again the next night.

Before the fourth night he knew that the cure was working. And sure enough, as she had said, on the eighth day after he had first seen her his fever had completely disappeared; and the good news was sent to Isabella that her Archbishop was on the way to recovery.

Ximenes was able to wander through the enchanting little courtyards of the Generalife. The sun warmed his bones and he remembered the wise woman's instructions that he should take nourishing food.

Often he expected to be confronted by her, demanding some payment for her services. But she did not come.

It was God's miracle, he told himself eventually. Perhaps she was a heavenly visitor who came in Moorish guise. Should I soften my attitude towards these Infidels because one of them has cured me? What a way of repaying God for His miracle!

Ximenes told himself that this was a test. His life had been saved, but he must show God that his life meant little to him compared with the great work of making an all-Christian Spain.

So when he was well he continued as harsh as ever towards the fellow countrymen of that woman who had saved his life; and as soon as he felt the full return of his vigour he resumed the hair shirt, the starvation diet and the wooden pillow.

≫ Chapter XV ≪

THE RETURN OF JUANA

At last Philip and Juana were on their way to Spain.

When Ferdinand received a letter from Philip he came raging into Isabella's apartments.

'They have begun the journey,' he said.

'Then that should be cause for rejoicing,' she answered him.

'They are travelling through France.'

'But they cannot do that.'

'They can and they are doing it. Has this young coxcomb no notion of the delicate relationship between ourselves and France? At this present time this might give rise to . . . I know not what.'

'And Charles?'

'Charles! They are not bringing him. He is too young.' Ferdinand laughed sharply. 'You see what this means? They are not going to have him brought up as a Spaniard. They are going to make a Fleming of him. But to go through France! And the suggestion is that there might be a betrothal of Charles and Louis's infant daughter, the Princess Claude.'

'They would not make such a match without our consent.'

Ferdinand clenched his fists in anger. 'I see trouble ahead. I fear these Habsburg alliances are not what I hoped for.'

Isabella answered: 'Still, we shall see our daughter. I long for that. I feel sure that when we talk together I shall know that all the anxiety she has caused us has been because she has obeyed her husband.'

'I shall make it my task to put this young Philip in his place,' growled Ferdinand.

After that Isabella eagerly awaited news of her daughter's progress. There were letters and dispatches describing the fêtes and banquets with which the King of France was entertaining them.

At Blois there had been a very special celebration. Here Philip had confirmed the Treaty of Trent between his father, the Emperor Maximilian, and the King of France; one of the clauses of this treaty was to the effect that the King's eldest daughter, Claude, should be affianced to young Charles.

It was a direct insult to Spain, Ferdinand grumbled. Had Philip forgotten that Charles was the heir of Spain? How dared he make a match for the heir of Spain without even consulting the Spanish Sovereigns!

The journey through France was evidently so enjoyable that Philip and Juana seemed in no hurry to curtail it.

Ferdinand suspected that the sly Louis was detaining them purposely to slight him and Isabella. Trouble was brewing between France and Spain over the partition of Naples, and both monarchs were expecting conflict to break out in the near future. So Louis amused himself by detaining Ferdinand's daughter and his son-in-law in France, and binding them to him by this Treaty of Trent and the proposed marriage of Charles and Claude.

But by the end of March news came that Philip and Juana with their train were approaching the Spanish border.

Soon I shall see my Juana, Isabella assured herself. Soon she would be able to test for herself how far advanced was this wildness of her daughter.

❧◈☙

As Isabella was preparing to go to Toledo, where she would meet Juana, there was news from England, disquieting news.

Catalina had written often to her mother and, although there had been no complaints, Isabella knew her daughter well enough to understand her deep longing for home. Etiquette would forbid her to compare her new country with that of her birth, or to mention her unhappiness, but Isabella knew how Catalina felt.

Arthur, Catalina's young husband, it seemed, was kind and gentle. So all would be well in time. In one year, Isabella assured herself, or perhaps in two, Spain will seem remote to her and she will begin to think of England as her home.

Then came this news which so disturbed her that she forgot even the perpetual anxiety of wondering what Juana would be like.

Catalina had travelled with her young husband to Ludlow, from which town they were to govern the Principality of Wales. They were to set up a Court there which was to be modelled on that of Westminster. Isabella had been pleased to picture her sixteen-year-old daughter and the fifteen-year-old husband ruling over such a Court. It would be good practice for them, she had said to Ferdinand, against that day when they would rule over England.

Catalina had written an account of the journey from

London to Ludlow; how she had ridden pillion behind her Master of Horse, and when she was tired of this mode of travelling had been carried in a litter. She had been delighted by the town of Ludlow; and the people, she wrote, seemed to have taken her to their hearts, for they cheered her and Arthur whenever she and he appeared among them.

'My little Catalina,' Isabella murmured, 'a bride of six months only!'

She wondered whether the marriage had yet been consummated or whether the King of England considered his son as yet too young. It would have been more suitable if Arthur had been a year older than Catalina instead of a year younger.

Ferdinand was with her when the news arrived. She read the dispatch, and the words danced before her eyes.

'Prince Arthur became stricken by a plague before he had been long in Ludlow. He fell into a rapid decline and, alas, the Infanta of Spain is now a widow.'

A widow! Catalina! Why, she was scarcely a wife.

Ferdinand's face had grown pale. 'But this is the Devil's own luck!' he cried. 'God in Heaven, are all our marriage plans for our children to come to nothing!'

Isabella tried to dismiss a certain exultation which had come to her. Catalina a widow! That meant that she could come home. She could be returned to her mother as her eldest sister, Isabella of Portugal, had been.

❧❧

Into Toledo rode Isabella and Ferdinand, there to await the arrival of Juana and Philip. The bells of the city were chiming; the people were crowding into the streets; they were ready to welcome not only their Sovereigns but their Sovereigns' heir.

Toledo cared nothing that Juana was a woman. She was the rightful successor to Isabella and they would accept her as their Queen when the time came.

The Queen's nervousness increased as the hour of the meeting with her daughter drew near.

I shall know, she told herself, as soon as I look at her. If there has been any change, it will immediately be visible to me. Oh, Juana, my dear daughter, be calm, my love. I pray you be calm.

Then she reminded herself that soon she would have Catalina home. What purpose could be served by her staying in England as the widow of the dead Prince? She must come home to her mother, so that she might more quickly recover from the shock her husband's death must have caused her.

It was a beautiful May day when Philip and Juana rode into Toledo. At the doors of the great Alcazar Ferdinand and Isabella stood waiting to receive them.

Isabella's eyes immediately went to her daughter. At first glance there appeared to be only that change which would seem inevitable after the ordeals of childbearing. Juana had given birth to a daughter, yet another Isabella, before she left Flanders. She had aged a little; and she had never been the most beautiful of their children.

And this was her husband. Isabella felt a tremor of fear as she looked at this fair young man who came forward with such arrogance. He was indeed handsome and fully aware of it. My poor Juana, thought Isabella. I hope it is not true that you love this man as distractedly as rumour tells me you do.

They were kneeling before the Sovereigns, but the Queen took her daughter and drew her into her arms. This was one of the rare occasions when Isabella disregarded etiquette. Love and anxiety were everything. She must hold this daughter in her arms, this one who had caused her more anxiety than any of the others, for she had discovered that she did not love her the less because of this.

Juana smiled and clung to her mother for a few seconds.

She is glad to be home! thought the Queen.

The brief ceremony was over, and Isabella said: 'I am going to have my daughter to myself for a little while. Give me this pleasure. Philip, your father-in-law will wish to talk with you.'

❧

Isabella took her daughter to that chamber in which, just over twenty years ago, she had been born.

'Juana,' Isabella held her daughter against her, 'I cannot tell you how glad I am to see you. We have had so much sorrow since you left us.'

Juana was silent.

'My dearest,' went on the Queen, 'you are happy, are you not? You are the happiest of my daughters. Your marriage has been fruitful, and you love your husband.'

Juana nodded.

'You are too overcome with happiness at being home to speak of it. That is so, is it not, my love? My happiness equals yours. How I have thought of you since you went away. Your husband . . . he is kind to you?'

Juana's face darkened, and the expression there set the Queen's heart leaping in terror.

'There are women . . . always women. There were women in Flanders. There have been women on the way. There will be women in Spain. I hate them all.'

'While he is in Spain,' said Isabella sternly, 'there must be no scandal.'

Juana laughed that wild laughter which was reminiscent of her grandmother.

'You would not be able to keep them away. They pursue him everywhere. Are you surprised? Is there a more handsome man in the world than my Philip?'

'He has good looks, but he should remember his dignity.'

'They won't let him. It is no fault of his. They are always there.' Juana clenched her hands together. 'Oh, how I hate women!'

'My dear, your father shall speak to him.'

Juana let out another peal of loud laughter. 'He would not listen.' She snapped her fingers. 'He cares not that for anyone . . . not for my father, nor the King of France. Oh, you should have seen him in France. The women of Blois, and indeed all the towns and villages through which we passed . . . they could not resist him . . . they followed him, imploring him to take them to his bed . . .'

'And he did not resist?'

Juana turned angrily on her mother. 'He is but human. He has the virility of ten ordinary men. It is no fault of his. It is the women . . . the cursed women.'

'Juana, my dear, you must be calm. You must not think too much of these matters. Men, who perforce must leave their wives now and then, often find consolation with others. That is but nature.'

'It is not only when he has to leave me,' said Juana slowly.

'There, my dear, you must not take these matters to heart. He has done his duty by you. There are children.'

'Do you think I care for that? Duty! Do I want duty as a

bedfellow? I want only Philip, I tell you. Philip . . . Philip . . . Philip . . .'

Isabella looked furtively about her. She was terrified that Juana's wild shouts might be heard. She must prevent rumour spreading through the Alcazar.

One thing was certain: marriage had done nothing to calm Juana.

❧❧

They must prepare now to take the oath as heirs to Castile. This ceremony would take place in the great Gothic Cathedral, and Isabella was afraid that Juana's wildness would show itself during the ceremony.

She sent for her son-in-law and she thought that, as he entered her apartment, his manner was insolent, but she quickly reminded herself that Flemish ways were not those of Spain; and she remembered how at times she had been faintly shocked by the manners of his sister, Margaret, who had been a good creature.

She dismissed all her attendants so that she might be quite alone with her son-in-law.

'Philip,' she said, 'I have heard rumours which disturb me.'

Philip raised his insolent and well-arched eyebrows. How handsome he is! she thought. Isabella had never seen a man so perfectly proportioned, of such clear skin, such arrogance, such an air of masculinity, such suggestion of power and knowledge that he could do everything better than anyone else.

If Juana had gone to Portugal, to gentle Emanuel, how much better that would have been.

'My daughter is devoted to you, but I understand you are less so to her. There have been unfortunate *affaires*.'

'I can assure Your Highness that they have been far from unfortunate.'

'Philip, I must ask you not to be flippant on a matter which to me is so serious. My daughter is . . . is not of a serene nature.'

'Ha!' laughed Philip. 'That is one way of describing it.'

'How would you describe it?' asked Isabella fearfully.

'Unbalanced, Madam, dangerous, tottering on the edge of madness.'

'Oh, no, no . . . that is not so. You are cruel.'

'If you wish me to make pretty speeches, I will do so. I thought you asked me for the truth.'

'So . . . that is how you have found her?'

'That is so.'

'She is so affectionate towards you.'

'Too affectionate by far.'

'Can you say that of your wife?'

'Her affection borders on madness, Madam.'

Isabella longed to dismiss this young man; she found herself loathing him. She was longing to go back in time and, if she could do that, she would never have allowed this marriage to take place.

'If you treated her with gentle kindness,' she began, 'as I always tried to do . . .'

'I am not her mother. I am her husband. She asks for more than gentle kindness from me.'

'More than you are prepared to give?'

He smiled at her sardonically. 'I have given her children. What more can you ask than that?'

It was no use pleading with him. He would continue with his

amours. Juana was nothing to him but the heiress of Spain. If only he were nothing to her but Maximilian's heir it would be better for her. To her he was the very meaning of her existence.

She said: 'I am anxious about the ceremony. This wildness of hers must not be visible. I do not know how the people would react. It is not only here in Castile that she must be calm. There will be the ceremony in Saragossa to follow. You will know that the people of Aragon were none too kind to her sister Isabella.'

'But they accepted her son Miguel as their heir. We have Charles to offer them.'

'I know. But Charles is a baby. I want them to accept you and Juana as our heirs. If she will be dignified before them, I believe they will. If not, I cannot answer for the consequences.'

Philip's eyes narrowed. Then he said: 'Your Highness need have no fear. Juana will behave with the utmost decorum before the Cortes.'

'How can you be sure of this?'

'I can be sure,' he answered arrogantly, 'I can command her.'

When he had left her Isabella thought: There is so much he could do for her. But he does not. He is cruel to her, my poor bewildered Juana.

Isabella found that she hated this son-in-law; she blamed his cruel treatment for the sad change in her daughter.

∽❦∼

Philip came into his wife's apartments in the Toledo Alcazar. Juana, who had been lying down, leapt to her feet, her eyes shining with delight.

'Leave us! Leave us!' she cried, fluttering her hands; and

Philip stood aside to let her women pass, smiling lasciviously at the prettiest one, calculatingly. He would remember her.

Juana ran to him and took his arm. 'Do not look at her. Do not look at her,' she cried.

He threw her off. 'Why not? She is a pleasant sight.'

'Pleasanter than I am?'

Her archness sickened him. He almost told her that he found her looks becoming more and more repulsive.

'Let me look at you,' he said; 'that will help me to decide.'

She lifted her face to his – all eagerness, all desire – pressing her body against him, her lips parted, her eyes pleading.

Philip held her off. 'I have had a talk with your mother. You have been telling her tales about me.'

Terror showed in her face. 'Oh no, Philip. Oh no . . . no, no! Someone has been carrying tales. I have said nothing but good of you.'

'In the eyes of your sainted mother I am a philanderer.'

'Oh . . . she is so prim, she does not understand.'

Philip gripped her wrist so tightly that she cried out, not in pain but in pleasure. She was happy for him to touch her, even though it might be in anger.

'But you understand, do you not, my dear wife? You do not blame me.'

'I don't blame you, Philip, but I hope . . .'

'You don't want another child yet, do you?'

'Yes, I do. We must have children . . . many, many children.'

He laughed. 'Listen,' he said, 'we have to undergo this ceremony with the Cortes. You know that?'

'Yes, to declare us heirs. That will please you, Philip. It is what you want. No one else could give you so much as that. I am the heiress of Castile and, as my husband, you share in my inheritance.'

'That is so. That is why I find you so attractive. Now listen to me. I want you to behave perfectly at the ceremony. Be quiet. Do not laugh, do not smile. Be serious. All the time. If you do not I shall never touch you again.'

'Oh, Philip. I will do everything you say. And if I do . . .'

'If you give satisfaction I will stay with you all through the night.'

'Philip, I will do anything . . . everything . . .'

He touched her cheek lightly. 'Do as I say, and I shall be with you.'

She threw herself against him, laughing, touching his face. 'Philip, my handsome Philip . . .' she moaned.

He put her from him.

'Not yet. You have not shown me that you'll give me what I want. After the ceremony we shall see. But one smile from you, one word out of place, and that is the end between us.'

'Oh, Philip!'

He shook himself free of her. Then he left her and went to find the pretty attendant.

The ceremonies both at Toledo and Saragossa had passed without a hitch. The people of Saragossa had accepted Juana without protest. She already had her son Charles, and it was unlikely that he would not be of an age to govern by the time Ferdinand was ready to pass on the Crown to him.

Isabella was delighted that the ceremonies had passed so smoothly. She had been terrified of an outburst from Juana.

On the other hand she knew that Philip had ordered his wife

to behave with decorum. Perhaps no one else had noticed the glance of triumph that Juana had given her husband once during the ceremony, but Isabella had seen it. It touched her deeply; it was almost like a child's saying: See how good I am.

So much she would do for him. What he could do for her if he would! She loved him with such abandon; if he were only good and kind he could save her from disaster.

Perhaps if Juana remained in Spain it might be possible to nurse her back to health. Isabella had been untiring in her watchfulness over her own mother. She had paid frequent visits to Arevalo to make sure that all that could be done was being done for that poor woman. If she had Juana with her she would watch over her even as she had watched over her mother.

She would suggest this at an appropriate time, but she did not believe for one moment that Philip would remain in Spain; and how could she persuade Juana to stay if he did not?

She tried to think of more pleasant matters. Soon she would have her little Catalina home. Negotiations were now going on with England. Half of Catalina's dowry had been paid, but Ferdinand had refused to pay the other half. Why should he when Catalina was now a widow and was coming home to her family?

Oh, to have her back! What joy that would be! It would compensate a little for all this trouble with Juana.

Perhaps good fortune is coming to me at last, thought the Queen. If I can keep Juana with me, if Catalina comes home, I shall have regained two of my daughters.

There was news from England. Isabella and Ferdinand received it together.

As Isabella read the letter a great depression came over her, but Ferdinand's expression was shrewd and calculating. The news in the letter, which filled Isabella with sadness, was to him good news.

'Why not?' cried Ferdinand. 'Why not? What could be better?'

'I had hoped to have her home with me,' sighed Isabella.

'That would be most unsettling for her. It is great good fortune that Henry has a second son. We must agree at once to this marriage with young Henry.'

'He is years younger than Catalina. Arthur was her junior by one year.'

'What matters that? Catalina can give Henry many children. This is excellent.'

'Let her come back home for a while. It seems to me somewhat indecent to talk of marrying her to her husband's brother almost before he is cold in his grave.'

'Henry is eager for this marriage. He hints here that, if we do not agree to Catalina's union with young Henry, it will be a French Princess for the boy. That is something we could not endure. Imagine! At this time. War over the partition of Naples pending, and who can know what that wily old Louis has up his sleeve! The English must be with us, not against us . . . and they would surely be against us if we refused this offer and young Henry married a French girl.'

'Agree to the marriage, but let there be an interval.'

'Indeed yes, there must be an interval. It will be necessary to get a dispensation from the Pope. He'll give it readily enough, but it will take a little time.'

'I wonder what our Catalina thinks of this?'

Ferdinand looked at his wife slyly. Then he took another letter from his pocket.

'She has written to me,' he said.

Eagerly Isabella seized the letter. She felt a little hurt because, on this important matter, Catalina had written to her father, but immediately she realised that it was the seemly thing to do. In this matter of disposing of his daughter it was Ferdinand, the father, who had the right to make the final decision.

'I have no inclination for a further marriage in England,' wrote Catalina, 'but I pray you do not take my tastes or desires into your consideration. I pray you act in all things as suits you best . . .'

Isabella's hand shook. She read between the lines. My little daughter is homesick . . . homesick for me and for Spain.

It was no use thinking of her return. Isabella knew that Catalina would not leave England.

She had a premonition then that when she had said goodbye to her daughter at Corunna that was the last she would see of her on Earth.

Almost immediately she had shaken off her morbid thoughts.

I am growing old, she told herself, and the events of the last years have dealt me great blows. But there is much work for me to do; and I shall have her letters for comfort.

'There should be no delay,' Ferdinand was saying. 'I shall write to England immediately.'

※

These journeys through Spain with the Court, that they might be acclaimed Heir and Heiress of Castile, quickly became irksome to Philip; and because he made no secret of his boredom this affected Juana also.

'How sickened I am by these ceremonies,' he exclaimed petulantly. 'You Spanish do not know how to enjoy life.'

Juana wept with frustration because her country did not please him. She too declared her desire to go back to Flanders.

'I will tell you this,' Philip said; 'as soon as all the necessary formalities are over, back we shall go.'

'Yes, Philip,' she answered.

Her attendants, some of whom were her faithful friends, shook their heads sadly over her. If only, they said to each other, she would not betray the depth of her need for him. He cared nothing for her and did not mind who knew it. It was shameful.

None felt this more deeply than the Queen. Often she shut herself in her apartments, declaring that matters of State occupied her. But when she was alone she often lay on her bed because she felt too exhausted to do anything else. The slightest exertion rendered her breathless, and her body was tortured by pain. She did not speak to her doctors about this, telling herself that she was merely tired and needed a little rest.

She prayed a great deal in the quietness of her apartments; and her prayers were for her children, for little Catalina who, with the serenity which she had learnt must be the aim of an Infanta of Spain, was accepting her betrothal to a boy who was not only five years her junior but also her brother-in-law. Isabella was glad that young Henry would not be ready for marriage for a few years.

She felt that Catalina would look after herself. The discipline of her childhood, the manner in which she had learned to accept what life brought her, would stand her in good stead. It was Juana who frightened her.

One day Juana burst in upon her when she was at prayer. She rose stiffly from her knees and looked at her daughter, who was wild-eyed and excited.

'My dear,' she said, 'I pray you sit down. Has something happened?'

'Yes, Mother. It has happened again. I'm going to have another child.'

'But this is excellent news, my darling.'

'Is it not! Philip will be pleased.'

'We shall all be pleased. You must rest more than you have been doing.'

Juana's lips trembled. 'If I rest he will be with other women.'

Isabella shrugged aside the remark as though she believed it was foolish.

'We must be more together,' she said. 'I feel the need to rest myself and, as you must do the same, we will rest together.'

'I do not feel the need of rest, Mother. I'm not afraid of childbirth. I've grown used to it, and my babies come easily.'

Yes, thought Isabella. You who are unsound of mind are sound enough of body. It is your children who are born strong, and those of darling Juan and my dearest Isabella who die.

She went to her daughter and put her arm about her. Juana's body was quivering with excitement; and Isabella knew that she was not thinking of the child she would have, but of the women who would be Philip's companions while she was incapacitated.

By December of that year Juana, six months pregnant, was growing large. Philip shuddered with distaste when he looked at her, and made no secret of his boredom.

He told her casually one day: 'I am leaving for Flanders next week.'

'For Flanders!' Juana tried to imagine herself in her condition making that long winter journey. 'But . . . how could I travel?'

'I did not say you. I said *I* was going.'

'Philip! You would leave me!'

'Oh come, you are in good hands. Your sainted mother wishes to watch over you when your child is born. She does not trust us in Flanders, you know.'

'Philip, wait until the child is born, then we will go together.'

'It's due in March. By God, do you expect me to stay in this place three more months? Then it will be another month or more before you are ready to leave. Four months in Spain! You couldn't condemn me to that. I thought you loved me.'

'With all my heart and soul I do.'

'Then do not make trouble.'

'I would give you everything I had to give.'

'No need to part with that, my dear. All you have to do is say a pleasant goodbye to me next week. That is what I want from you.'

'Oh Philip . . . Philip . . .' She sank to her knees and embraced his legs. He threw her off, and she lay sprawling on the floor, grotesque in her condition.

He closed his eyes so that he need not look at her, and hurried away.

Nothing could make him change his mind. Isabella had begged him to stay with a humility which was rare with her, but he was adamant. His duty lay in Flanders, he declared.

He turned to Ferdinand. 'I shall return by way of France,' he said.

'Would that be wise?' Ferdinand asked.

'Most wise. The King of France is a friend *of mine*.'

While Isabella deplored his insolence, Ferdinand did not, because he could not stop wondering what advantage might accrue through this journey of his son-in-law's into French territory.

'It might be possible,' said Ferdinand, 'for you to negotiate with the King of France on my behalf.'

'Nothing would please me better,' answered Philip, secretly deciding that any negotiations he concluded with Louis were going to be to his own advantage rather than Ferdinand's.

'We could ask for certain concessions,' said Ferdinand, 'since Charles is affianced to Claude; and why should these two not be given the titles of King and Queen of Naples?'

'It is an excellent idea,' answered Philip. 'In the meantime let the King of France appoint his own governor for his portion, and I will govern on behalf of yourself. As Charles's father, how could you make a better choice?'

'This needs a little consideration,' said Ferdinand.

Philip smiled and answered:' You have a week in which to make up your mind.'

Juana had sunk into deepest melancholy. All the wildness had gone out of her. This was a mood which Isabella had not seen before. Her daughter scarcely ate; Isabella did not believe she slept very much. She thought of nothing but the fact that Philip was returning to Flanders and leaving her in Spain.

January and February had passed, and Juana did not rouse herself from her dejection. She would sit for hours at her window, looking out as though she were hoping for the return of Philip.

She appeared to loathe all things Spanish, and when she did speak, which was rarely, it was to complain of her room, her surroundings, her attendants.

Isabella visited her often, but Juana had nothing to say, even to her mother. Oddly enough, in spite of her refusal to eat what was brought to her and the fact that she took scarcely any exercise, she remained healthy.

It was a cold March day when her pains began, and Isabella, who had demanded to be told as soon as this happened, was close at hand when the child was born.

Another boy, a healthy, lusty boy.

How strange life was. Here was another healthy child for this poor deluded girl.

Juana quickly recovered from the ordeal, and now that her body was light again she seemed a little happier.

When her parents came to her she held the child in her arms and declared that he was very like his father. 'But I see my own father in him,' she added. 'We shall call him Ferdinand.'

Ferdinand was delighted with the boy. He seemed to be quite unaware of the strangeness of his daughter. She was capable of bearing sturdy sons – that was enough for him.

❧ Chapter XVI ❧

JUANA THE MAD

Isabella had hoped that when the child was born Juana would cease to fret for Philip and turn her interest to the baby. This was not so. Juana did not change. She scarcely looked at the child. Her one desire was to rejoin Philip.

'You are not strong enough,' said her mother. 'We could never allow you to make the long journey in your present condition.'

'What is he doing while I am not there?' demanded Juana.

'Much the same as he would do if you were there, I doubt not,' replied Isabella grimly.

'I *must* go,' cried Juana.

'Your father and I will not allow it until you are stronger.'

So Juana sank once more into melancholy. Sometimes for whole days she said nothing. At other times she could be heard shouting her resentment in her apartments.

Isabella gave instructions that she must be watched.

'She so longs to rejoin her husband,' she explained, 'that she may attempt to leave. The King and I are determined that she must be fully recovered before she does so.'

A month after the birth of little Ferdinand, Philip in Lyons had made the treaty between the Kings of Spain and France; but it was clear that it meant very little and, as the armies moved in to take possession of their portions of the divided Kingdom of Naples, it became obvious that conflict was close.

It broke out later that year; and the minds of the Sovereigns were concentrated on the new war.

Isabella however contrived to spend as much time as possible with Juana. She was growing increasingly afraid of leaving her, for since the departure of Philip Juana's affliction was becoming more and more apparent. Now it was no use pretending that she was normal. The Court was aware of her mental instability; in a very short time the rumours would be spreading throughout the country.

Juana had written many pleading letters to her husband. 'They will not let me come to you,' she told him. 'It is for you to bid me come. Then they cannot stand in my way.'

It was on a November day when she received the letter from Philip. It was ungracious, but it was nevertheless an invitation to return to Flanders. If she thought it worth while making a sea journey at this time; or if she was ready to come through France, a country which was hostile to Spain, why should she not do so?

Juana read the letter and kissed it. Philip's hand had touched the paper. That made it sacred in her mind.

She threw off her melancholy.

'I am leaving,' she cried. 'I am leaving at once for Flanders.'

Her attendants, terrified of what she would do, sent word to the Queen of her new mood.

The Court was then in residence at Medina del Campo, and Isabella had insisted that Juana follow the Court that she herself might be near her daughter whenever possible. Shortly she must leave for Segovia, and when she heard this news she was thankful that she had not already left.

She went at once to Juana's apartments and found her daughter with her hair loose about her shoulders and her eyes wild.

'What has happened, my child?' asked the Queen gently.

'Philip has sent for me. He commands me to go.' Holy Mother, prayed the Queen, does he then wish to rid himself of her? To suggest she should go at this time of the year, with the weather at sea as it is! And how could she travel through France at such a time?

'My dearest,' she said, 'he does not mean now. He means that when the spring comes you must go to him.'

'He says *now*.'

'But you could not go in this inclement weather. You would probably be shipwrecked.'

'I could go across France.'

'Who knows what would happen to you? We are at war with France.'

'The King is Philip's friend. He would not harm Philip's wife.'

'He would not forget that you are your father's daughter.'

Juana twisted a strand of her long hair and pulled it hard in her vehemence. 'I will go. I will go.'

'No, my darling. Be calm. Let your mother decide.'

'You are against me,' cried Juana. 'You are all against me. It is because you are jealous, it is because I am married to the handsomest man in the world.'

'My dearest, I pray you be silent. Do not say such things. You do not mean them. Oh, my Juana, I know you do not mean them. You are overwrought. Let me help you to your bed.'

'Not to bed. To Flanders!'

'In the spring, my dear, you shall go.'

'Now!' screamed Juana, her eyes dilating. 'Now!'

'Then wait here awhile.'

'You will help me?'

'I would always help you. You know that.'

Juana suddenly flung herself into her mother's arms. 'Oh Mother, Mother, I love him so much. I want him so much. You, who are so cold . . . so correct . . . how can you understand what he is to me?'

'I understand,' said the Queen. She led her daughter to her bed. 'You must rest tonight. You could not set off on a journey tonight, could you?'

'Tomorrow.'

'We will see. But tonight you must rest.'

Juana allowed herself to be led to her bed. She was murmuring to herself: 'Tomorrow I will go to him. Tomorrow . . .'

Isabella laid the coverlet over her daughter.

'Where are you going?' demanded Juana.

'To order a soothing drink for you.'

'Tomorrow,' whispered Juana.

Isabella went to the door of the apartment and commanded that her physician be brought to her.

When he came she said: 'A sleeping draught for my daughter.'

The physician brought it and Juana drank it eagerly.

She longed for sleep. She was exhausted with her longing, and sleep would bring tomorrow nearer.

Isabella sat by the bed until she slept.

It has come at last, she told herself. I can no longer hide the truth. Everyone will know. I must have a guard set over her. This is the first step to Arevalo.

Her face was pale, almost expressionless. The greatest blow of all had fallen She was surprised that she could accept it with such resignation.

∽∾

It was past midday when Juana awoke from her drugged sleep.

She immediately remembered the letter which she had received from Philip.

'I am going home to Flanders,' she said aloud. 'It is today that I go.'

She made to rise, but a feeling of great lassitude came over her and she lay back on her pillows contemplating, not the journey to Flanders, but the end of it, the reunion with Philip.

The thought was so intoxicating that she threw off her lassitude and leaped out of bed.

She shouted to her attendants: 'Come! Help me to dress. Dress me for a journey. I am leaving today.'

The women came in. They looked different, a little furtive perhaps. She noticed this and wondered why.

'Come along,' she ordered. 'Be quick. We are leaving today. You have much to do.'

'Highness, the Queen's orders were that you were to rest in your apartment today.'

'How can I do that when I have a journey to make?'

'The Queen's instructions were . . .'

'I do not obey the Queen's instructions when my husband bids me go to him.'

'Highness, the weather is bad.'

'It will take more than weather to keep me from him. Where is the Queen?'

'She left for Segovia, and she has given all here these instructions: We are to look after you until her return, and then she will talk with you about your journey.'

'When does she return?'

'She said that we were to tell you that as soon as her State duties were done at Segovia she would be with you.'

'And she expects me to wait until she returns?'

Juana was pulling at the stuff of the robe which she had wrapped about her when she rose from her bed.

'We fear, Highness, that there is no alternative. Instructions have been given to all.'

Juana was silent. A cunning look came into her eyes, but she composed herself and she noticed that the attendants showed an immense relief.

'I will speak with the Queen on her return,' she said. 'Come, help me to dress and do my hair.'

She was quiet while they did this; she ate a little food; then she took her seat at the window, and for hours she looked out on the scene below.

By that time the melancholy mood had returned to her.

❧

It was night. Juana woke suddenly and there were tears on her cheeks.

Why was she crying? For Philip. They were keeping her from Philip when he had asked her to return. They made excuses to keep her here. Her mother was still in Segovia. She did not hurry to Medina del Campo because she knew that when she did come she must make arrangements for her daughter's departure.

It was a plot, a wicked, cruel plot to keep her from Philip. They were all jealous because she had married the most handsome man in the world.

She sat up in bed. There was pale moonlight in the room. She got out of bed. She could hear the even breathing of her attendants in the adjoining room.

'I must not wake them,' she whispered. 'If I do they will stop me.'

Stop her? From doing what?

She laughed inwardly. She was not going to wait any longer. She was going . . . now.

There was no time to waste. There was no time to dress. She put a robe about her naked body and, her feet still bare, she crept from the room.

No one heard her. Down the great staircase . . . out to the hall.

One of the guards at the door gasped as though he saw a ghost, and indeed she looked strange enough to be one, with her hair flowing wildly about her shoulders and the robe flapping about her naked body.

'Holy Mother . . .' gasped the guard.

She ran past him.

'Who is it?' he demanded.

'It is I,' she answered. 'Your Sovereign's daughter.'

'It is indeed. It is the Lady Juana herself. Your Highness, my lady, what do you here? And garbed thus! You will die of the cold. It is a bitter night.'

She laughed at him. 'Back to your post,' she commanded. 'Leave me to my duty. I am on my way to Flanders.'

The frightened guard shouted to his sleeping companions, and in a few seconds he was joined by half a dozen of them.

They saw the flying figure of their heiress to the throne running across the grounds towards the gates.

'They're locked,' said one of the men. 'She'll not get any farther.'

'Raise the alarm,' said one. 'My God, she's as mad as her grandmother.'

Juana stood facing them, her back against the buttress, her head held high in defiance.

'Open the gates,' she screamed at the Bishop of Burgos who had been brought hurrying from his apartments in the Palace to deal with this situation.

'Highness,' he told her, 'it is impossible. The Queen's orders are that they shall not be opened.'

'I give you orders,' shouted Juana.

'Highness, I must obey the orders of my Sovereign. Allow me to call your attendants that they may help you back to your bed.'

'I am not going back to my bed. I am going to Flanders.'

'Later, Your Highness. For tonight . . .'

'No, no,' she screamed. 'I'll not go back. Open the gates and let me be on my way.'

The Bishop turned to one of the men and said: 'Go to Her Highness's apartments and get her women to bring warm clothes.'

The man went away.

'What are you whispering?' cried Juana. 'You are jealous of

me . . . all of you. That is why you keep me here. Open those gates or I will have you flogged.'

One of her women now approached.

'Highness,' she wailed, 'you will die of the cold if you stay here. I pray you come back to bed.'

'You want to stop me, do you not? You want to keep me away from him. Do not think I cannot understand. I saw your lascivious eyes upon him.'

'Highness, please, Highness,' begged the woman.

Another woman arrived with some warm clothing. She tried to slip a heavy cloak about Juana's shoulders. Juana seized it and with a wild cry threw it at them.

'I'll have you all flogged,' she cried. 'All of you. You have tried to keep me from him.'

'Come inside the Palace, Highness,' implored the Bishop. 'We will send immediately for the Queen, and you can discuss your departure with her.'

But Juana's mood had again changed. She sat down and stared ahead of her as though she did not see them. To all their entreaties she made no reply.

The Bishop was uncertain what to do. He could not *command* Juana to return to her apartments, yet feared for her health and even her life, if she remained out of doors during this bitter night.

He went into the Palace and sent for one of his servants.

'Leave at once for Segovia. You cannot go by the main gates. You will be quietly conducted through a secret door. Then with all haste go to the Queen. Tell her what has happened . . . everything you have seen. Ask her for instructions as to how I shall proceed. Go quickly. There is not a moment to lose.'

All through that night Juana remained at the gates of the Palace. The Bishop pleaded with her, even so far forgot her rank as to storm at her. She took no notice of him and at times seemed unaware of him.

The distance between Medina del Campo and Segovia was some forty miles. He could not expect the Queen to arrive that day, nor perhaps the next. He believed that if Juana spent another night in the open, inadequately clothed, she would freeze to death.

All through the next day she refused to move but, as night fell again, he persuaded her to go into a small dwelling on the estate, a hut-like place in which it would be impossible for them to imprison her. There she might have some shelter against the bitter cold.

This Juana eventually agreed to do, and the second night she stayed there; but as soon as it was light she took her place at the gates once more.

When the news of what was happening was brought to Isabella she was overcome with grief. Since her arrival at Segovia she had been feeling very ill; the war, her many duties, the disappointment about Catalina and the persistently nagging fear for Juana were taking their toll of her.

She would return to Medina at once, but she feared that feeble as she was she would be unable to make enough speed.

She called Ximenes to her and, because she feared his sternness towards her daughter, she sent also for Ferdinand's cousin Henriquez.

'I want you to ride with all speed to Medina del Campo,' she said. 'I shall follow, but necessarily more slowly. My daughter is behaving . . . strangely.'

She explained what was happening, and within an hour of

leaving her the two set off, while Isabella herself made preparations to depart.

When Ximenes and Henriquez arrived at Medina, the Bishop received them with the utmost relief. He was frantic with anxiety, for Juana still remained, immobile, her features set in grim purpose, her feet and hands blue with cold, seated on the ground with her back against the buttress by the gate of the Palace.

When the gates were opened to admit Ximenes and Henriquez she tried to rise, but she was numb with the cold and the gates had been shut again before she could reach them.

Ximenes thundered at her; she must go to her apartments at once. It was most unseemly, most immodest for a Princess of the royal House to be seen wandering about half clad.

'Go back to your University,' she cried. 'Go and get on with your polyglot Bible. Go and torture the poor people of Granada. But leave me alone.'

'Your Highness, it would seem that all sense of decency has deserted you.'

'Save your words for those who need them,' she spat at him. 'You have no right to torture me, Ximenes de Cisneros.'

Henriquez tried with softer words.

'Dearest cousin, you are causing us distress. We are anxious on your account. You will become ill if you stay here thus.'

'If you are so anxious about me, why do you stop my joining my husband?'

'You are not stopped, Highness. You are only asked to wait until the weather is more suited to the long journey you must make.'

'Leave me alone,' she snarled.

Then she hung her head and stared at the ground, and would not answer them.

Ximenes was pondering whether he would not have her taken in by force, but it was not easy to find those who would be ready to carry out such instructions. This was the future Queen of Spain.

He shuddered when he thought of her. She was inflicting suffering on her body as he himself had so many times. But for what different purpose! He had mortified his flesh that he might grow to greater saintliness; she mortified hers out of defiance because she was denied the gratification of her lust.

Juana spent the next night in the hut, and again at daybreak she was at her post at the gates. And that morning Isabella arrived.

As soon as the Queen entered she went straight to her daughter. She did not scold her, or speak of her duty; she merely took Juana into her arms, and for the first time Isabella broke down. The tears ran down her cheeks as she embraced her daughter. Then, still weeping, she took off her heavy cloak and wrapped it about Juana's cold form.

Then Juana seemed to forget her purpose. She gave a little cry and whispered: 'Mother, oh my dear Mother.'

'I am here now,' said Isabella. 'All is well. Mother is here.'

It was as though she were a child again. The years seemed to drop from her. She was the wild Juana who had been guilty of some mischief, who had been punished, and who was frightened and uncertain and wanted only the comfort and reassurance her mother could give.

'We are going inside now,' said the Queen. 'Then you and I will talk. We will make plans and discuss all that you wish to discuss. But, my darling, you are so cold and you are so weak.

You must do what your mother says. Then you will be strong and well enough to join your husband in Flanders. If you are sick you could not, could you? Nor would he want a sick wife.'

Isabella, with those few words, had been able to do what the fire of Ximenes, the persuasion of Henriquez and the entreaties of Burgos had failed to do.

Her arm about her daughter, the Queen led Juana into the Palace.

Now that the final blow had fallen on Isabella – that which she had dreaded for so long and which could now not be denied – her health gave way.

She was so ill that for days she could do nothing but keep to her bed. She was unable to make her journeys with Ferdinand, and this was indeed an anxious time for Spain, for the French were threatening invasion.

With the coming of the spring Juana left for Flanders. Isabella said a fond farewell to her daughter, certain that she would never see her again. She did not attempt to advise her, because any advice she gave would not be heeded.

Isabella was aware that her grip on life was no longer very strong.

Even as she embraced Juana she was telling herself that she must put her affairs in order.

Juana rode joyfully to the coast. The people cheered as she went. There were many in the country villages who did not know of her madness, and who believed that she had been cruelly kept a prisoner, separated from her husband.

As she went, smiling graciously, there was nothing of the mad woman about her. When she was peacefully happy, Juana appeared to be completely sane; and she was happy now because she was going to be with Philip.

There was a delay at Laredo before the sea journey could be attempted, and during that time Juana began to show signs of stress, but before her madness could take a grip of her she was at sea.

What joy it was to be in Brussels again. She was a little worried when Philip did not come to the coast to meet her. Those of her attendants who knew the signs of wildness watched her intently and waited.

In the Palace Philip greeted her casually as though they had not been separated for months. But if she were disappointed she was so delighted to be near him again that she did not show this.

He spent the first night of her arrival with her and she was ecstatically happy; but it was not long before she discovered that his attention was very much occupied elsewhere.

He had a new mistress, one on whom he doted, and it did not take Juana very long to discover who this was. There were many malicious tongues eagerly waiting for the opportunity to point the woman out to her.

When Juana saw her, waves of anger rose within her. This woman had the physique of a Juno. She was a typical Flemish beauty, big-hipped, big-breasted, with a fresh complexion, but the most startling thing about her was her wonderful golden hair; abundant, it fell curling about her shoulders to beyond her waist, and it was clear that she was so proud of it that she invariably wore it loose and was actually setting a new fashion at the Court.

For days Juana watched that woman, hatred growing within her. For nights when she lay alone hoping that Philip would come to her she thought of that woman and what she would do to her if she could lay her hands upon her.

Philip neglected her completely now and the frustration of being so near him and yet denied his company was as great as that of being a prisoner in Medina del Campo.

Philip had to leave Court for a few days, and to Juana's great joy he did not take his golden-haired mistress with him.

With Philip away Juana could give her orders. She was his wife, the Princess of Spain, the Archduchess of Flanders. He could not take that away from her and give it to the long-haired wanton.

Juana was wild with excitement. She summoned her women to her, and demanded that her husband's mistress be brought before her.

There she stood, insolent, knowing her power, fully realising Juana's love and need of Philip; in her eyes was a look of pitying insolence as though she were remembering all that she enjoyed with Philip, which favours were denied to his wife.

Juana cried: 'Have you brought the cords I asked for?'

And one of the women answered that she had.

'Then send for the men,' ordered Juana. And several of the men servants, who had been waiting for this summons, having been warned that it would come, entered the apartment.

Juana pointed to Philip's mistress. 'Bind her. Bind her, hand and foot.'

'Do no such thing,' cried the woman. 'It will be the worse for you if you do.'

Juana in her frenzy assumed all the dignity which her mother had always been at great pains to teach her. 'You will obey *me*!' she said quietly. 'I am the mistress here.'

The men looked at each other and, as the flaxen-haired beauty was about to run from the apartment, one of them caught her and held her fast. The others, following his lead, did as Juana had commanded, and in a few minutes the struggling woman was pinioned, and the stout cords wound about her body. Trussed, she lay at the feet of Juana, her great blue eyes wide with horror.

'Now,' said Juana, 'send for the barber.'

'What are you going to do?' cried the woman.

'You will see,' Juana told her; and she felt the wild laughter shake her body; but she controlled it. If she were going to take her revenge she must be calm.

The barber entered, carrying the tools of his trade.

'Place this woman on a chair,' said Juana.

Again that wild laughter surged up within her. Often she had imagined what she would do with one of Philip's women if she ever had one at her mercy. She had imagined torture, mutilation, even death for one of those who had caused her so much suffering.

But now she had a brilliant idea. This was going to be the best sort of revenge.

'Cut off her hair,' said Juana. 'Shave her head.'

The woman screamed, while the barber stood aghast, staring at that rippling golden glory.

'You heard what I said,' screeched Juana. 'Do as I say, or I will have you taken to prison. I will have you tortured. I will have you executed. Obey me at once.'

The barber muttered: 'Yes, yes . . . Your Grace . . . yes, yes, my lady.'

'She is mad, mad,' screamed the frightened woman, who could imagine few greater tragedies than the loss of her beautiful hair.

But the barber was at work and there was little she could do about it. Juana commanded two of the other men to hold her still, and soon the beautiful locks lay scattered on the floor.

'Now shave her head,' cried Juana. 'Let me see her completely bald.'

The barber obeyed.

Juana was choking with laughter. 'How different she looks! I do not recognise her. Do you? She's no beauty now. She looks like a chicken.'

The woman who had shrieked her protests in a manner almost as demented as Juana's now lay gasping in her chair. She was clearly suffering from shock.

'You may release her,' said Juana. 'You may take her away. Bring a mirror. Let her see how much she owed to those beautiful golden curls of which I have robbed her.'

As the woman was carried out, Juana gave way to paroxysms of laughter.

❦

Philip strode into his wife's apartments.

'Philip!' she cried and her eyes shone with delight.

He was looking at her coldly and she thought: So he went to her first; he has seen her.

Then a terrible fear came to her. He was angry, and not with his mistress for the loss of the beautiful hair which he had found so attractive, but with the one who had been responsible for cutting it off.

She stammered: 'You have seen her?' And in spite of herself, gurgling, choking laughter rose in her throat. 'She . . . she looks like . . . a chicken.'

Philip took her by the shoulders and shook her. Yes, he had seen her. He had been thinking of her during the journey to Brussels, thinking with pleasure of the moment of reunion; and then to find her . . . hideous. That shaved head instead of those soft flaxen curls! He had found her repulsive and had not been able to hide it. He had seen the deep humiliation in her face and had but one desire – to get away from her.

She had said to him: 'I was tied up, made helpless, and my hair was cut off, my head shaved. Your wife did it . . . your mad wife.'

Philip said: 'It will grow.' And he was thinking: My wife . . . my mad wife.

He had come straight to her and there was loathing within him.

She was mad. She was more repulsive to him than any woman he had ever known. She dared to do this while he was away. She believed she had some power in his Court. This was because her arrogant parents had reminded her that she was the heiress of Spain.

'Philip,' she cried, 'I did it because she maddened me.'

'You did not need her to madden you,' he answered sharply. 'You were mad already.'

'Mad? No, Philip, no. Mad only with love for you. If you will be kind to me I will be calm always. It was only because I was jealous of her that I did this. Say you are not angry with me. Say you will not be cruel. Oh, Philip, she looked so queer . . . that head . . .' The laughter bubbled up again.

'Be silent!' Philip said coldly.

'Philip, do not look at me like that. I did it only because . . .'

'I know why you did it. Take your hands off me. Never come near me again.'

'You have forgotten. I am your wife. We must get children . . .'

He said: 'We have children enough. Go away from me. I never want you near me again. You are mad. Have a care or I will put you away where you belong.'

She was pulling at his doublet, her face turned up to his, the tears beginning to run down her cheeks.

He threw her off and she fell to the floor as he walked quickly from the room.

Juana remained on the floor, sobbing; then suddenly she began to laugh again, remembering that grotesque shaven head.

None came near her. Outside the apartment her attendants whispered together.

'Leave her. It is best when the madness is upon her. What will become of her? She grows more mad every day.'

And after a while Juana rose and went to her bed. She lay down and when her women came to her she said: 'Prepare me for my bed. My husband will be coming to me soon.'

All through the night she waited; but he did not come. She waited through the days and nights that followed, but she did not see him.

She would sit waiting, a melancholy expression on her face; but occasionally she would burst into loud laughter; and each day someone in the Brussels Palace said: 'She grows a little more insane each day.'

Chapter XVII

ISABELLA'S END

I sabella lay ill at Medina de Campo. She was suffering from the tertian fever, it was said, and there were signs of dropsy in her legs.

It was June when news was brought to her of that disgraceful episode at the Brussels Court.

'Oh, my daughter,' she murmured, 'what will become of you?'

What could she do? she asked herself. What could she do for any of her daughters? Catalina was in England; she was afraid for Catalina. It was true that she had been formally betrothed to Henry, now Prince of Wales and heir of Henry VII, but she was anxious concerning the bull of dispensation which she had heard had come from Rome and which alone could make legal a marriage between Catalina and Prince Henry. She had not seen the dispensation. Could she trust the wily King of England? Might it not be that he wished to get his greedy hands on Catalina's dowry, and not care whether the marriage to her late husband's brother was legal or not?

'I must see the bull,' she told herself. 'I must see it before I die.'

Maria as Queen of Portugal would be happy enough. Emanuel could be trusted. Maria the calm one, unexciting and unexcitable, had never given her parents any anxiety. Her future seemed more secure than that of any other of Isabella's daughters.

But Isabella could cease to fret about Catalina when she contemplated Juana. What terrible tragedy did the future hold in store for Juana?

But, sick as she was, she was still the Queen. She must not forget her duties. There were always visitors from abroad to be received; the rights of her own people to protect. Ferdinand was unable to be with her. The French had attempted an invasion of Spain itself, but this Ferdinand had quickly frustrated.

Now that she was ill, Ferdinand himself was ill and unable to come to her; her anxiety for him increased her melancholy.

What will happen when I and Ferdinand have gone? Charles is a baby, Juana is mad. Philip will rule Spain. That must not be. Ferdinand must not die.

She prayed for her husband, prayed that he might be given strength to recover, to live until that time when Charles was grown into a strong man; and she prayed that her grandson might not have inherited his mother's taint. Then she remembered Ximenes, her Archbishop; and a great joy came to her. He must stand beside Ferdinand; together they would rule Spain.

She thanked God for the Archbishop.

News came that Ferdinand had recovered from his sickness and, as soon as he was well enough to travel, he would be with her. With a lightened heart she made her will.

She wished to lie, she said, in Granada, in the Franciscan monastery of Santa Isabella in the Alhambra, with no memorial, only a plain inscription.

But I must lie beside Ferdinand, she thought, and it may be that he will wish to lie in a different place. So often during their lives she had felt herself forced to disagree with him. In death she would do as he wished.

She wrote somewhat unsteadily: 'Should the King, my lord, prefer a sepulchre in another place, then my will is that my body be transported thither and laid at his side.'

She went on to write that the crown was to be settled on Juana, as Queen Proprietor, and the Archduke Philip, her husband; but she appointed Ferdinand, her husband, sole regent of Castile until the majority of her grandson Charles, for she must make arrangements respecting the government in the absence or incapacity of her daughter Juana.

Then she wept a little thinking of Ferdinand. She could remember clearly how he had looked when he had first come to her. In those days she had thought him perfect, the materialization of an ideal. Had she not determined to be the wife of Ferdinand many years before she had seen him? Young, handsome, virile – how many women had been fortunate enough to have such a husband?

'If we had been humble people,' she murmured, 'if we had always been together, life would have been different for us. The children he begot on other women would have been my children. What a fine, big family I should have then!'

She wrote: 'I beseech the King, my lord, that he will accept all my jewels or such as he shall select so that, seeing them, he may be reminded of the singular love I always bore him while living, and that I am now waiting for him in a better world; by which remembrance he may be encouraged to live the more justly and holily in this.'

She made the two principal executors of this will the King and Ximenes.

And when it was in order she prepared herself for death, for she knew there was very little time left to her on Earth.

❧❦

On that dark November day in the year 1504, a deep sadness settled on the land. Throughout Spain it was known that the Queen was dying.

Isabella lay back on her bed; she was ready now to go. She had made her peace with God; she had lived her life. She could do no more for her beloved daughters, but in these last minutes she prayed for them.

She was conscious of Ferdinand, and she did not see him as the man he had become, but the young husband. She thought of the early days of their marriage when the country was divided and bands of robbers roamed the mountains and the plains. She could catch at that happiness now, that glorious feeling of certainty.

In those days she had said: 'We will make a great Spain, Ferdinand, you and I together.'

And had they? To them was the honour of the re-conquest. To them was the glory of an all-Christian Spain. They had rid the country of Jews and Moors. In every town the fires of the Inquisition were blazing. A great New World across the sea was theirs.

'And yet . . . and yet . . .' she murmured.

She was clinging to life, because there were so many tasks yet to be completed.

'Catalina . . .' her lips formed the name of her youngest daughter. 'Catalina, what will become of you in England?'

And then: 'Juana . . . oh, my poor mad Juana, what lies ahead for you?'

These things she would never know; and now she was slipping away.

'Ximenes,' she whispered; 'you must stand with Ferdinand. You must forget your dislike of each other and stand together.'

Then she seemed to hear Ferdinand's voice close, filled with contempt: '*Your* Archbishop!'

But she was too tired, too weak; and these problems were no longer for her to solve. She was fifty-four and she had reigned for thirty years. It had been a good, long life.

Those about her bed were weeping, and she said: 'Do not weep for me, nor waste your time in prayers for my recovery. I am going. Pray then for the salvation of my soul.'

They gave her Extreme Unction then; and shortly before noon on that November day Isabella, the Queen, slipped quietly away.

BIBLIOGRAPHY

Altamira, Rafael, translated by P. Volkov. *A History of Spanish Civilization*.

Adams, Nicholson B., *The Heritage of Spain: An Introduction to Spanish Civilization*.

Bertrand, Louis and Petrie, Sir Charles, MA, FRHistS. *The History of Spain*.

Burke, Ulick Ralph, MA, with additional Notes and Introduction by Martin A. S. Hume, *A History of Spain from Earliest Times to the Death of Ferdinand the Catholic*. Two volumes.

Ellis, Havelock, *The Soul of Spain*.

Hope, Thomas, *Torquemada, Scourge of the Jews*.

Hume, Martin A. S., *Spain: Its Greatness and Decay* (1479–1788).

Hume, Martin A. S., *Queens of Old Spain*.

Merton, Reginald, *Cardinal Ximenes and the Making of Spain*.

Prescott, William H., edited by John Foster Kirk, *History of the Reign of Ferdinand and Isabella the Catholic*. Two volumes.

Sabatini, Rafael, *Torquemada and the Spanish Inquisition*.

Sedgwick, Henry Dwight, *Spain*.

Spain and Portugal. Edited by Doré Ogrizek, translated by Paddy O'Hanlon and H. Iredale Nelson.

Spain: A Companion to Spanish Studies. Edited by E. Allison Peers.

Sitwell, Sacheverell, *Spain*.